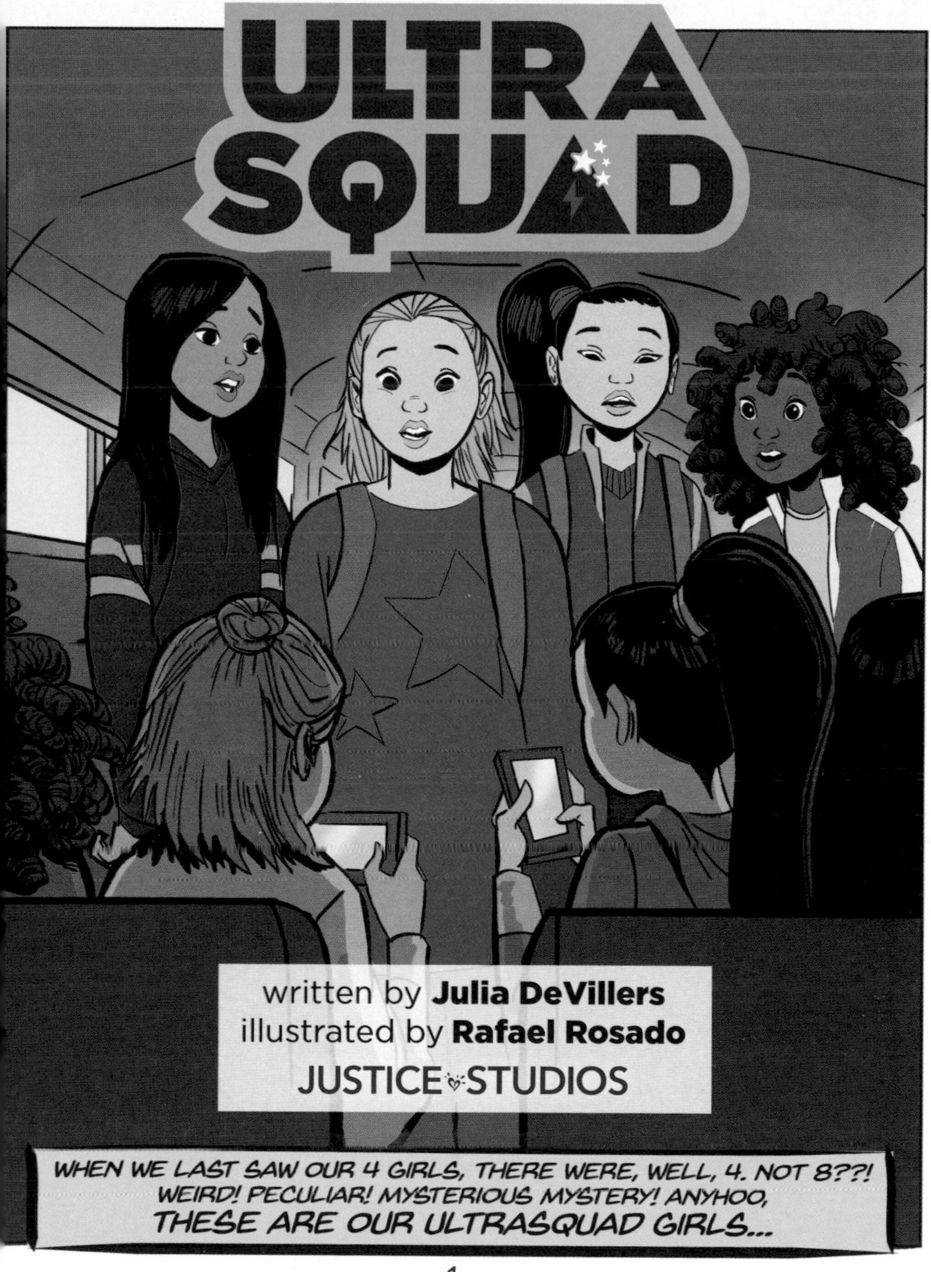
ULTRA SQUAD
written by Julia DeVillers
illustrated by Rafael Rosado
JUSTICE STUDIOS
WHEN WE LAST SAW OUR 4 GIRLS, THERE WERE, WELL, 4. NOT 8??! WEIRD! PECULIAR! MYSTERIOUS MYSTERY! ANYHOO, THESE ARE OUR ULTRASQUAD GIRLS...

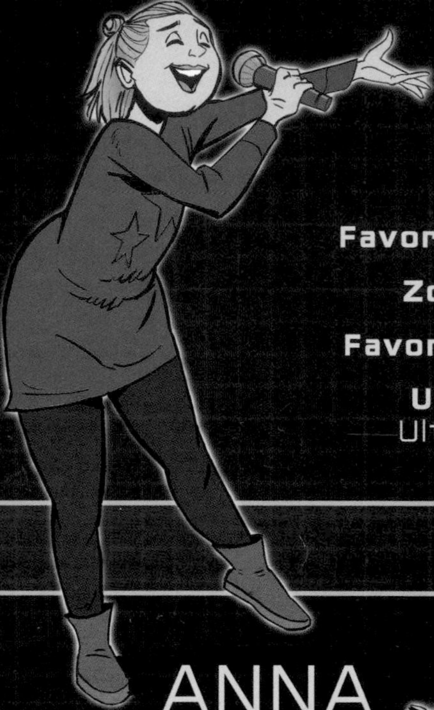

POSEY

Passion: Acting

Color: Pink

Favorite Snack: Yogurt

Zodiac Sign: Libra

Favorite Scent: Vanilla

Ultra-Super-Power:
Ultra-Sparkle bracelet!

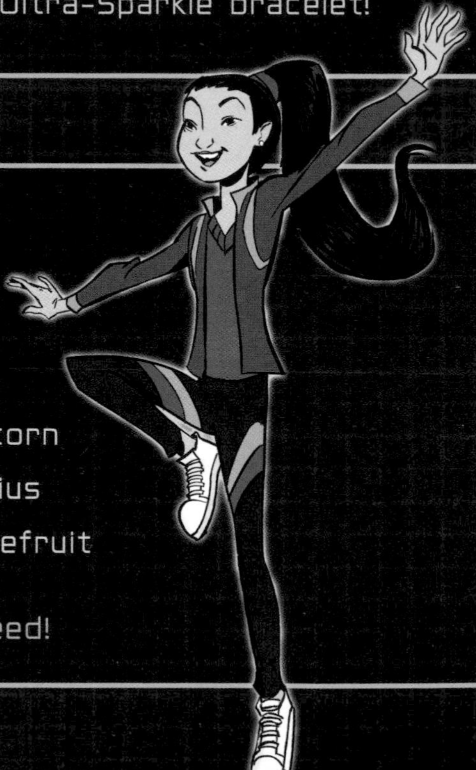

ANNA

Passion: Gymnastics

Color: Turquoise

Favorite Snack: Popcorn

Zodiac Sign: Sagittarius

Favorite Scent: Grapefruit

Ultra-Super-Power:
Ultra-Boost super speed!

LYRIC

Passion: Music

Color: Purple

Favorite Snack: Chips

Zodiac Sign: Scorpio

Favorite Scent: Cinnamon

Ultra-Super-Power:
Ultra-Sonic guitar!

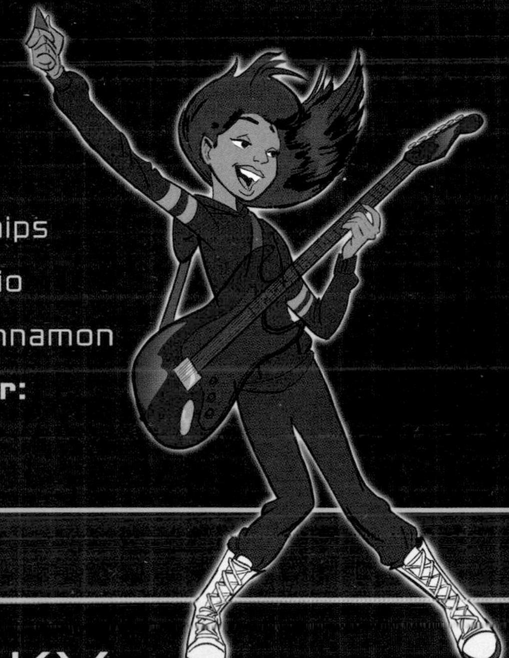

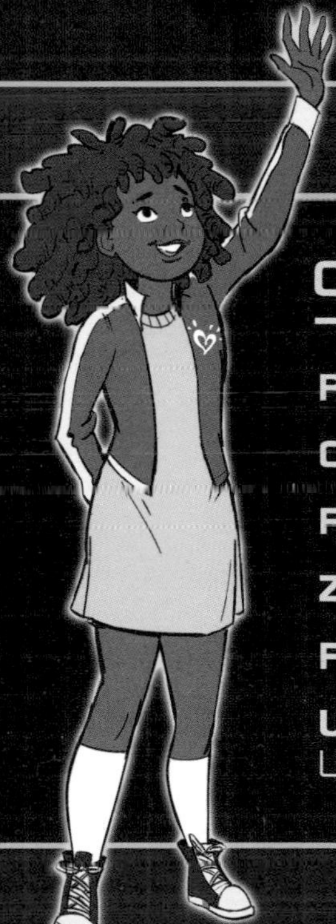

SKY

Passion: Computers

Color: Green

Favorite Snack: Sour Gummies

Zodiac Sign: Virgo

Favorite Scent: Sugar cookies

Ultra-Super-Power:
Ultra-Brainz super smarts!

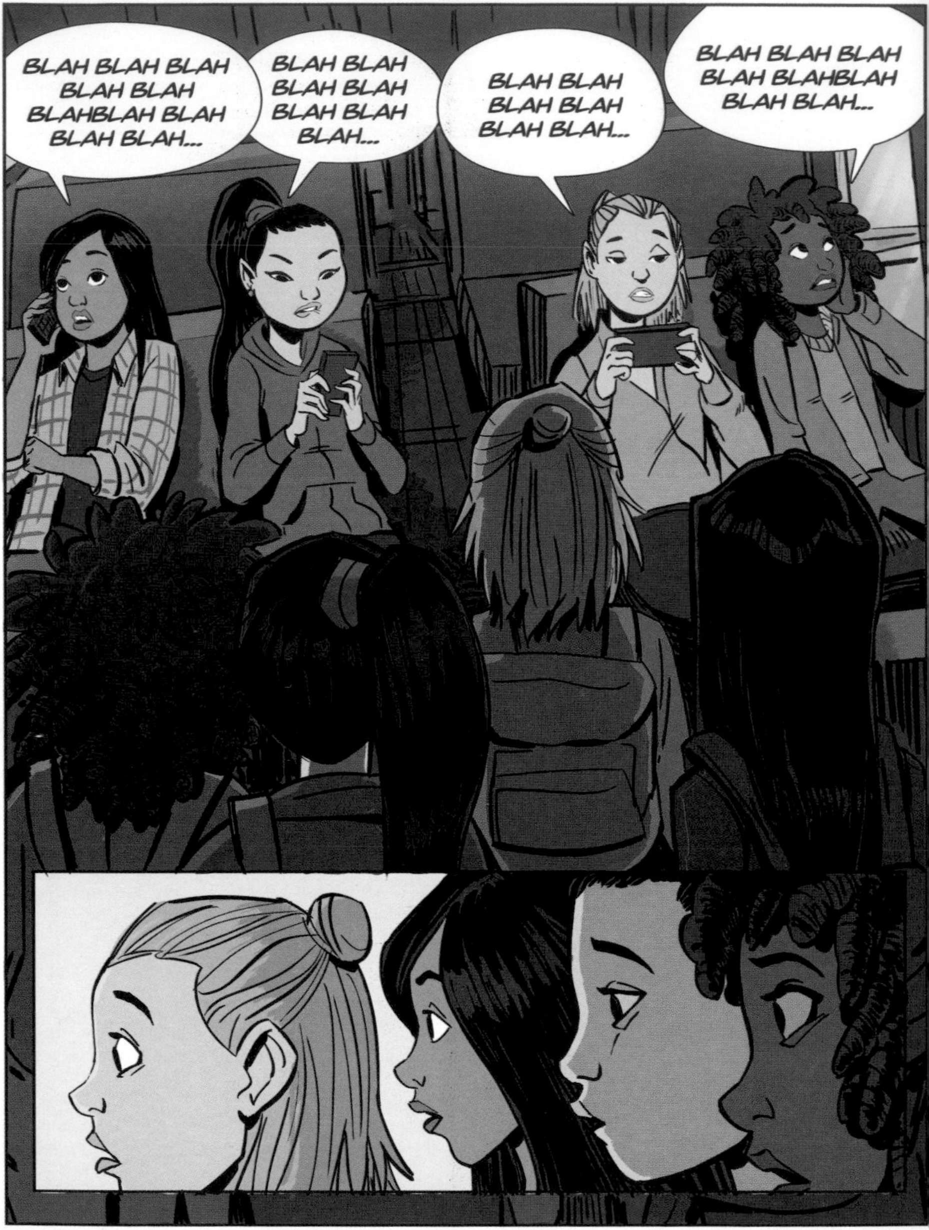
BLAH BLAH BLAH BLAH BLAH BLAHBLAH BLAH BLAH BLAH...
BLAH BLAH BLAH BLAH BLAH BLAH BLAH...
BLAH BLAH BLAH BLAH BLAH BLAH...
BLAH BLAH BLAH BLAH BLAHBLAH BLAH BLAH...

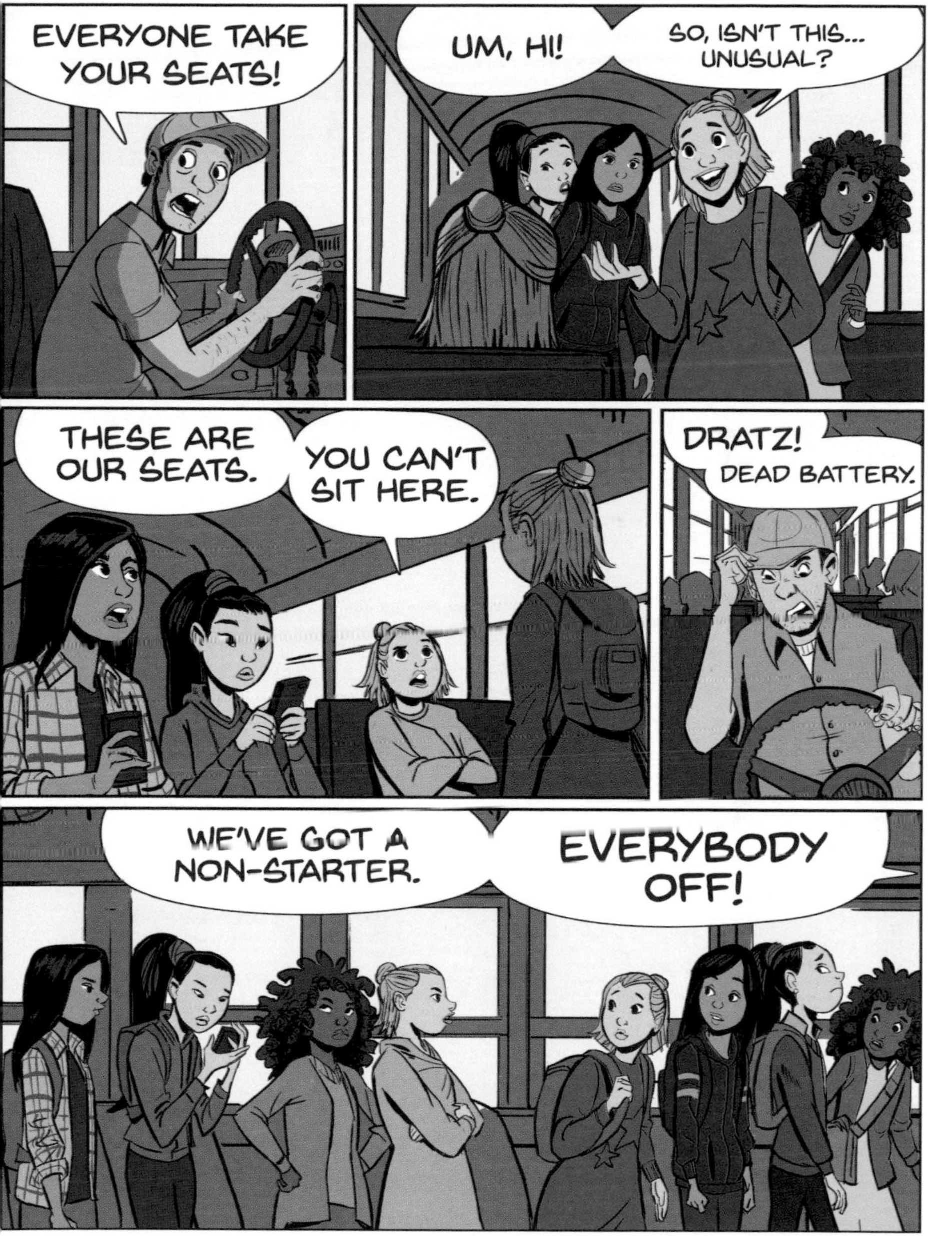
EVERYONE TAKE YOUR SEATS!
UM, HI!
SO, ISN'T THIS... UNUSUAL?
THESE ARE OUR SEATS.
YOU CAN'T SIT HERE.
DRATZ!
DEAD BATTERY.
WE'VE GOT A NON-STARTER.
EVERYBODY OFF!

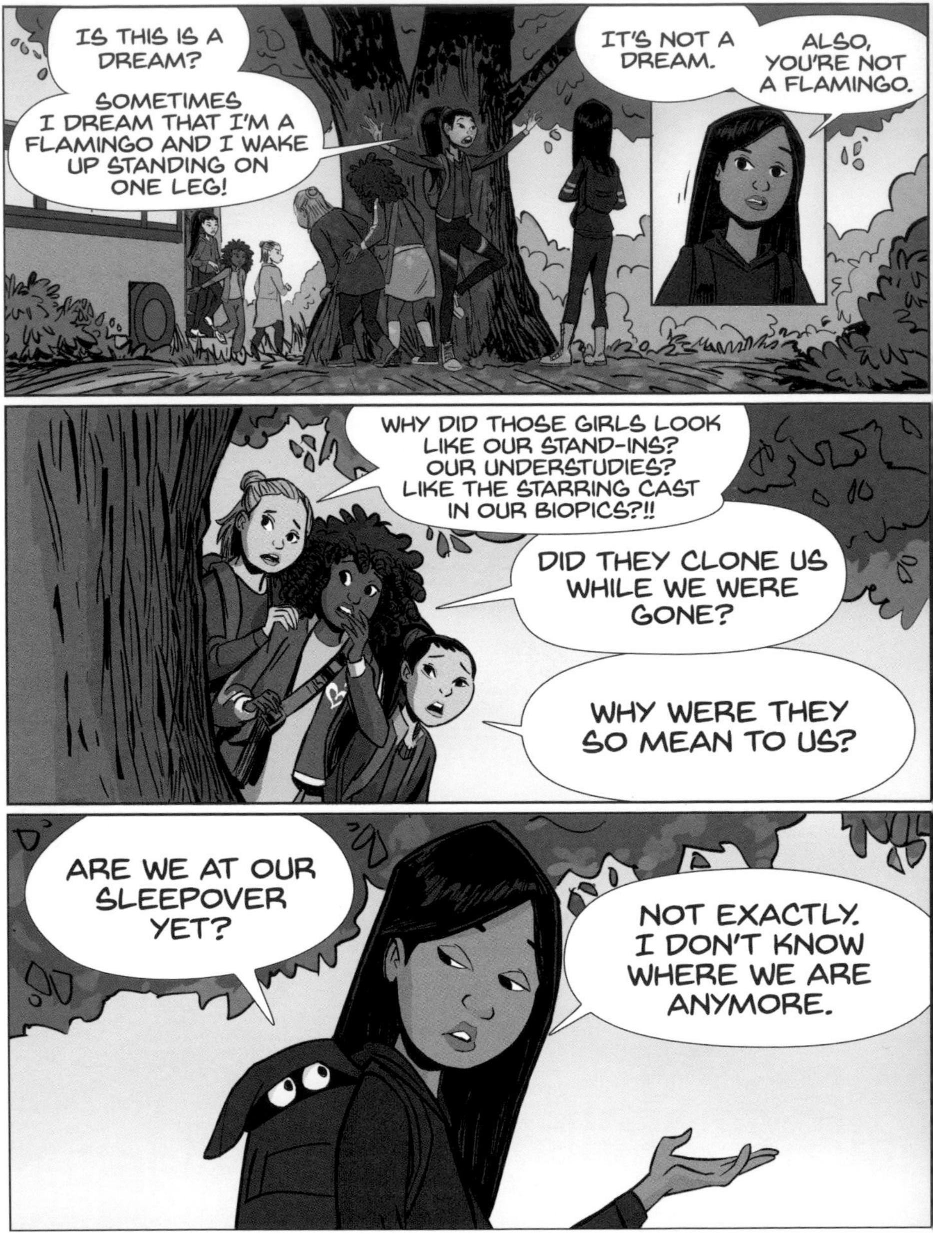
IS THIS IS A DREAM?
SOMETIMES I DREAM THAT I'M A FLAMINGO AND I WAKE UP STANDING ON ONE LEG!
IT'S NOT A DREAM.
ALSO, YOU'RE NOT A FLAMINGO.
WHY DID THOSE GIRLS LOOK LIKE OUR STAND-INS? OUR UNDERSTUDIES? LIKE THE STARRING CAST IN OUR BIOPICS?!!
DID THEY CLONE US WHILE WE WERE GONE?
WHY WERE THEY SO MEAN TO US?
ARE WE AT OUR SLEEPOVER YET?
NOT EXACTLY. I DON'T KNOW WHERE WE ARE ANYMORE.

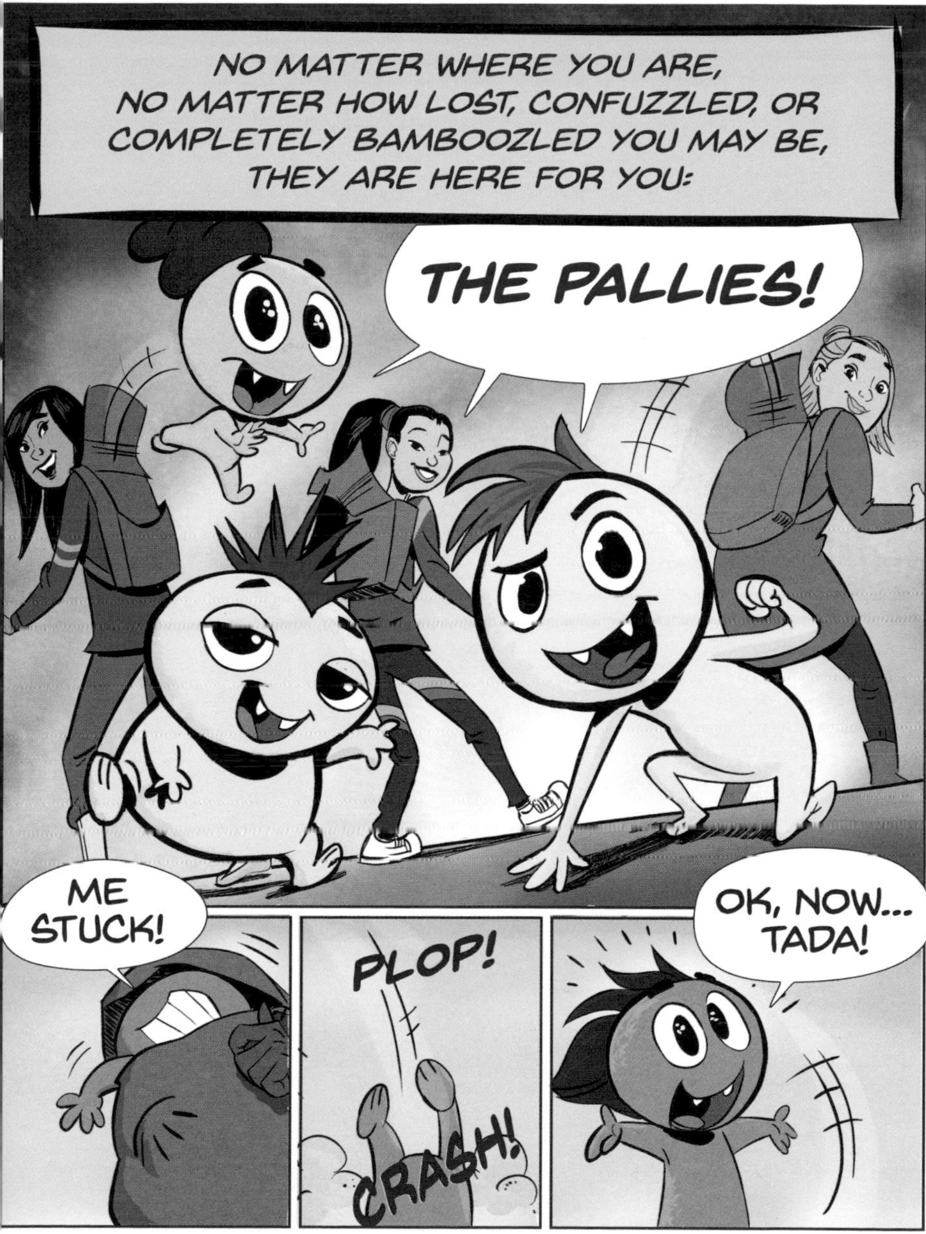
NO MATTER WHERE YOU ARE, NO MATTER HOW LOST, CONFUZZLED, OR COMPLETELY BAMBOOZLED YOU MAY BE, THEY ARE HERE FOR YOU:
THE PALLIES!
ME STUCK!
PLOP!
CRASH!
OK, NOW... TADA!

Captain Bardo Babu
"BOB"

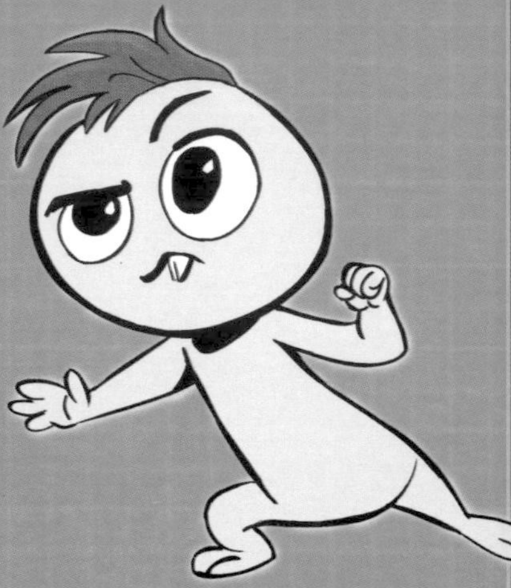

Want a pal who will stick by your side?

Captain Bob is here to protect and support you! And he is always up for imagination and adventures. Just tell Bob where and he'll lead the way! His Zodiac sign is a Capricorn!

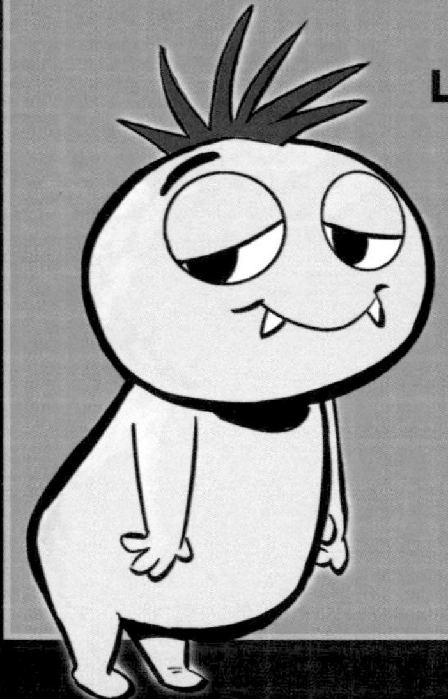

Lieutenant Cruzob Shlunk
"Shlunk"

Want a pal to relax with?

Sleepy Shlunk is always up for a snuggly night in, watching videos. Don't forget his super-soft blanky! Shlunk is a Taurus.

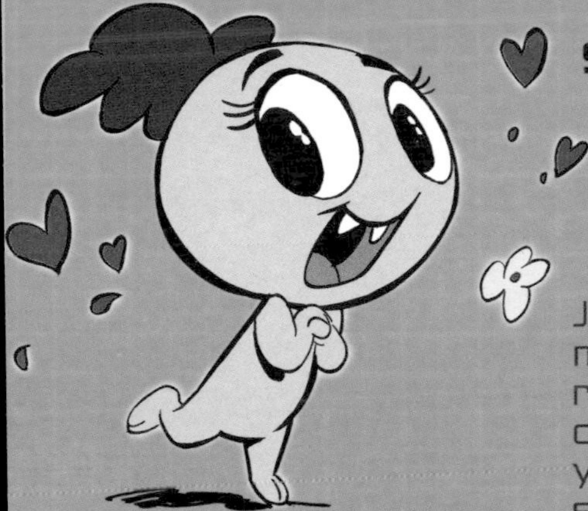

Sergeant Lo-Jane
"JANE"

Want a pal who will cheer you up?

Jane loves to watch and make funny videos: Get ready to lip synch, funny dances and giggle until your cheeks hurt! Jane's sign is Pisces!

Airman Darval Loofah
"Louie"

Want a pal who will cook, bake, and whip up some yummies?

Louie is a foodie! His secret dream is to become a chef with his own cooking show! Louie is a Capricorn!

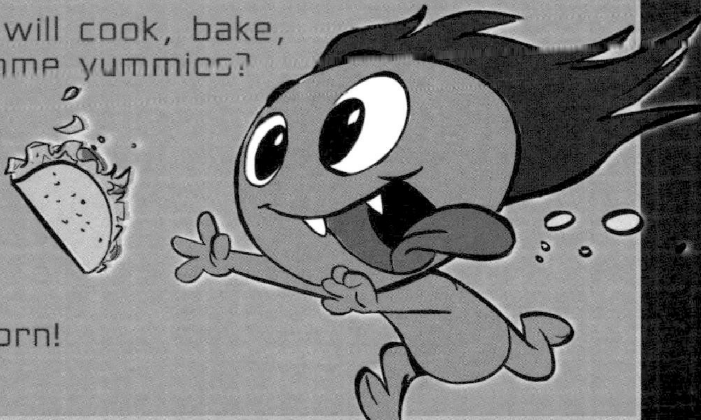

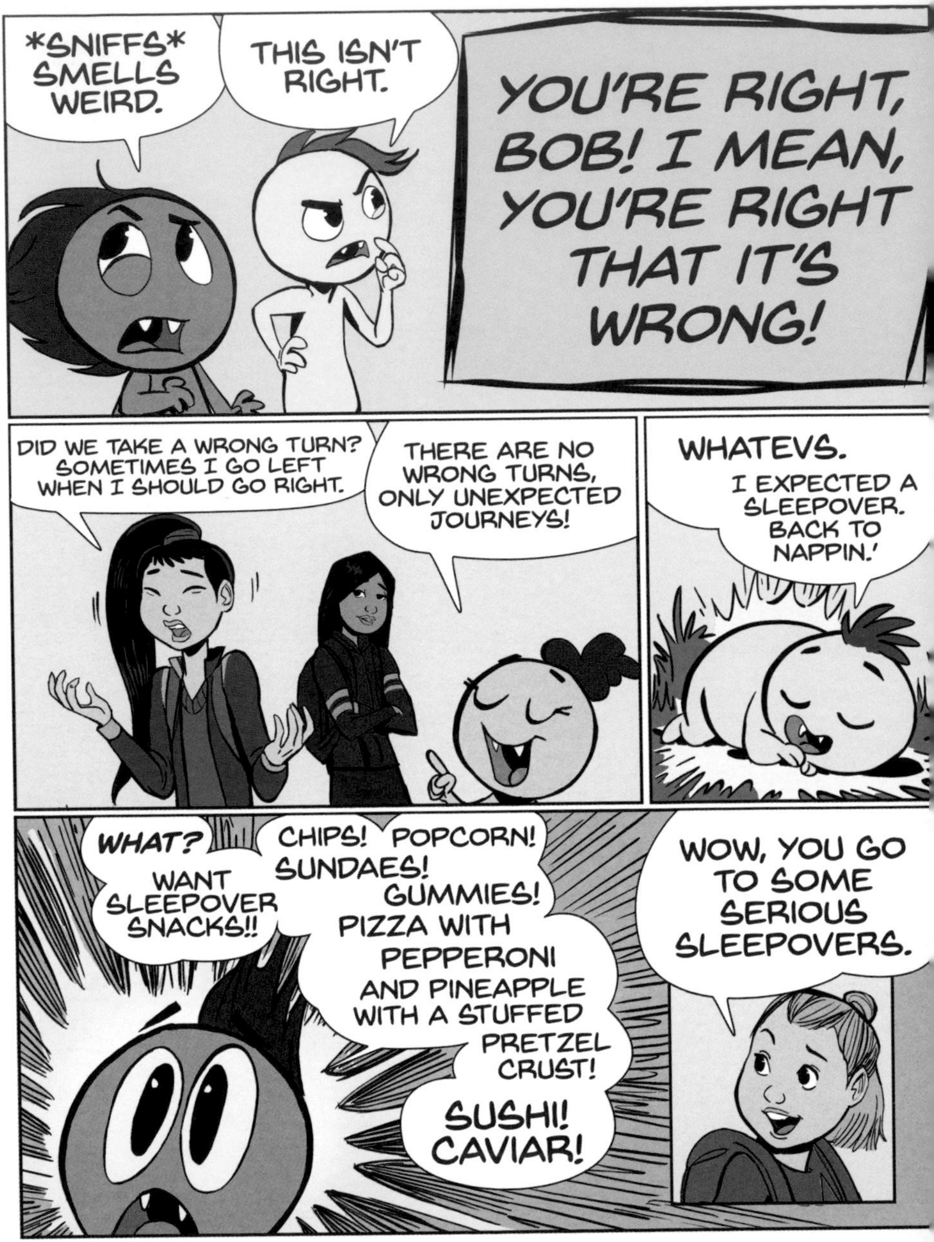
SNIFFS SMELLS WEIRD.
THIS ISN'T RIGHT.
YOU'RE RIGHT, BOB! I MEAN, YOU'RE RIGHT THAT IT'S RIGHT THAT IT'S WRONG!
DID WE TAKE A WRONG TURN? SOMETIMES I GO LEFT WHEN I SHOULD GO RIGHT.
THERE ARE NO WRONG TURNS, ONLY UNEXPECTED JOURNEYS!
WHATEVS.
I EXPECTED A SLEEPOVER. BACK TO NAPPIN.'
WHAT?
WANT SLEEPOVER SNACKS!!
CHIPS! POPCORN! SUNDAES! GUMMIES! PIZZA WITH PEPPERONI AND PINEAPPLE WITH A STUFFED PRETZEL CRUST!
SUSHI! CAVIAR!
WOW, YOU GO TO SOME SERIOUS SLEEPOVERS.

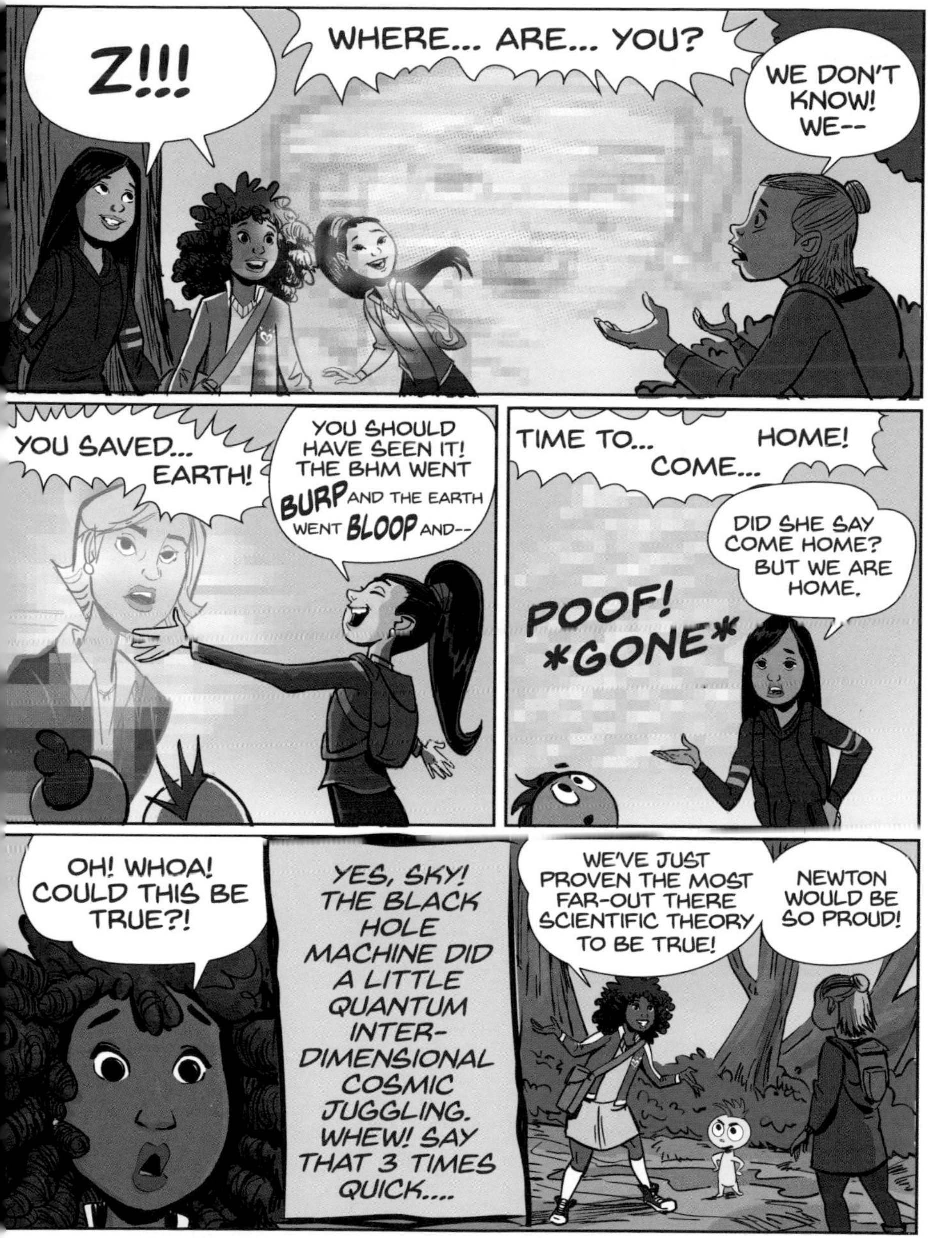
Z!!!
WHERE... ARE... YOU?
WE DON'T KNOW! WE--
YOU SAVED... EARTH!
YOU SHOULD HAVE SEEN IT! THE BHM WENT BURP AND THE EARTH WENT BLOOP AND--
TIME TO... COME... HOME!
DID SHE SAY COME HOME? BUT WE ARE HOME.
POOF! *GONE*
OH! WHOA! COULD THIS BE TRUE?!
YES, SKY! THE BLACK HOLE MACHINE DID A LITTLE QUANTUM INTER-DIMENSIONAL COSMIC JUGGLING. WHEW! SAY THAT 3 TIMES QUICK....
WE'VE JUST PROVEN THE MOST FAR-OUT THERE SCIENTIFIC THEORY TO BE TRUE!
NEWTON WOULD BE SO PROUD!

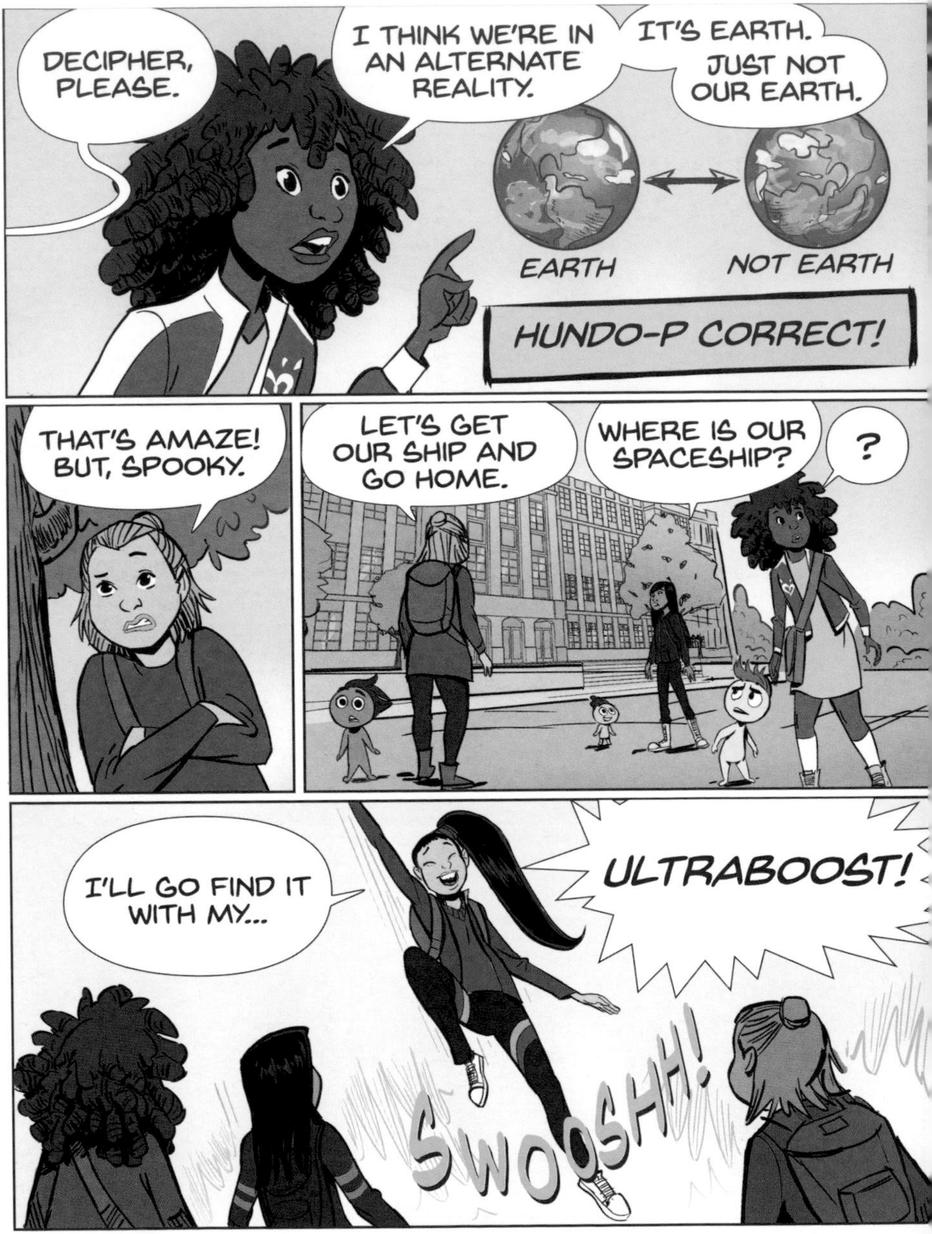
DECIPHER, PLEASE.
I THINK WE'RE IN AN ALTERNATE REALITY.
IT'S EARTH.
JUST NOT OUR EARTH.
EARTH
NOT EARTH
HUNDO-P CORRECT!
THAT'S AMAZE! BUT, SPOOKY.
LET'S GET OUR SHIP AND GO HOME.
WHERE IS OUR SPACESHIP?
?
I'LL GO FIND IT WITH MY...
ULTRABOOST!
SWOOSHH!

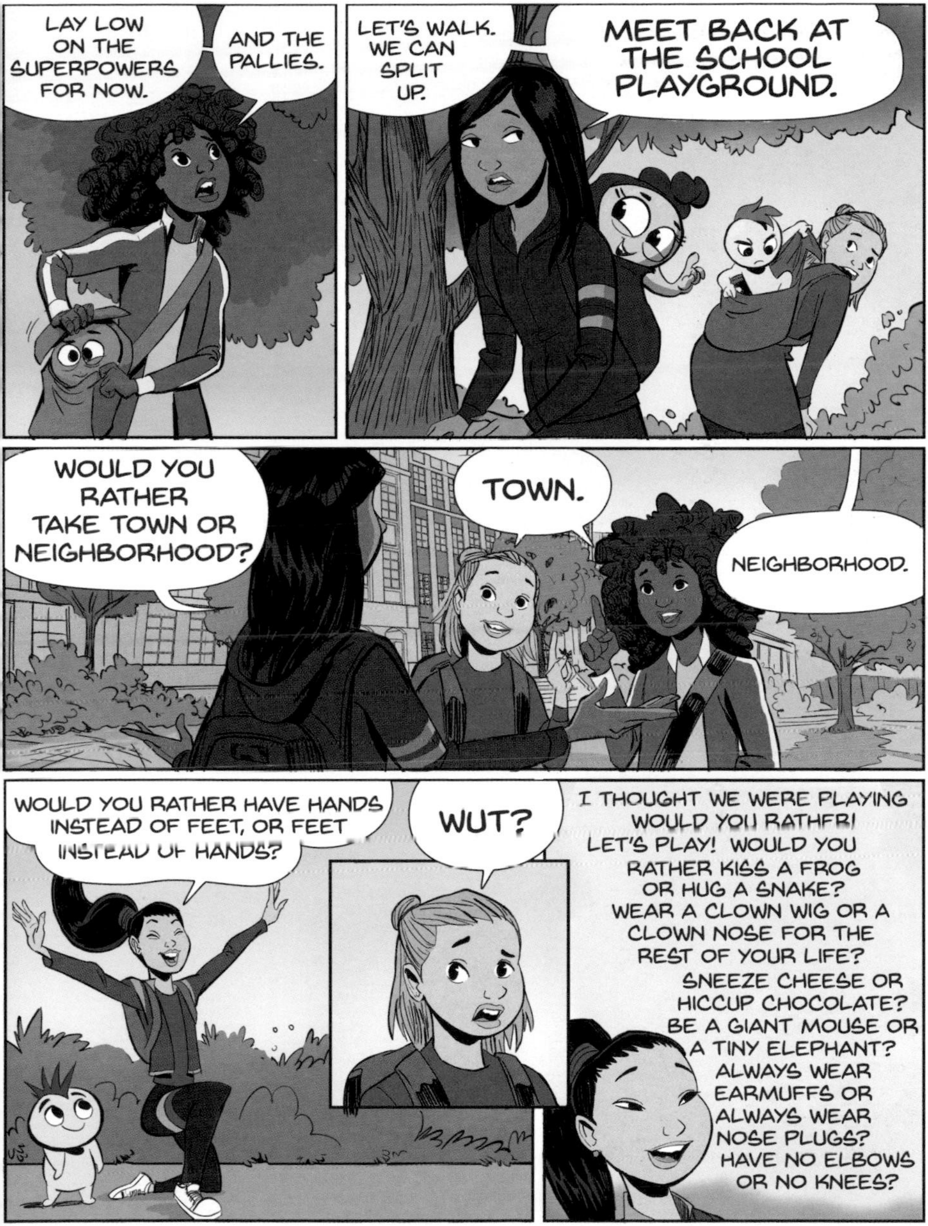
LAY LOW ON THE SUPERPOWERS FOR NOW.
AND THE PALLIES.
LET'S WALK. WE CAN SPLIT UP.
MEET BACK AT THE SCHOOL PLAYGROUND.
WOULD YOU RATHER TAKE TOWN OR NEIGHBORHOOD?
TOWN.
NEIGHBORHOOD.
WOULD YOU RATHER HAVE HANDS INSTEAD OF FEET, OR FEET INSTEAD OF HANDS?
WUT?
I THOUGHT WE WERE PLAYING WOULD YOU RATHER!
LET'S PLAY! WOULD YOU RATHER KISS A FROG OR HUG A SNAKE?
WEAR A CLOWN WIG OR A CLOWN NOSE FOR THE REST OF YOUR LIFE?
SNEEZE CHEESE OR HICCUP CHOCOLATE?
BE A GIANT MOUSE OR A TINY ELEPHANT?
ALWAYS WEAR EARMUFFS OR ALWAYS WEAR NOSE PLUGS?
HAVE NO ELBOWS OR NO KNEES?

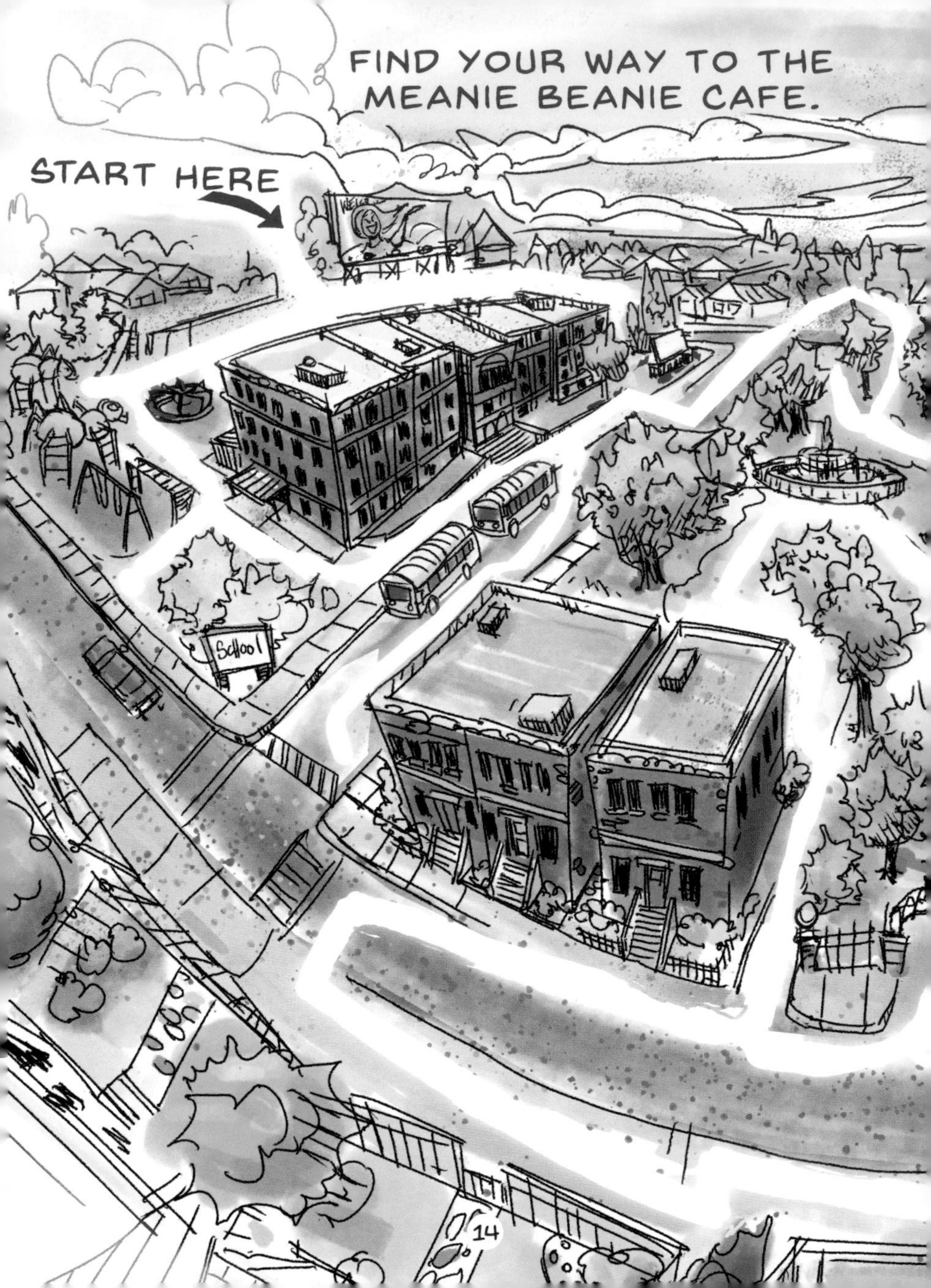
FIND YOUR WAY TO THE
MEANIE BEANIE CAFE.
START HERE
School

BUT DON'T CROSS THE LINES!

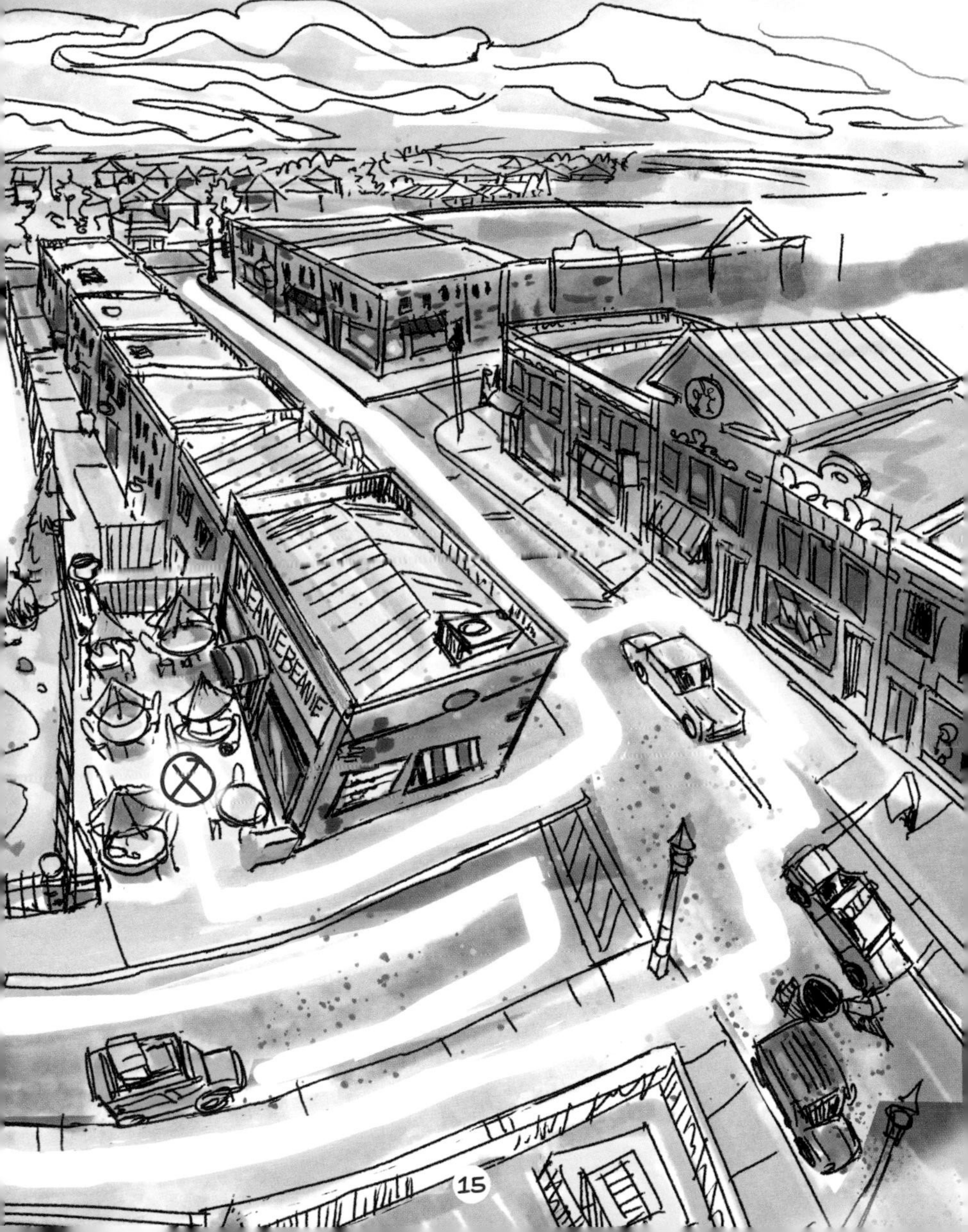
BEANIE BEANIE

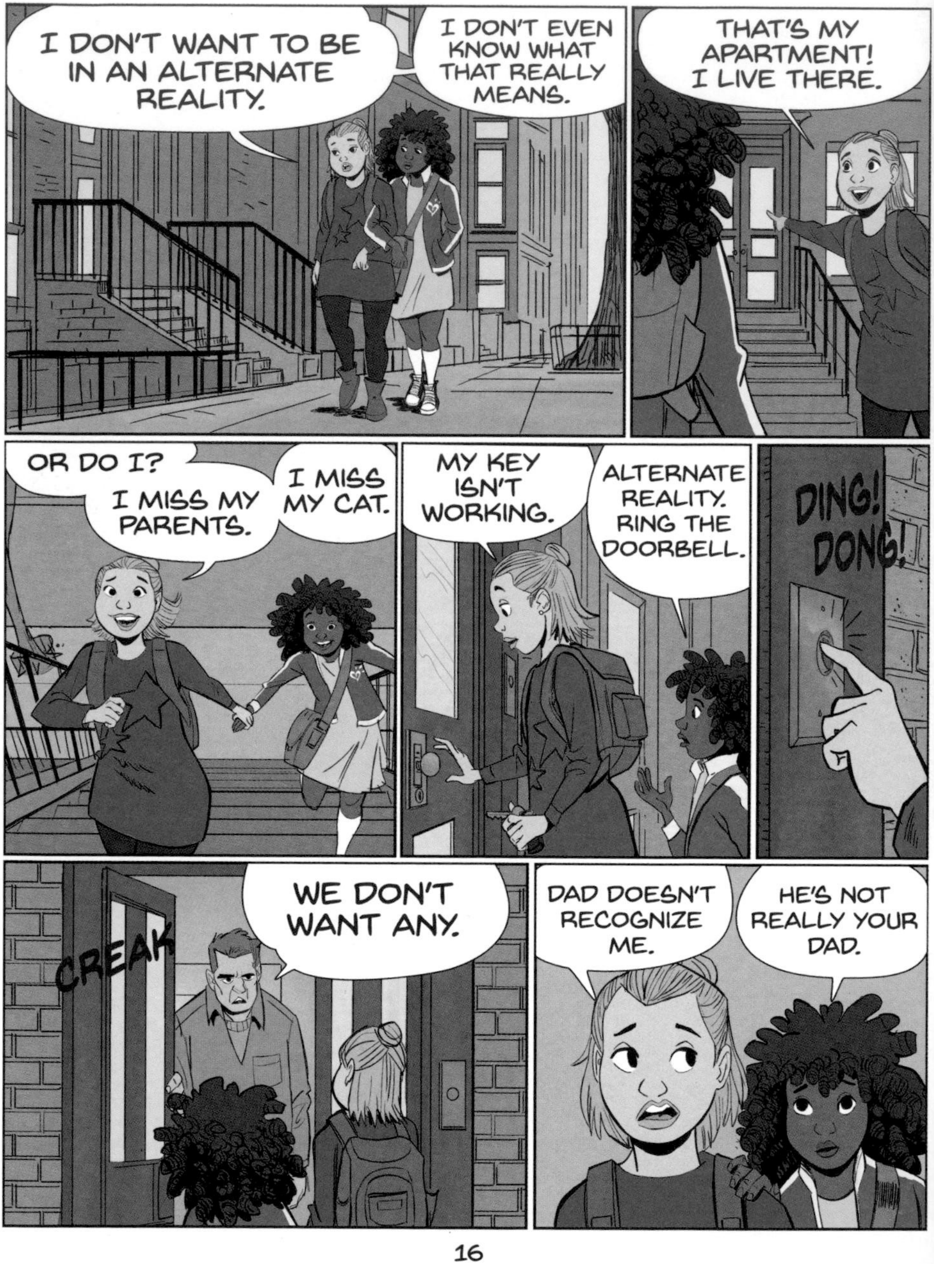
I DON'T WANT TO BE IN AN ALTERNATE REALITY.
I DON'T EVEN KNOW WHAT THAT REALLY MEANS.
THAT'S MY APARTMENT! I LIVE THERE.
OR DO I?
I MISS MY PARENTS.
I MISS MY CAT.
MY KEY ISN'T WORKING.
ALTERNATE REALITY. RING THE DOORBELL.
DING! DONG!
CREAK
WE DON'T WANT ANY.
DAD DOESN'T RECOGNIZE ME.
HE'S NOT REALLY YOUR DAD.

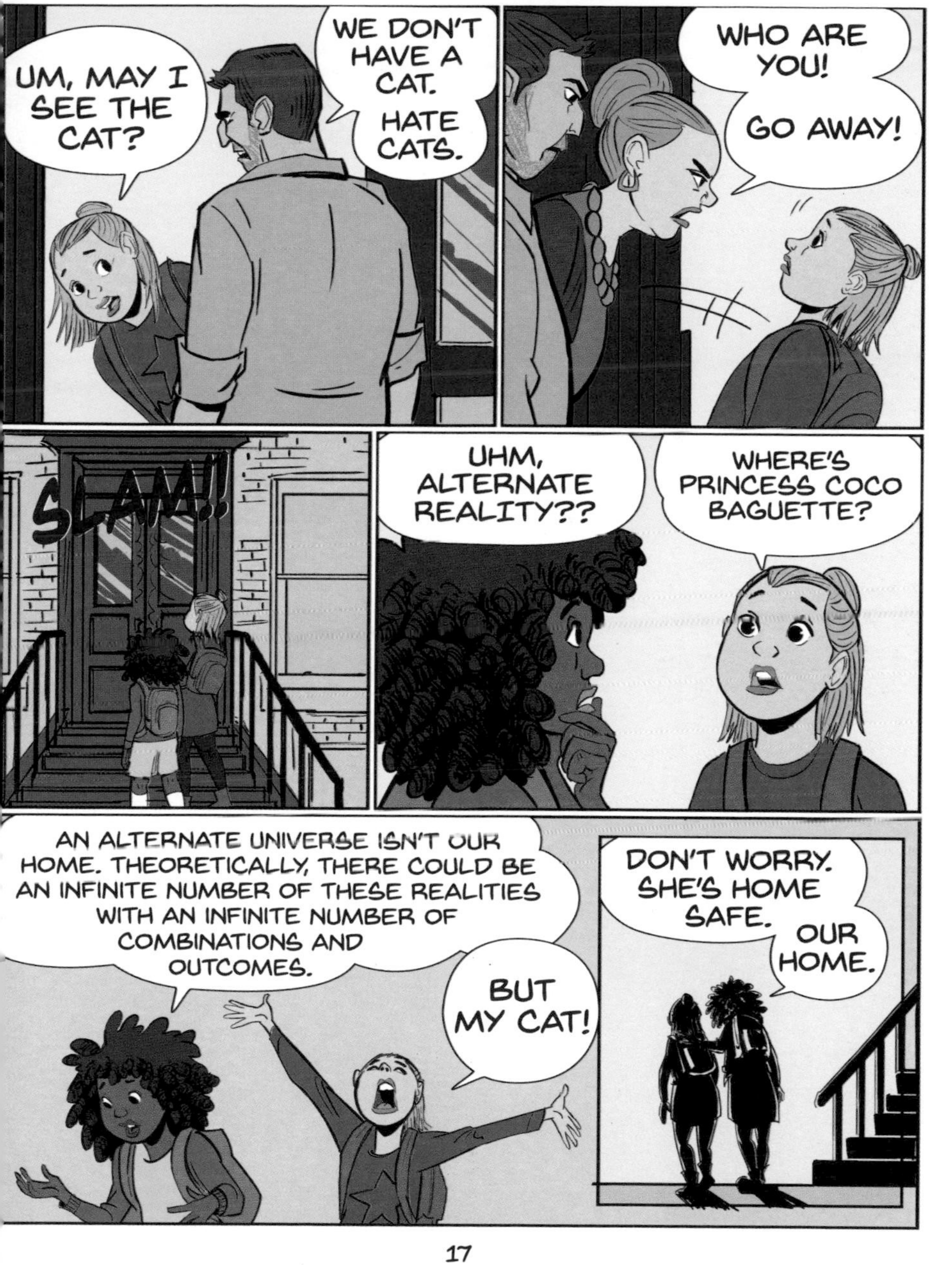
UM, MAY I SEE THE CAT?
WE DON'T HAVE A CAT.
HATE CATS.
WHO ARE YOU!
GO AWAY!
SLAM!!
UHM, ALTERNATE REALITY??
WHERE'S PRINCESS COCO BAGUETTE?
AN ALTERNATE UNIVERSE ISN'T OUR HOME. THEORETICALLY, THERE COULD BE AN INFINITE NUMBER OF THESE REALITIES WITH AN INFINITE NUMBER OF COMBINATIONS AND OUTCOMES.
BUT MY CAT!
DON'T WORRY. SHE'S HOME SAFE.
OUR HOME.

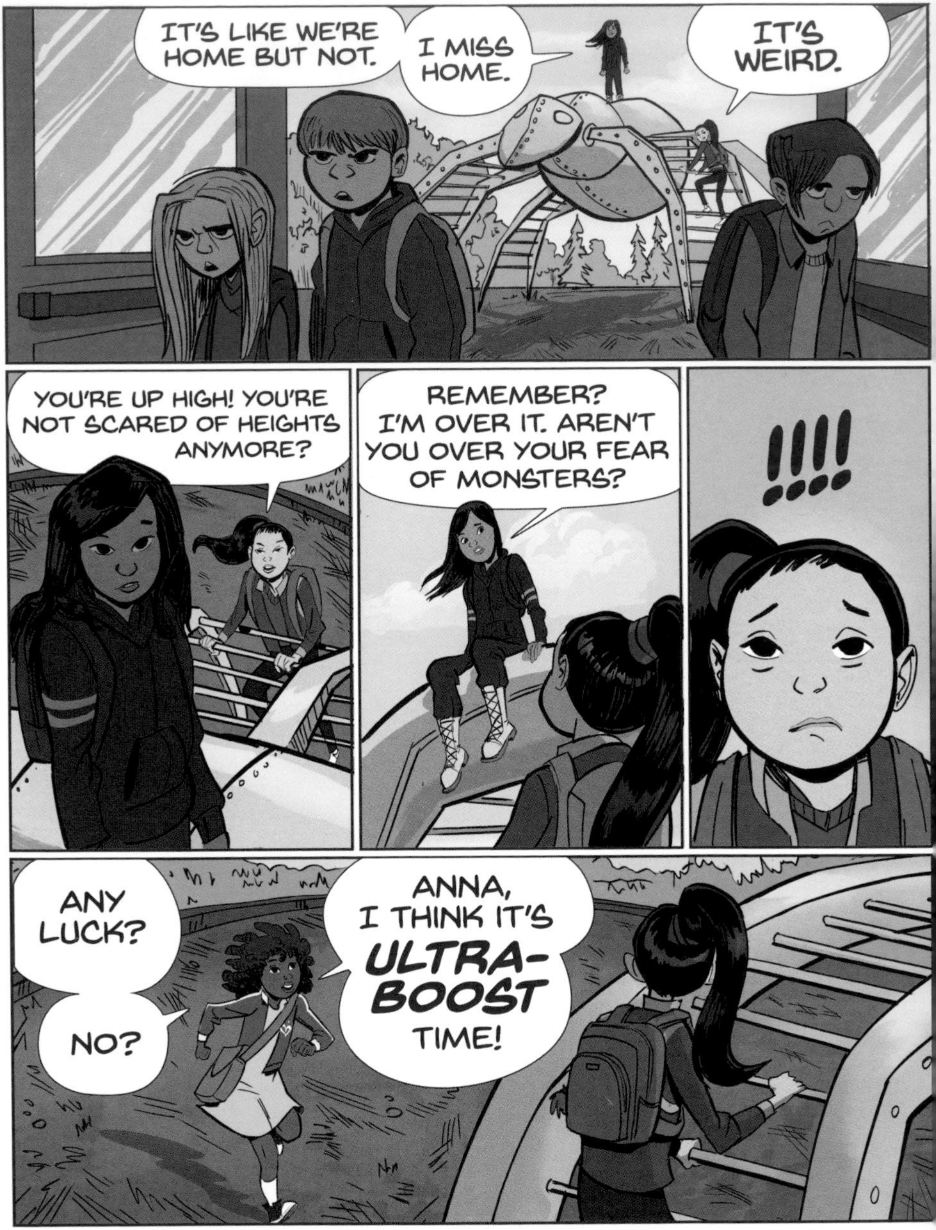
IT'S LIKE WE'RE HOME BUT NOT.
I MISS HOME.
IT'S WEIRD.
YOU'RE UP HIGH! YOU'RE NOT SCARED OF HEIGHTS ANYMORE?
REMEMBER? I'M OVER IT. AREN'T YOU OVER YOUR FEAR OF MONSTERS?
!!!!
ANY LUCK?
NO?
ANNA, I THINK IT'S ULTRA-BOOST TIME!

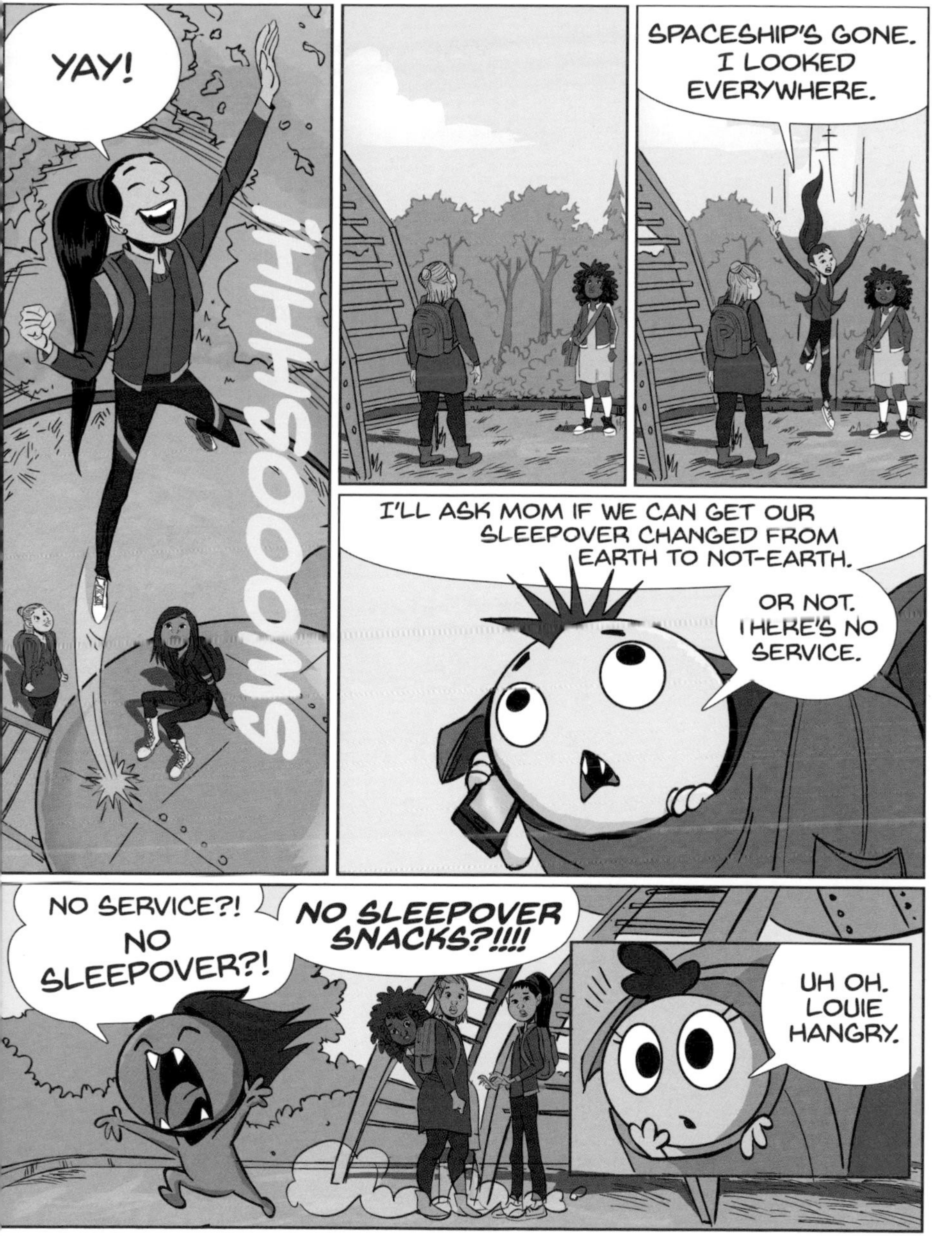
YAY!
SWOOOSHHH!
SPACESHIP'S GONE. I LOOKED EVERYWHERE.
I'LL ASK MOM IF WE CAN GET OUR SLEEPOVER CHANGED FROM EARTH TO NOT-EARTH.
OR NOT. THERE'S NO SERVICE.
NO SERVICE?! NO SLEEPOVER?!
NO SLEEPOVER SNACKS?!!!!
UH OH. LOUIE HANGRY.

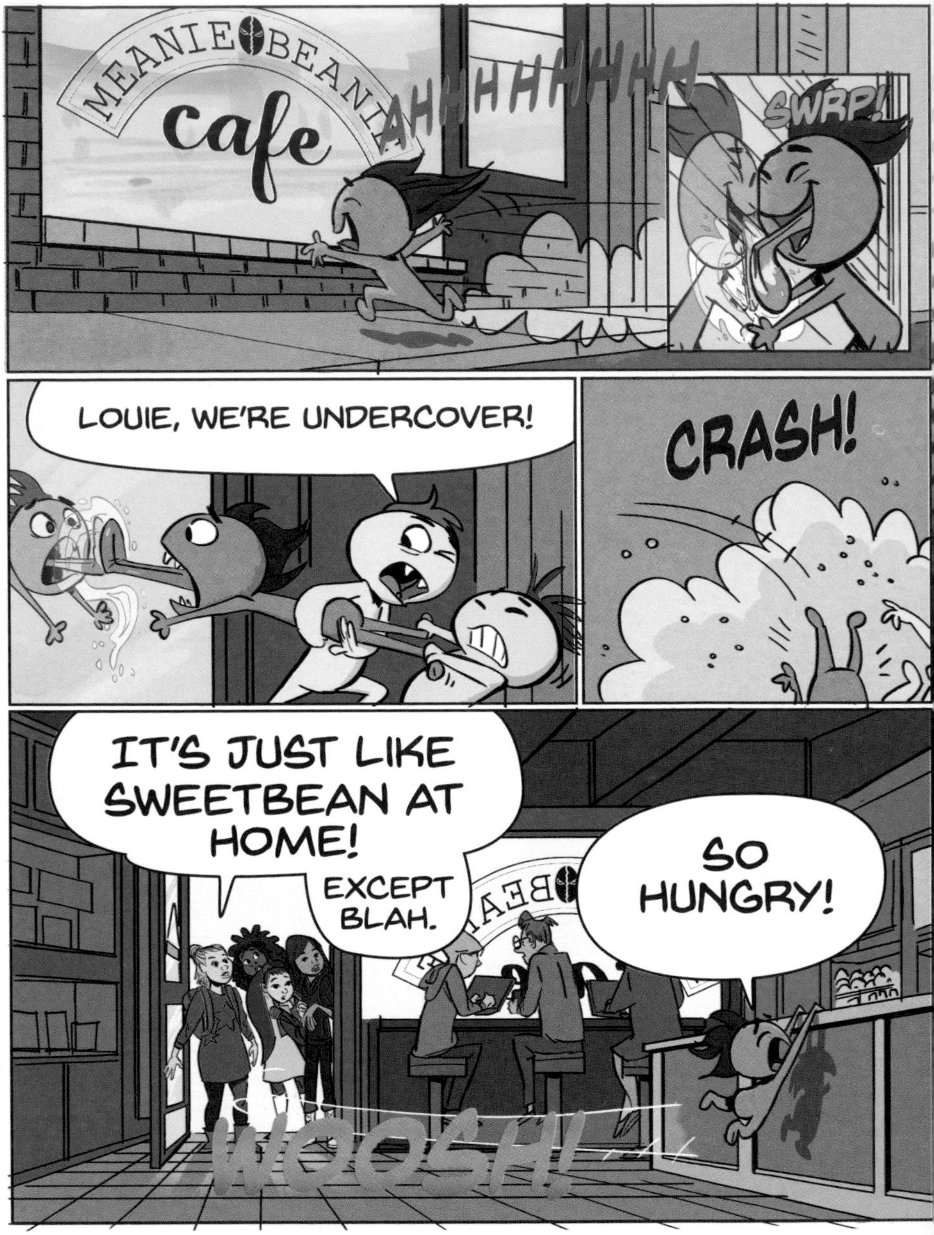

MEANIE BEANIE
cafe
AHHHHHHHHH
SWRP!
LOUIE, WE'RE UNDERCOVER!
CRASH!
IT'S JUST LIKE SWEETBEAN AT HOME!
EXCEPT BLAH.
SO HUNGRY!
WOOSH!

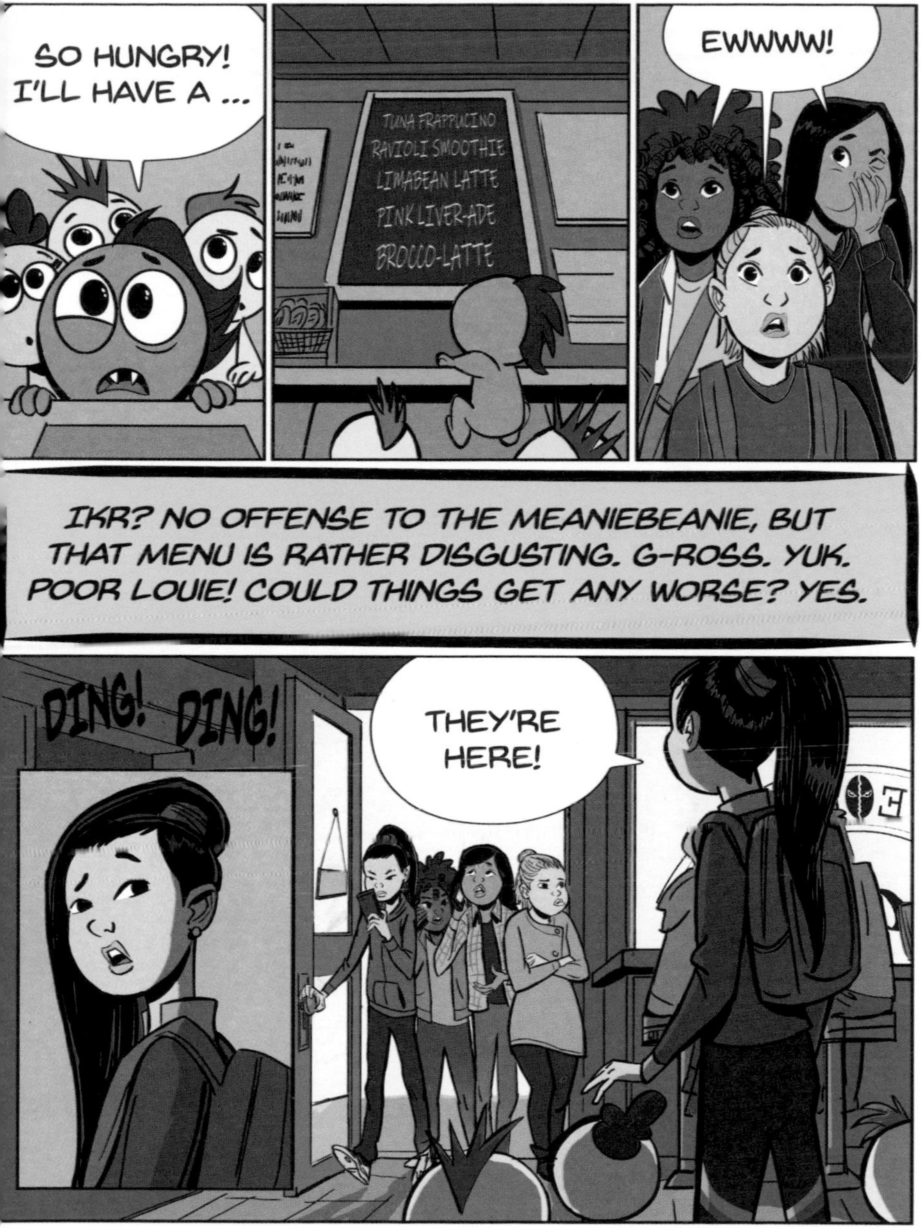
SO HUNGRY! I'LL HAVE A ...
TUNA FRAPPUCINO
RAVIOLI SMOOTHIE
LIMABEAN LATTE
PINK LIVER-ADE
BROCCO-LATTE
EWWWW!
IKR? NO OFFENSE TO THE MEANIEBEANIE, BUT THAT MENU IS RATHER DISGUSTING. G-ROSS. YUK. POOR LOUIE! COULD THINGS GET ANY WORSE? YES.
DING! DING!
THEY'RE HERE!

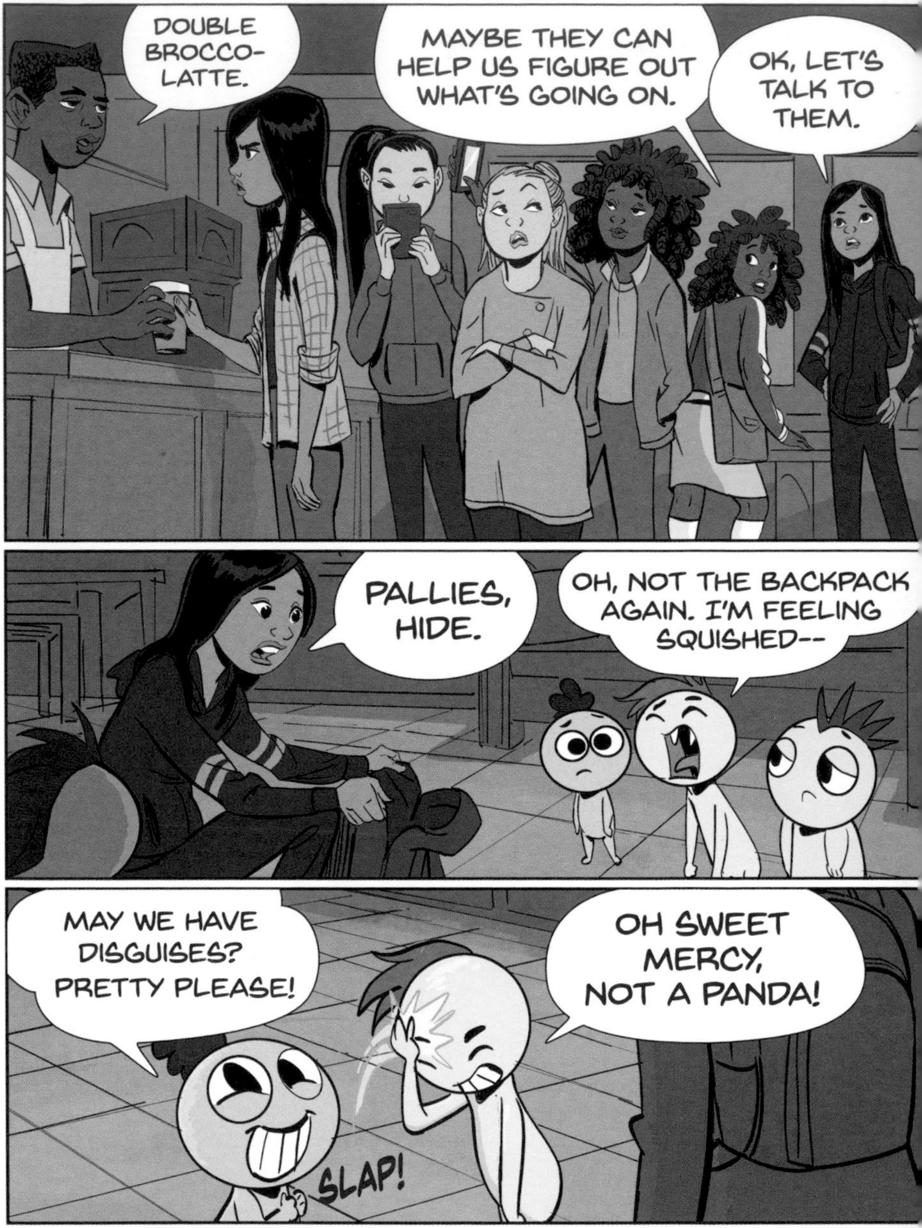
DOUBLE BROCCO-LATTE.
MAYBE THEY CAN HELP US FIGURE OUT WHAT'S GOING ON.
OK, LET'S TALK TO THEM.
PALLIES, HIDE.
OH, NOT THE BACKPACK AGAIN. I'M FEELING SQUISHED--
MAY WE HAVE DISGUISES? PRETTY PLEASE!
OH SWEET MERCY, NOT A PANDA!
SLAP!

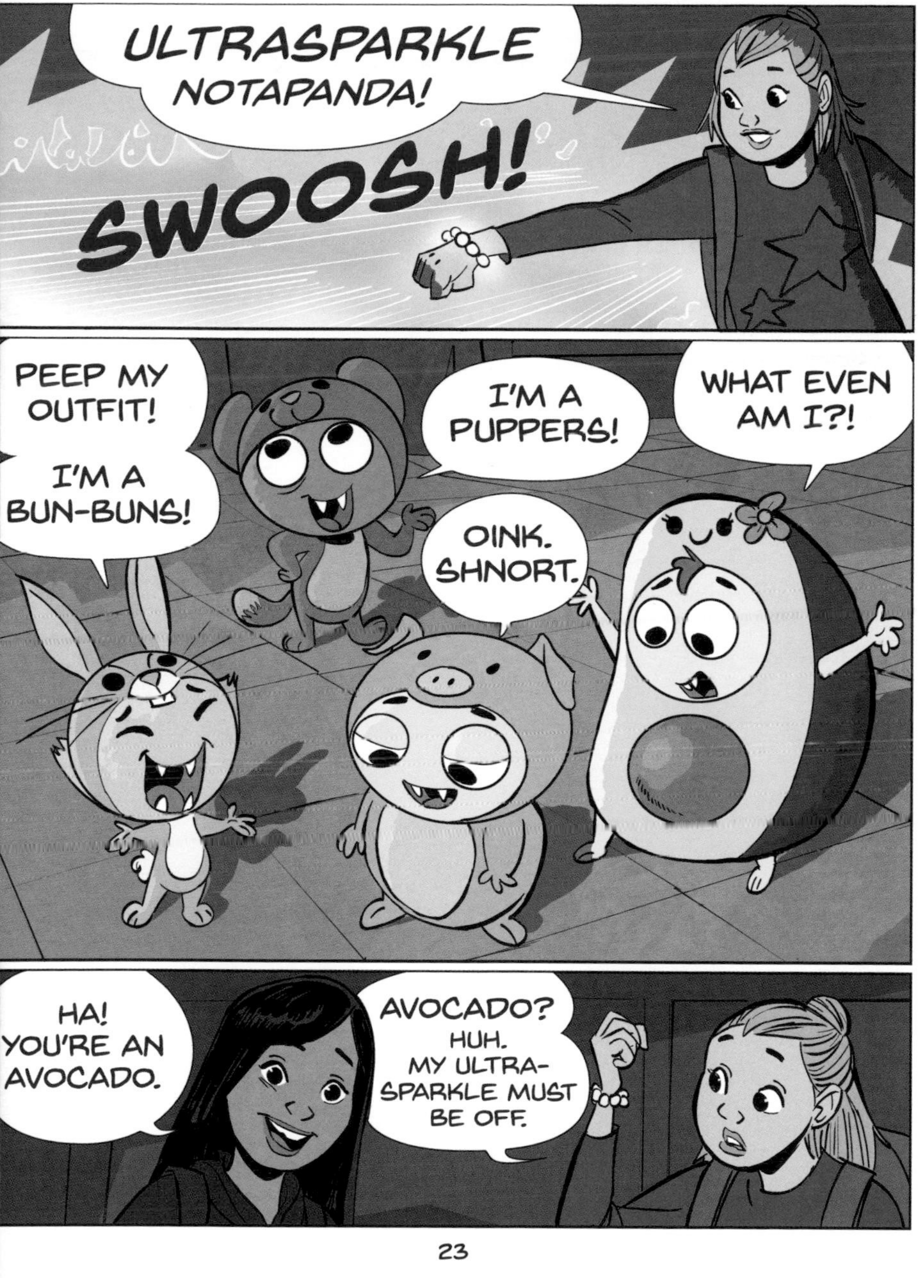
ULTRASPARKLE NOTAPANDA!
SWOOSH!
PEEP MY OUTFIT! I'M A BUN-BUNS!
I'M A PUPPERS!
WHAT EVEN AM I?!
OINK. SHNORT.
HA! YOU'RE AN AVOCADO.
AVOCADO? HUH. MY ULTRA-SPARKLE MUST BE OFF.

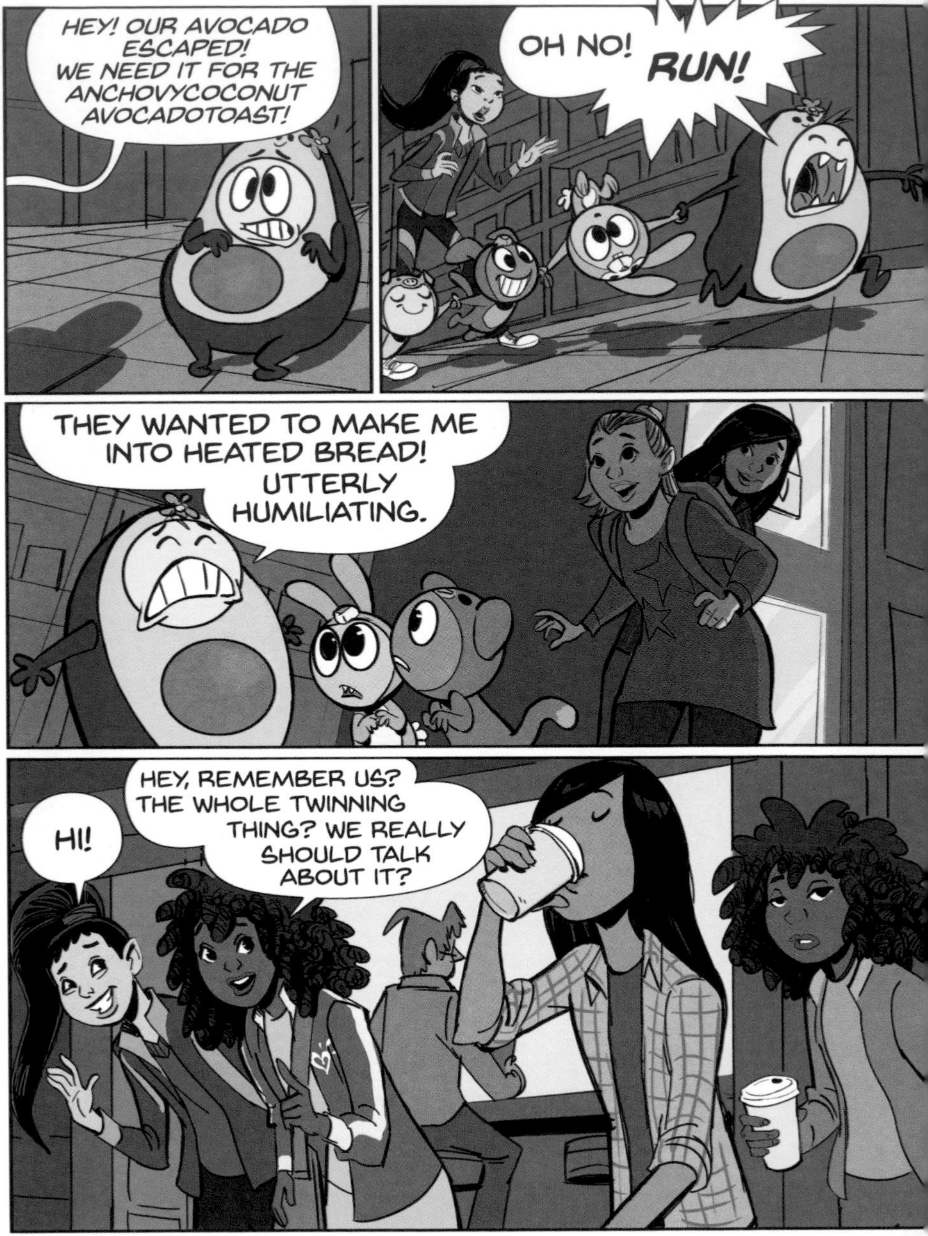
HEY! OUR AVOCADO ESCAPED! WE NEED IT FOR THE ANCHOVYCOCONUT AVOCADOTOAST!
OH NO!
RUN!
THEY WANTED TO MAKE ME INTO HEATED BREAD! UTTERLY HUMILIATING.
HI!
HEY, REMEMBER US? THE WHOLE TWINNING THING? WE REALLY SHOULD TALK ABOUT IT?

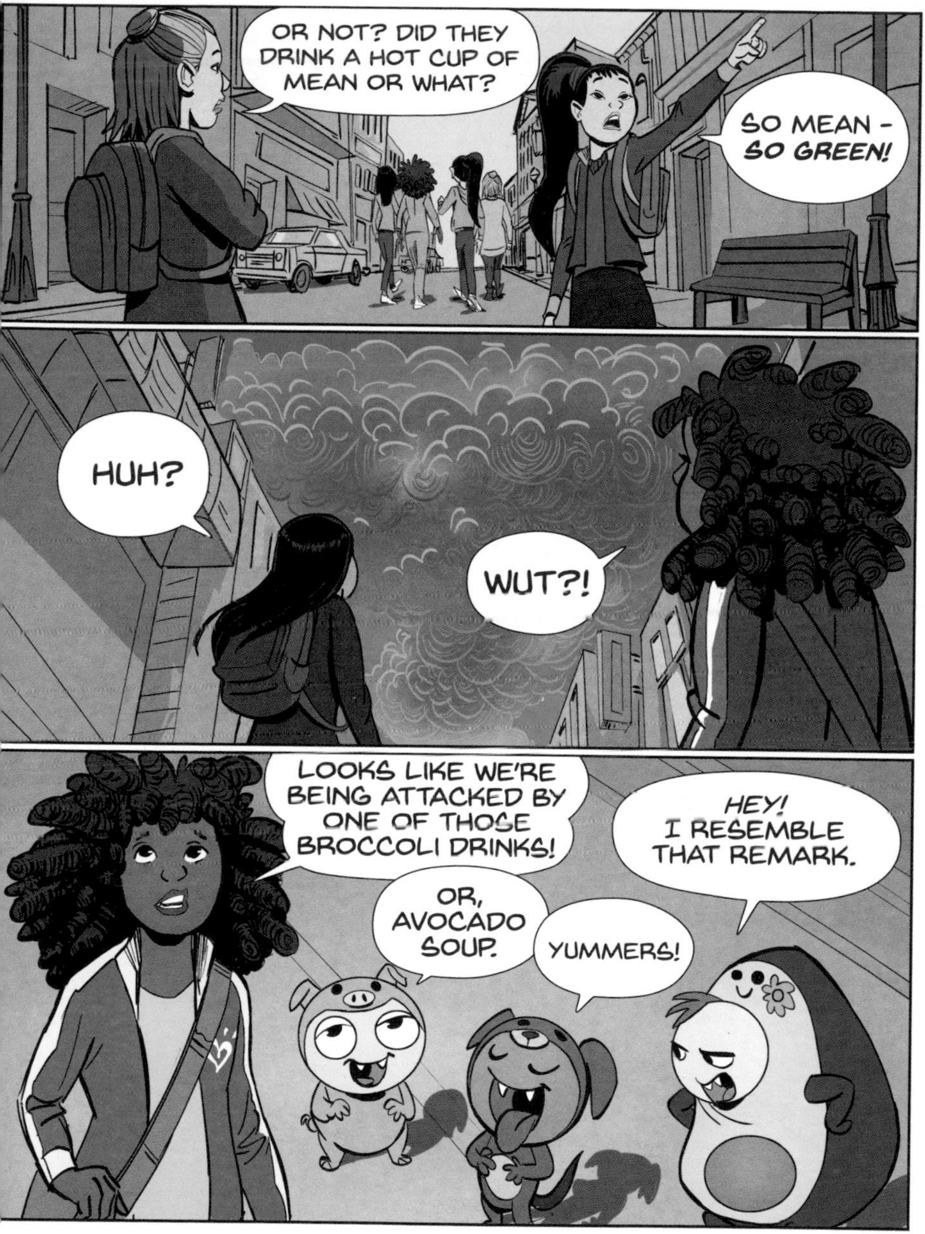
OR NOT? DID THEY DRINK A HOT CUP OF MEAN OR WHAT?
SO MEAN - SO GREEN!
HUH?
WUT?!
LOOKS LIKE WE'RE BEING ATTACKED BY ONE OF THOSE BROCCOLI DRINKS!
OR, AVOCADO SOUP.
YUMMERS!
HEY! I RESEMBLE THAT REMARK.

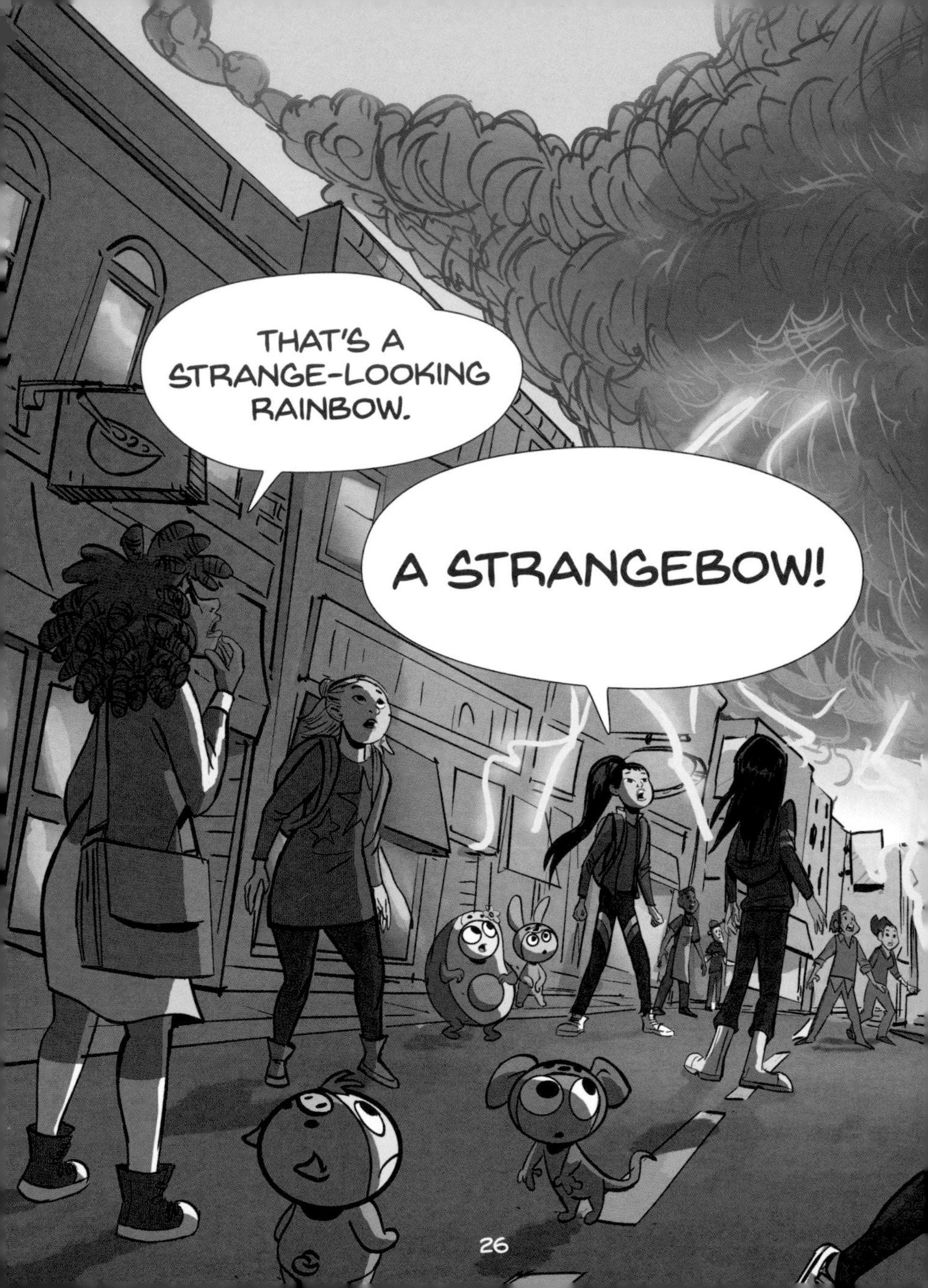
THAT'S A STRANGE-LOOKING RAINBOW.
A STRANGEBOW!

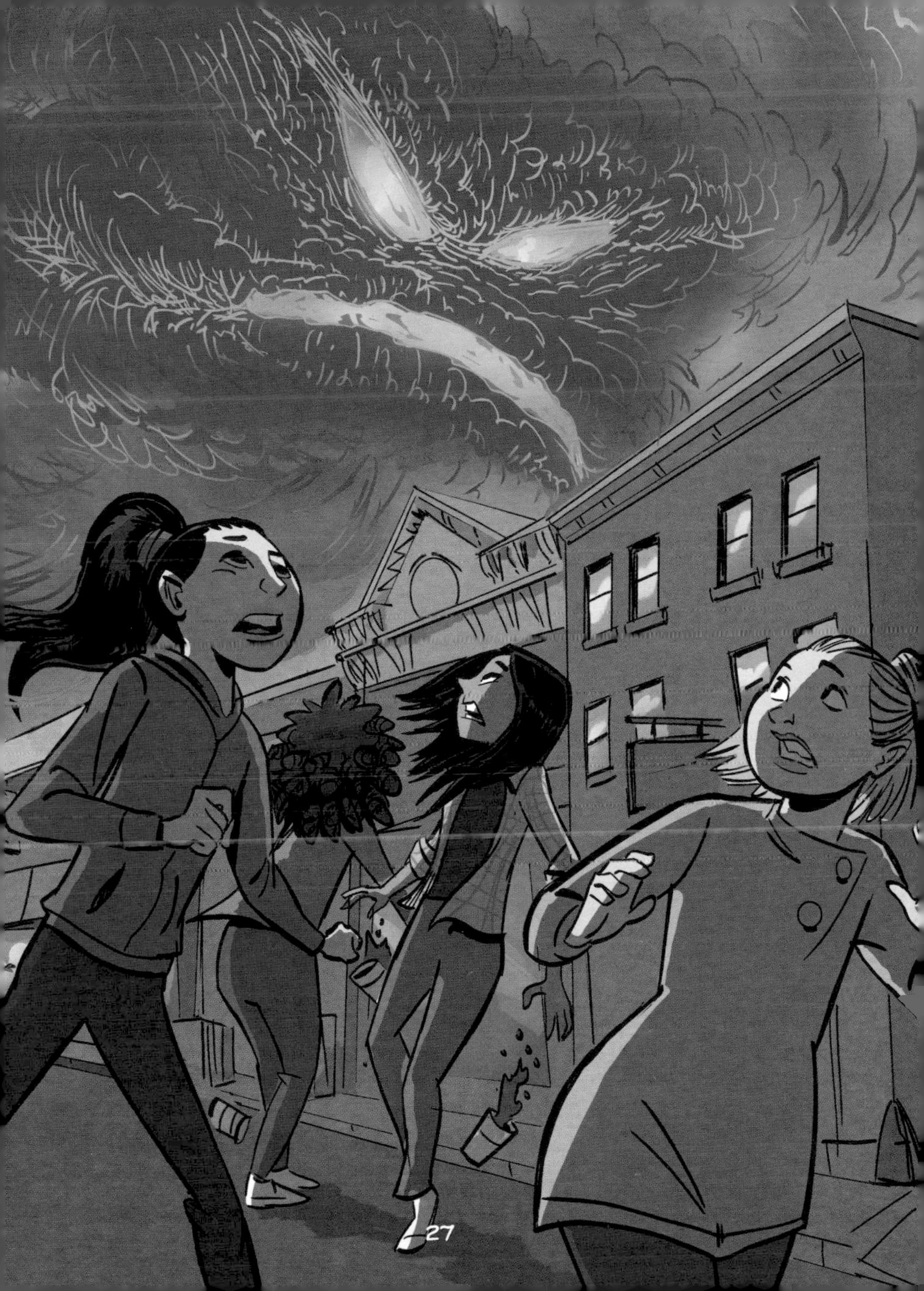

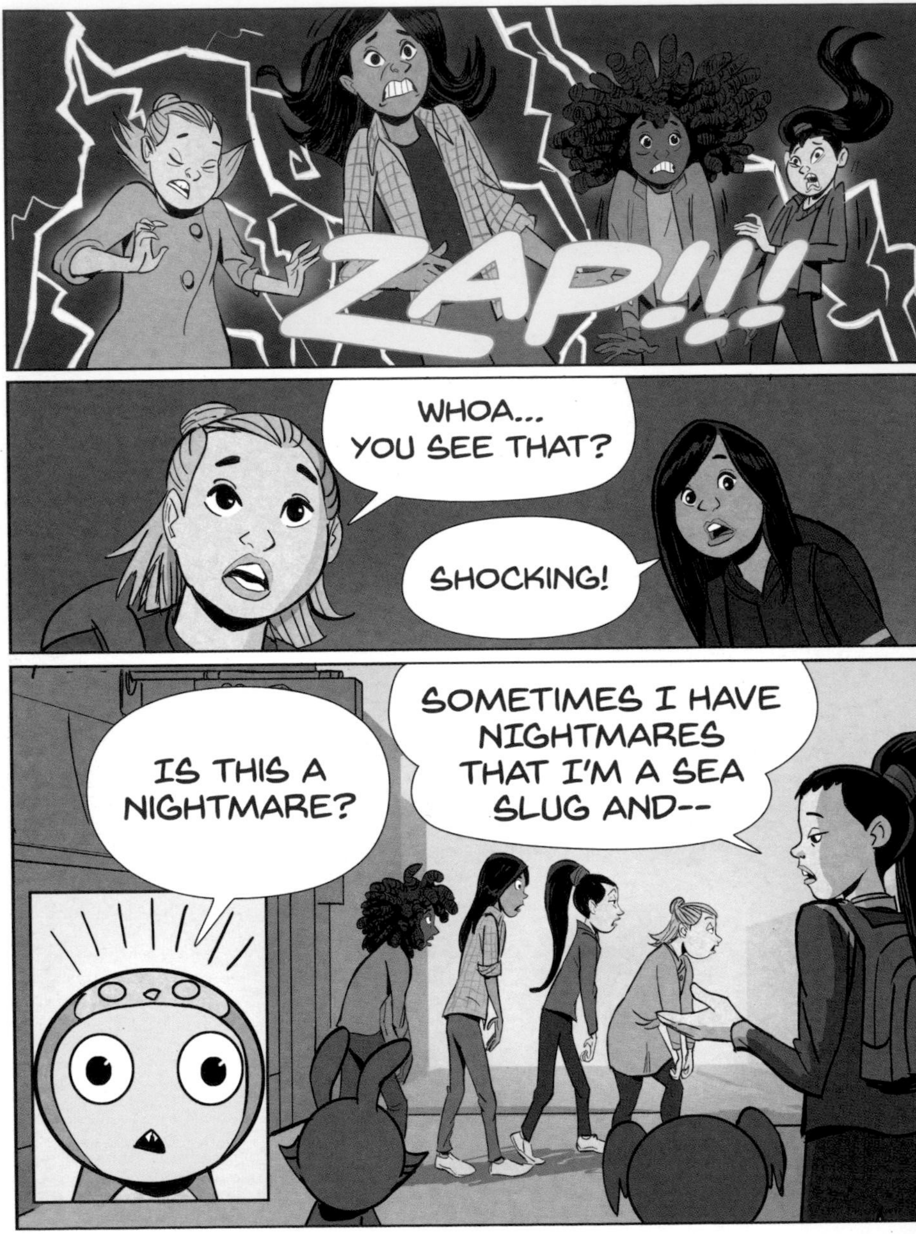
ZAP!!!
WHOA... YOU SEE THAT?
SHOCKING!
IS THIS A NIGHTMARE?
SOMETIMES I HAVE NIGHTMARES THAT I'M A SEA SLUG AND--

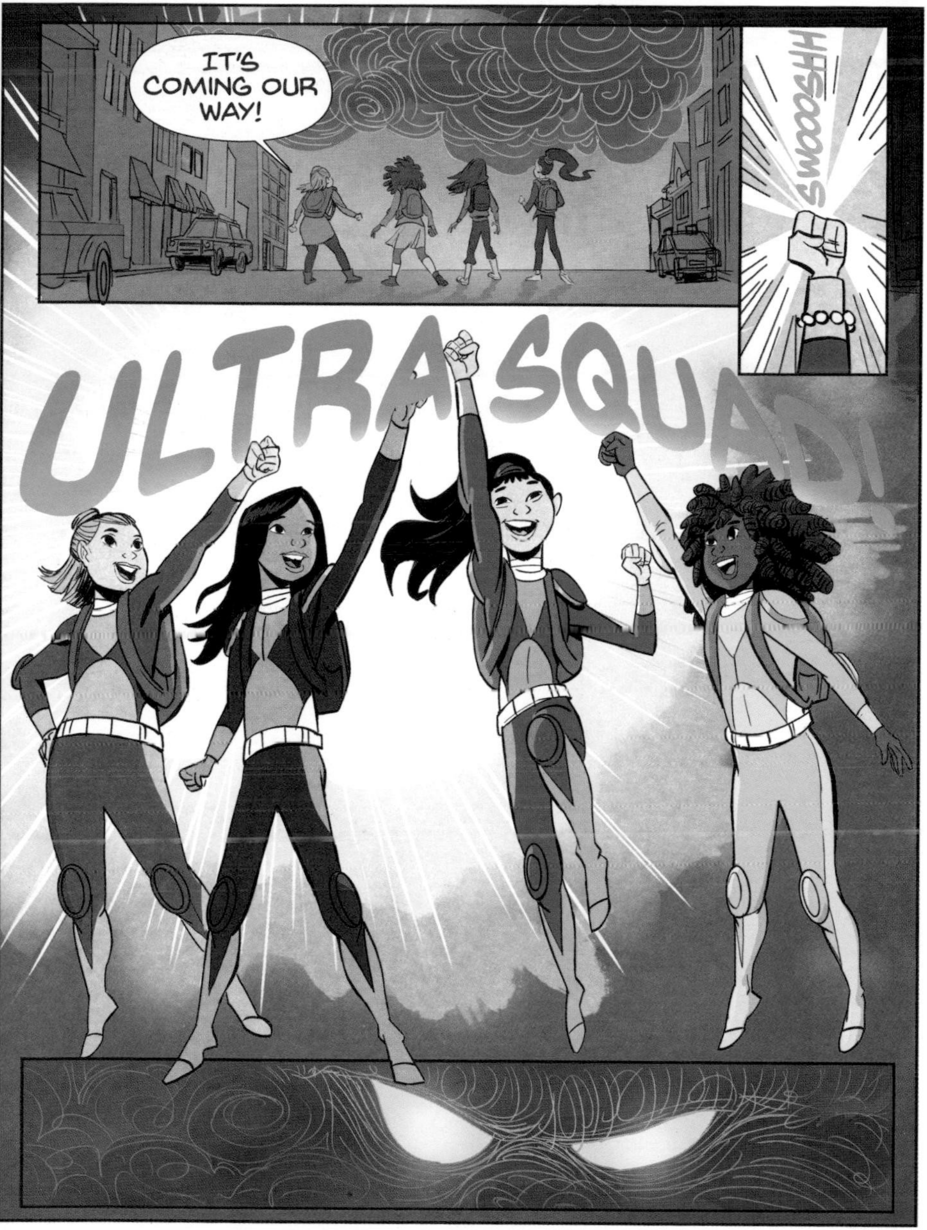
IT'S COMING OUR WAY!
SWOOOSH
ULTRA SQUAD!

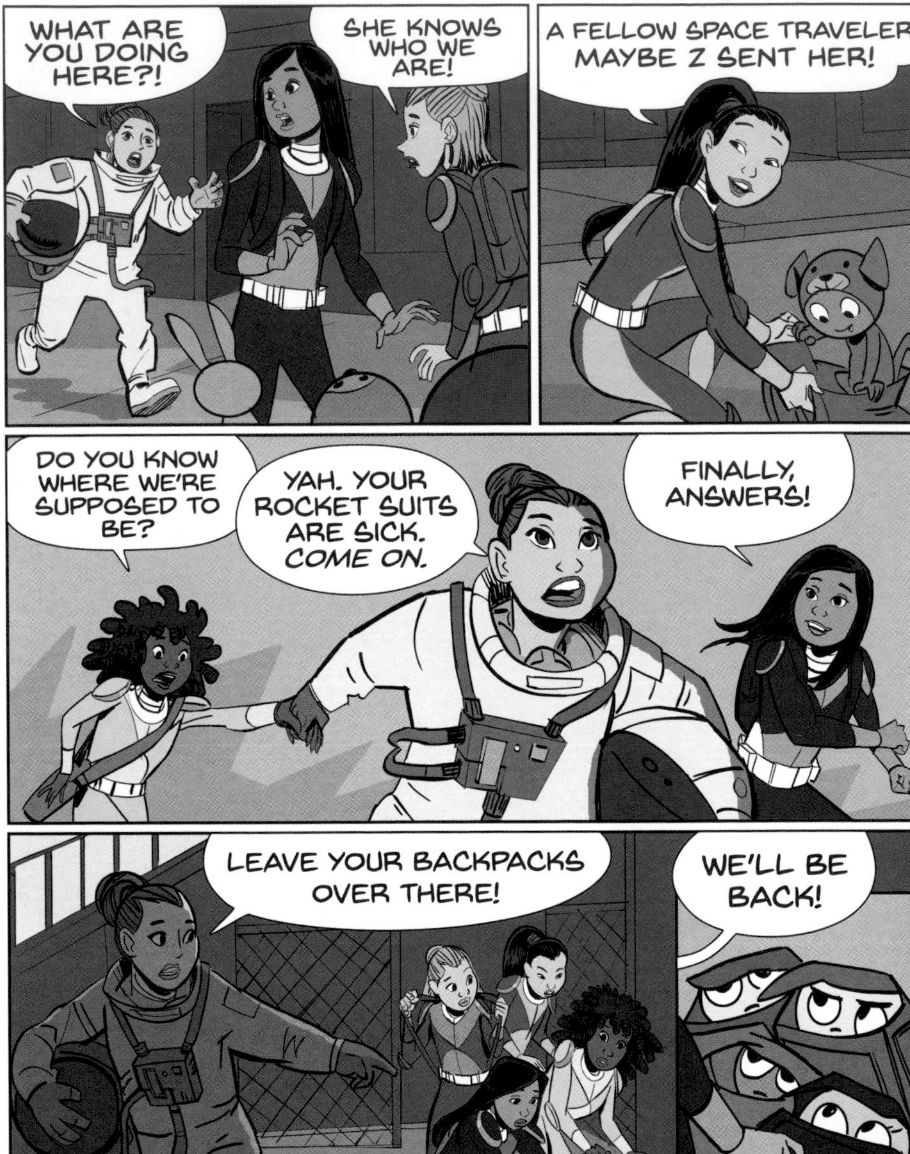
WHAT ARE YOU DOING HERE?!
SHE KNOWS WHO WE ARE!
A FELLOW SPACE TRAVELER! MAYBE Z SENT HER!
DO YOU KNOW WHERE WE'RE SUPPOSED TO BE?
YAH. YOUR ROCKET SUITS ARE SICK. COME ON.
FINALLY, ANSWERS!
LEAVE YOUR BACKPACKS OVER THERE!
WE'LL BE BACK!

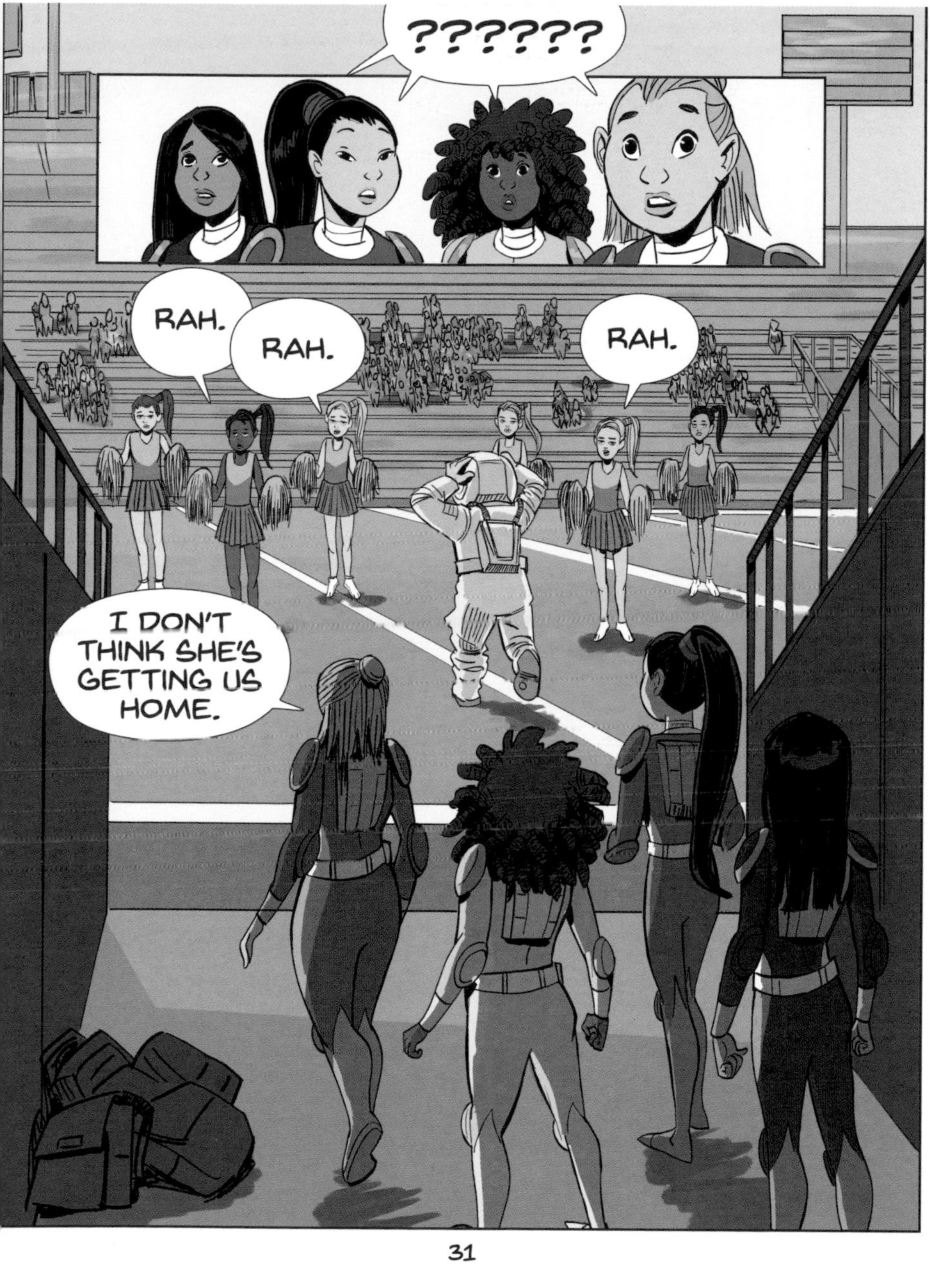
??????
RAH.
RAH.
RAH.
I DON'T THINK SHE'S GETTING US HOME.

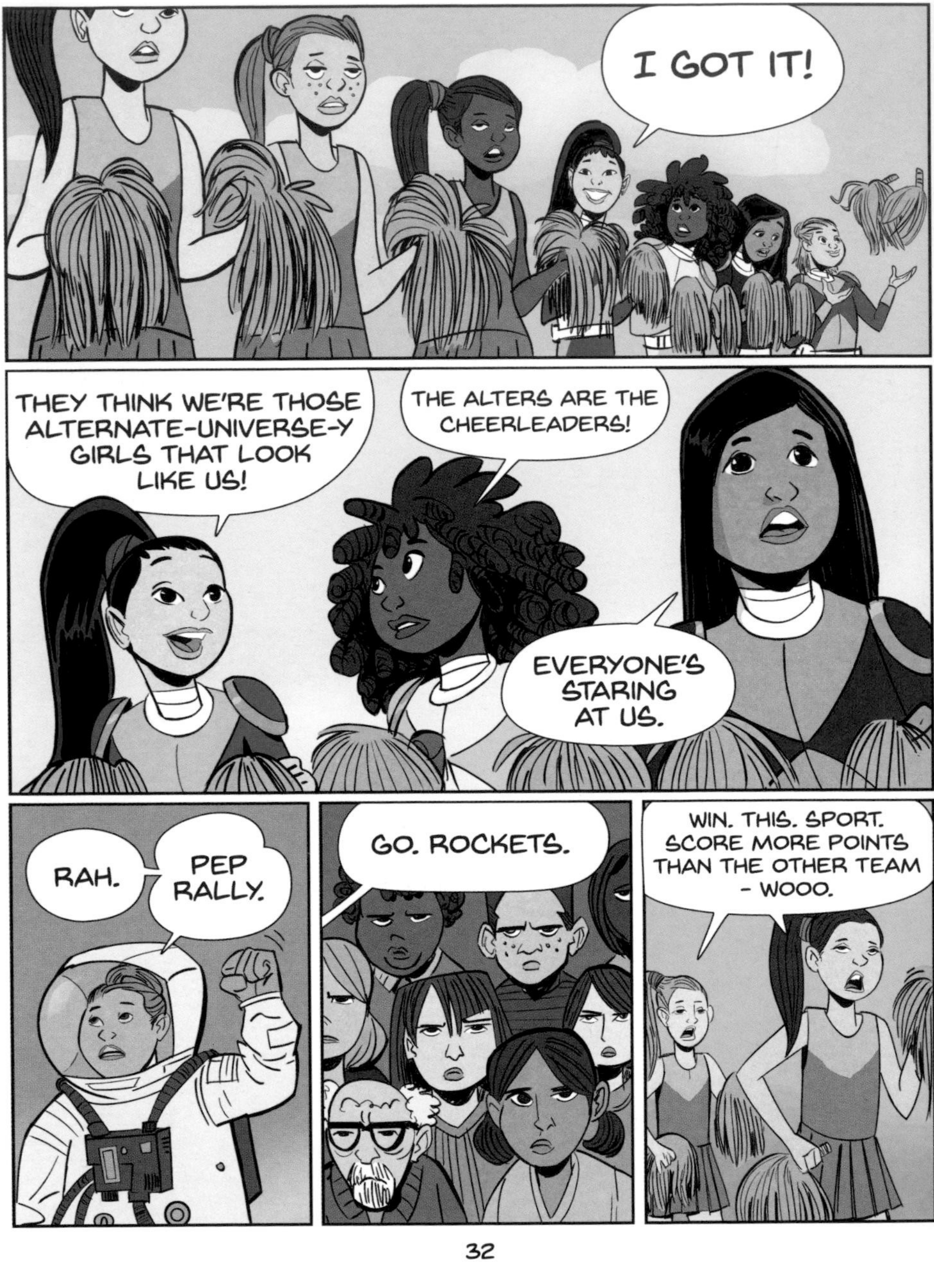
I GOT IT!
THEY THINK WE'RE THOSE ALTERNATE-UNIVERSE-Y GIRLS THAT LOOK LIKE US!
THE ALTERS ARE THE CHEERLEADERS!
EVERYONE'S STARING AT US.
RAH.
PEP RALLY.
GO. ROCKETS.
WIN. THIS. SPORT. SCORE MORE POINTS THAN THE OTHER TEAM - WOOO.

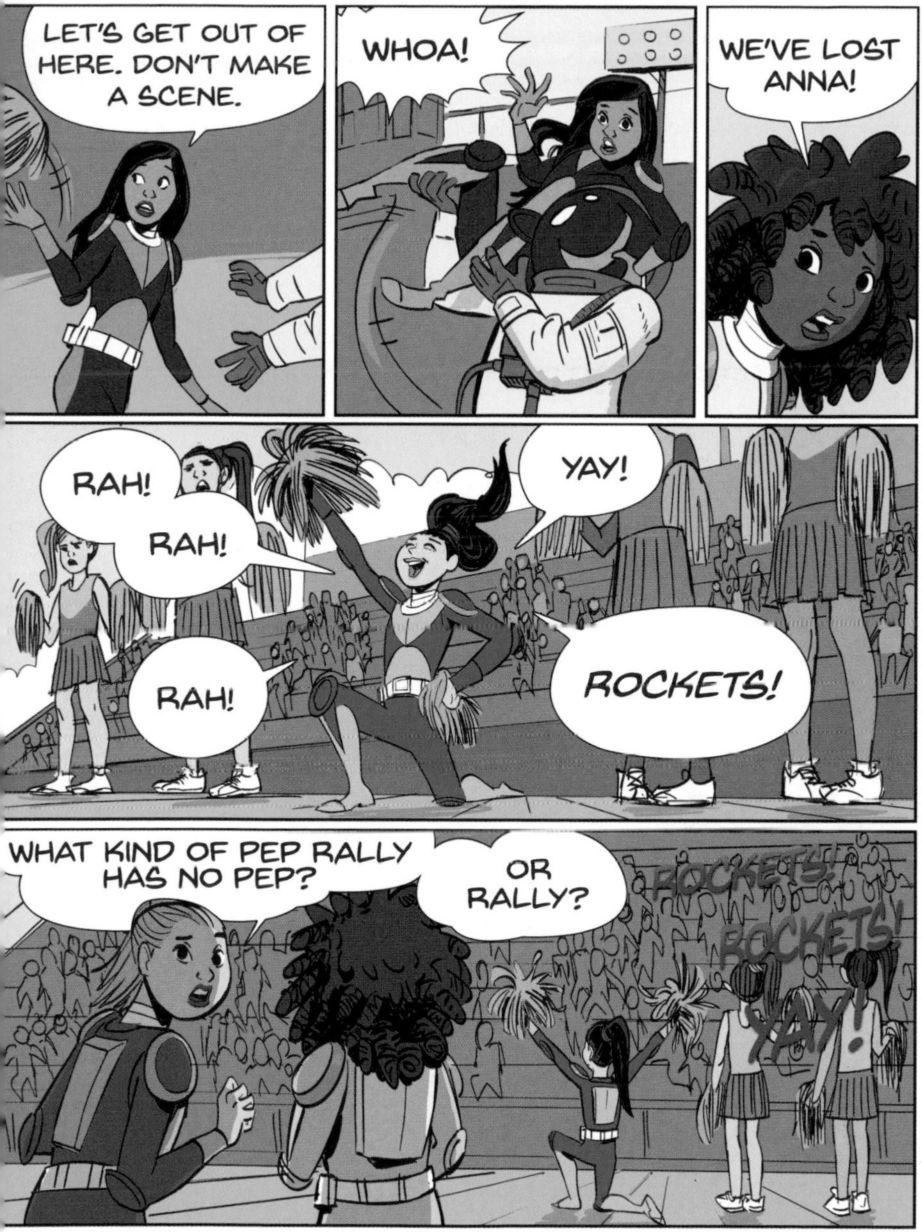
LET'S GET OUT OF HERE. DON'T MAKE A SCENE.
WHOA!
WE'VE LOST ANNA!
RAH!
RAH!
YAY!
RAH!
ROCKETS!
WHAT KIND OF PEP RALLY HAS NO PEP?
OR RALLY?
ROCKETS!
ROCKETS!
YAY!

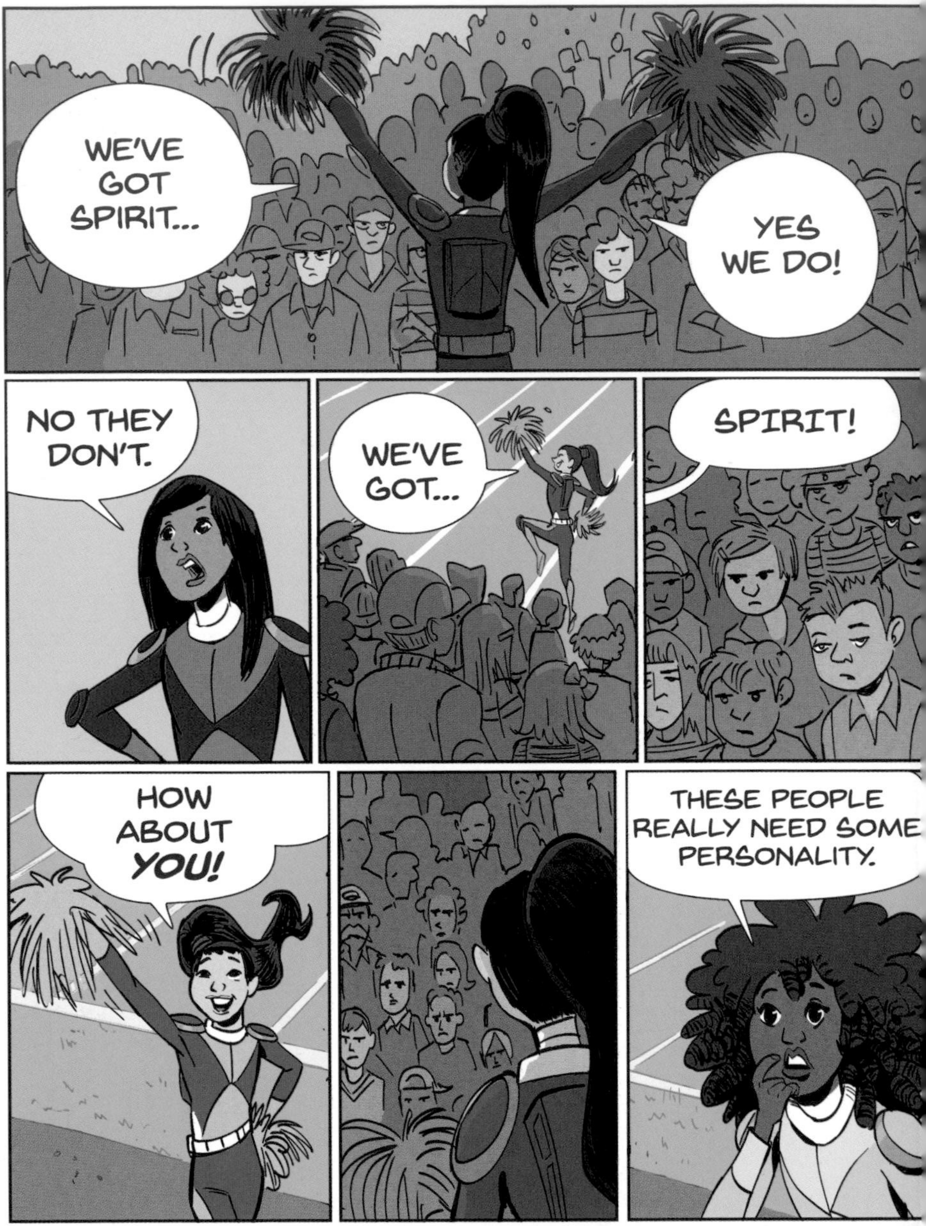
WE'VE GOT SPIRIT...
YES WE DO!
NO THEY DON'T.
WE'VE GOT...
SPIRIT!
HOW ABOUT *YOU!*
THESE PEOPLE REALLY NEED SOME PERSONALITY.

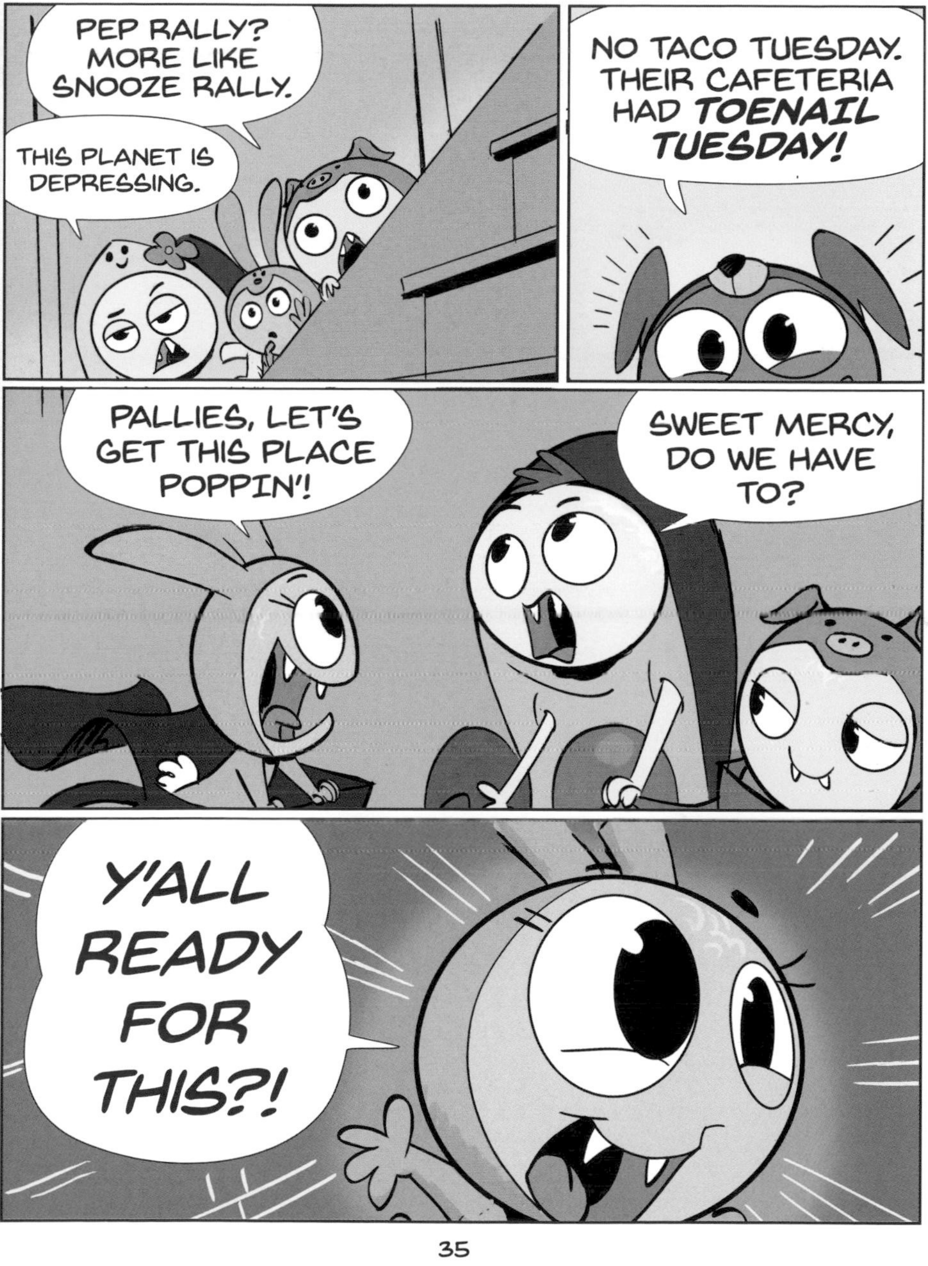
PEP RALLY? MORE LIKE SNOOZE RALLY.
THIS PLANET IS DEPRESSING.
NO TACO TUESDAY. THEIR CAFETERIA HAD ***TOENAIL TUESDAY!***
PALLIES, LET'S GET THIS PLACE POPPIN'!
SWEET MERCY, DO WE HAVE TO?
Y'ALL READY FOR THIS?!

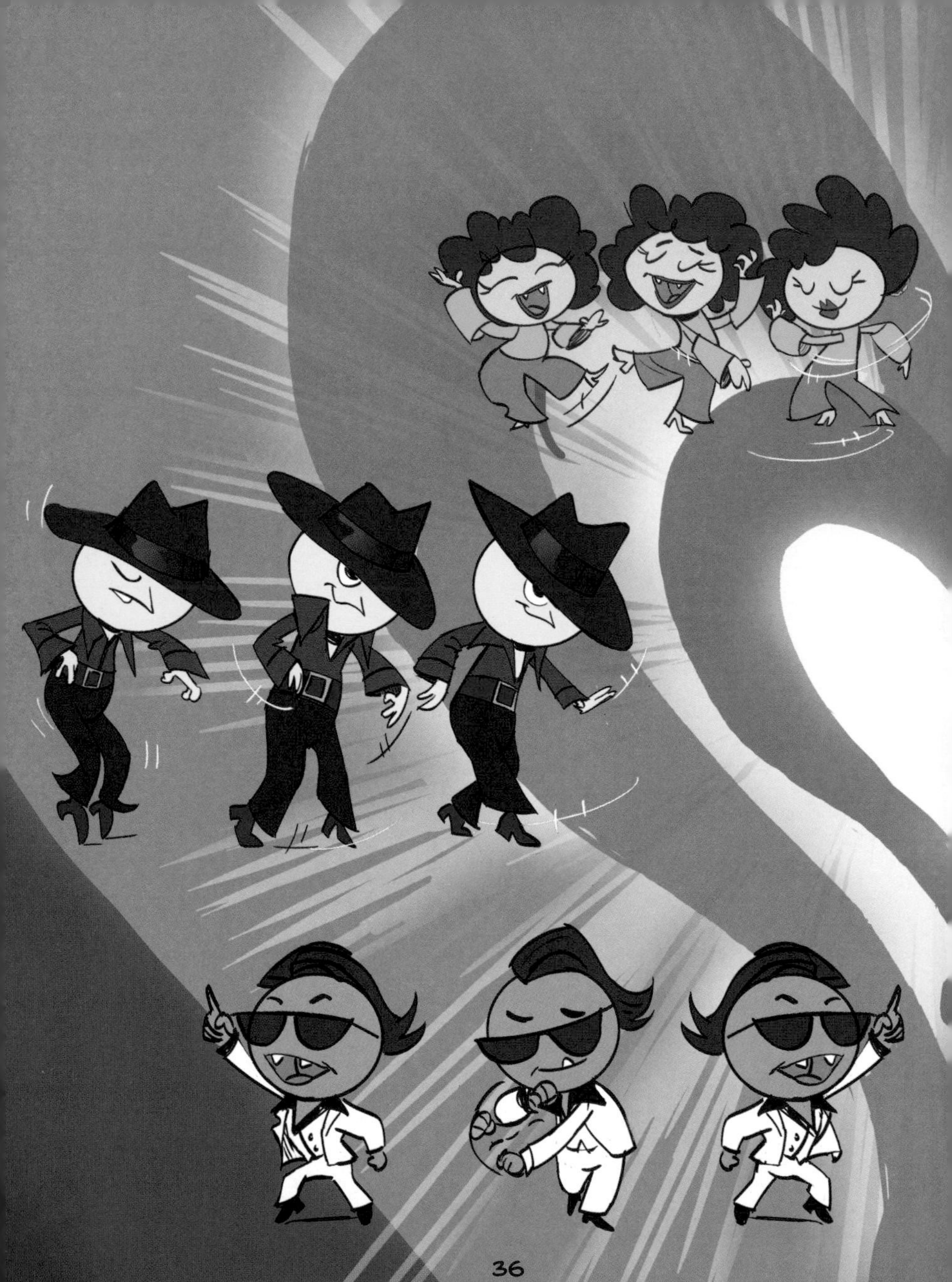

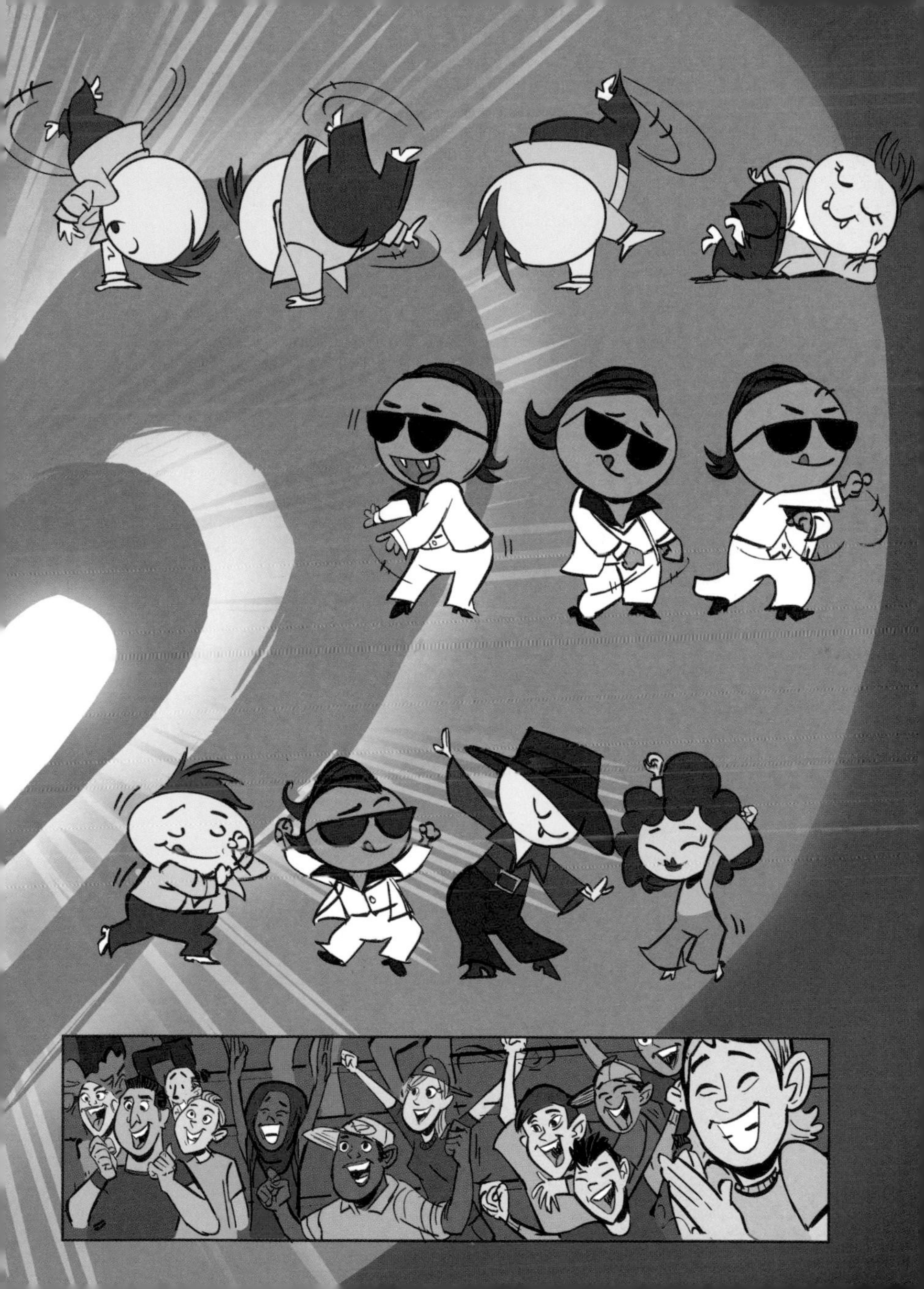

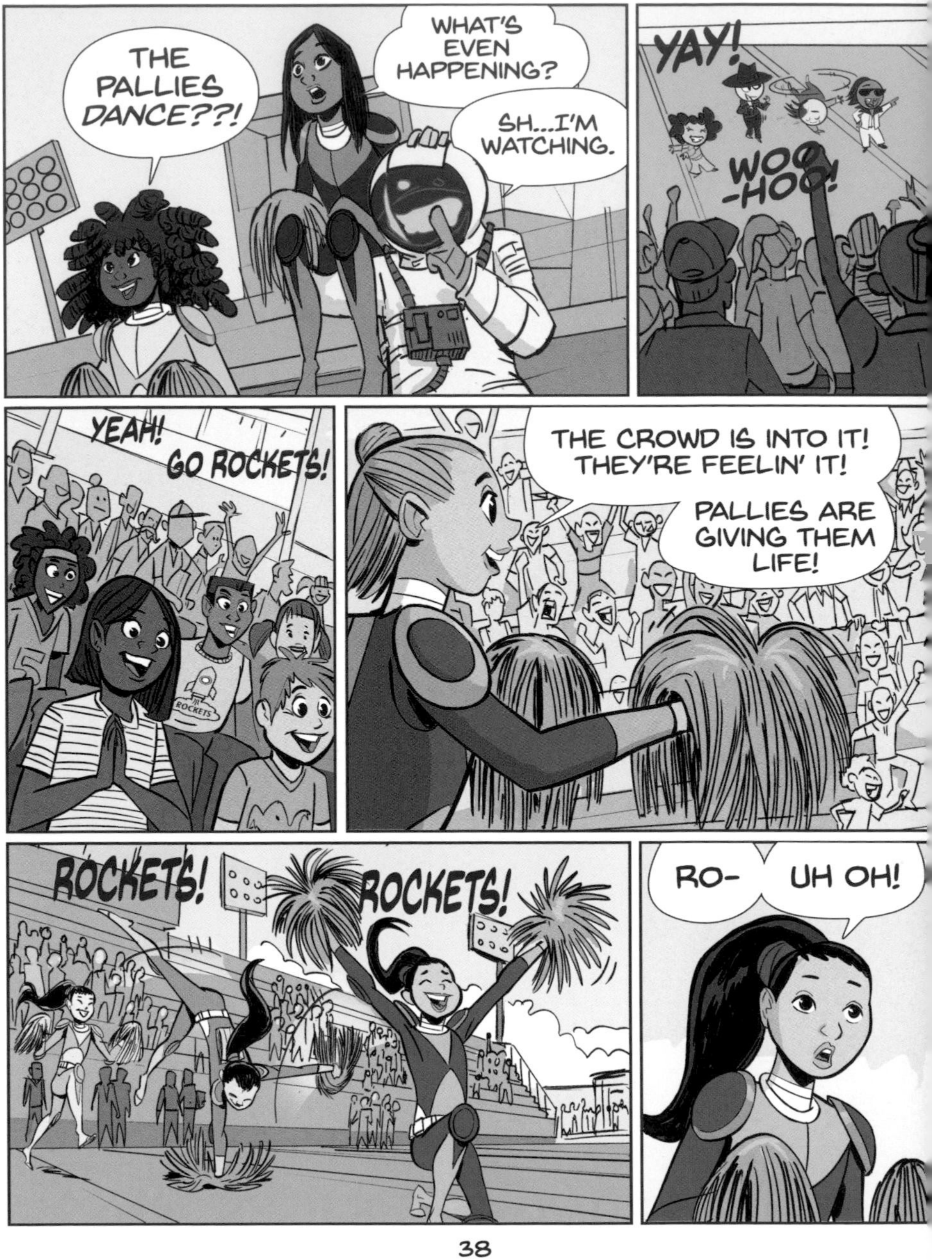
THE PALLIES DANCE??!
WHAT'S EVEN HAPPENING?
SH...I'M WATCHING.
YAY!
WOO -HOO!
YEAH!
GO ROCKETS!
ROCKETS
THE CROWD IS INTO IT! THEY'RE FEELIN' IT!
PALLIES ARE GIVING THEM LIFE!
ROCKETS!
ROCKETS!
RO-
UH OH!

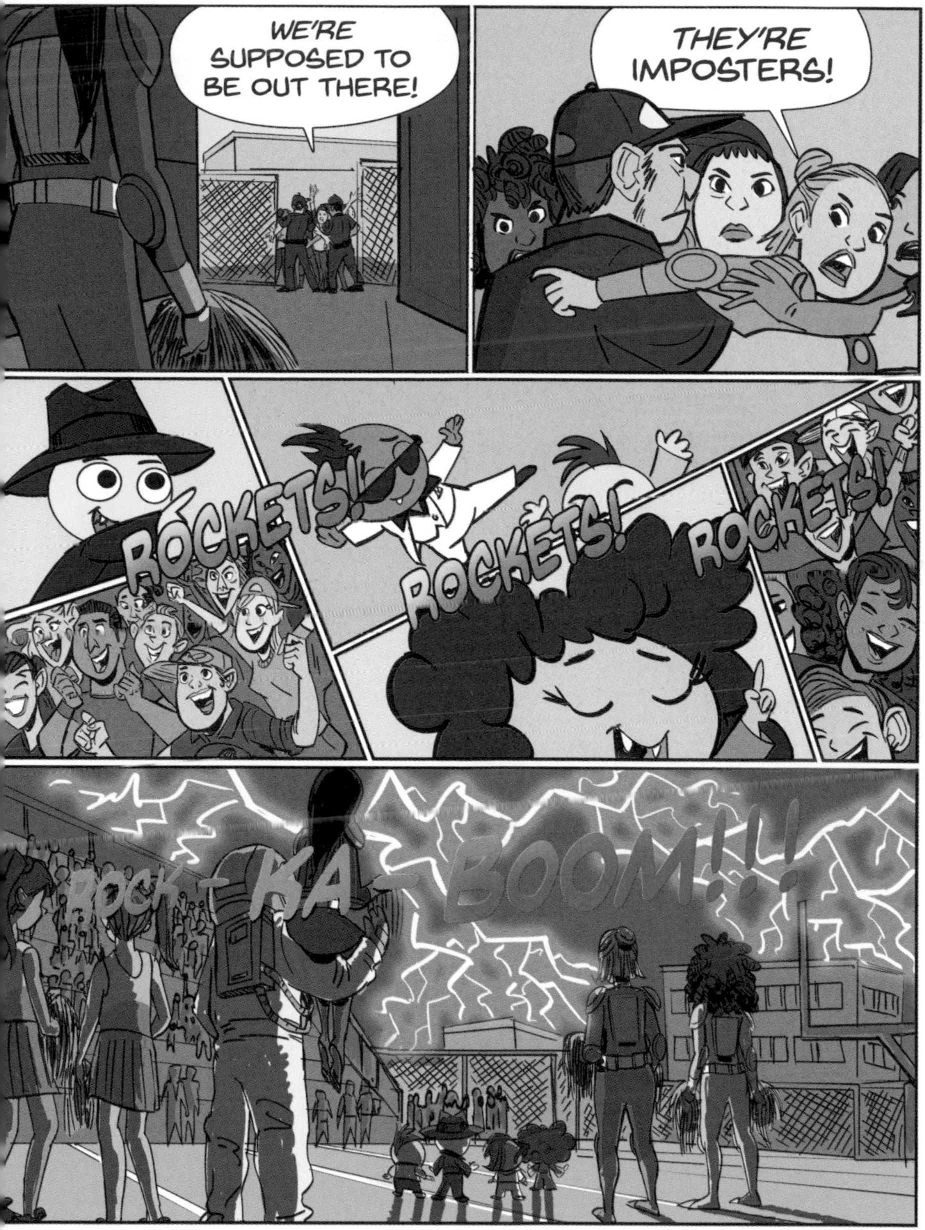
WE'RE SUPPOSED TO BE OUT THERE!
THEY'RE IMPOSTERS!
ROCKETS!
ROCKETS!
ROCKETS!
ROCK-KA-BOOM!!!

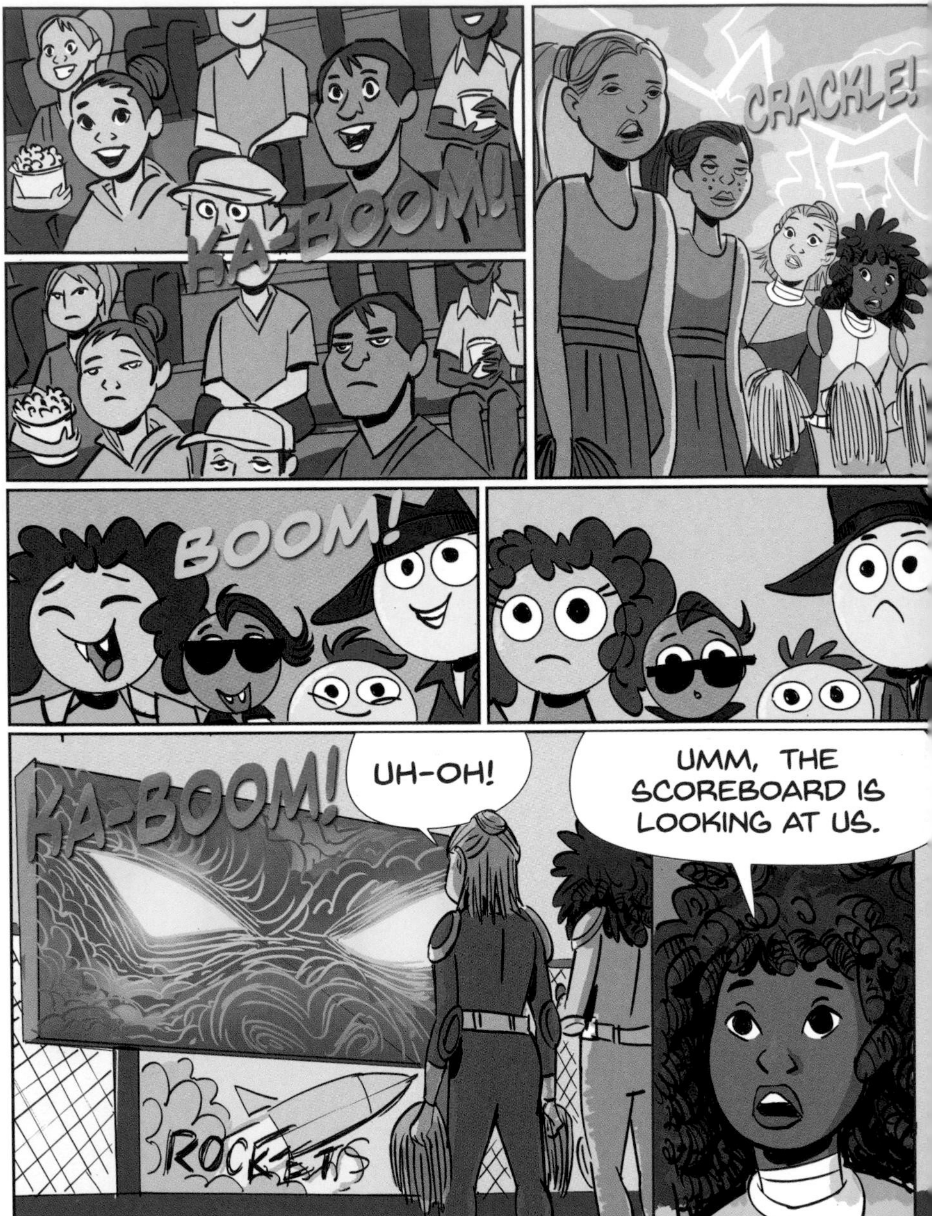
KA-BOOM!
CRACKLE!
BOOM!
KA-BOOM!
UH-OH!
UMM, THE SCOREBOARD IS LOOKING AT US.
ROCKETS

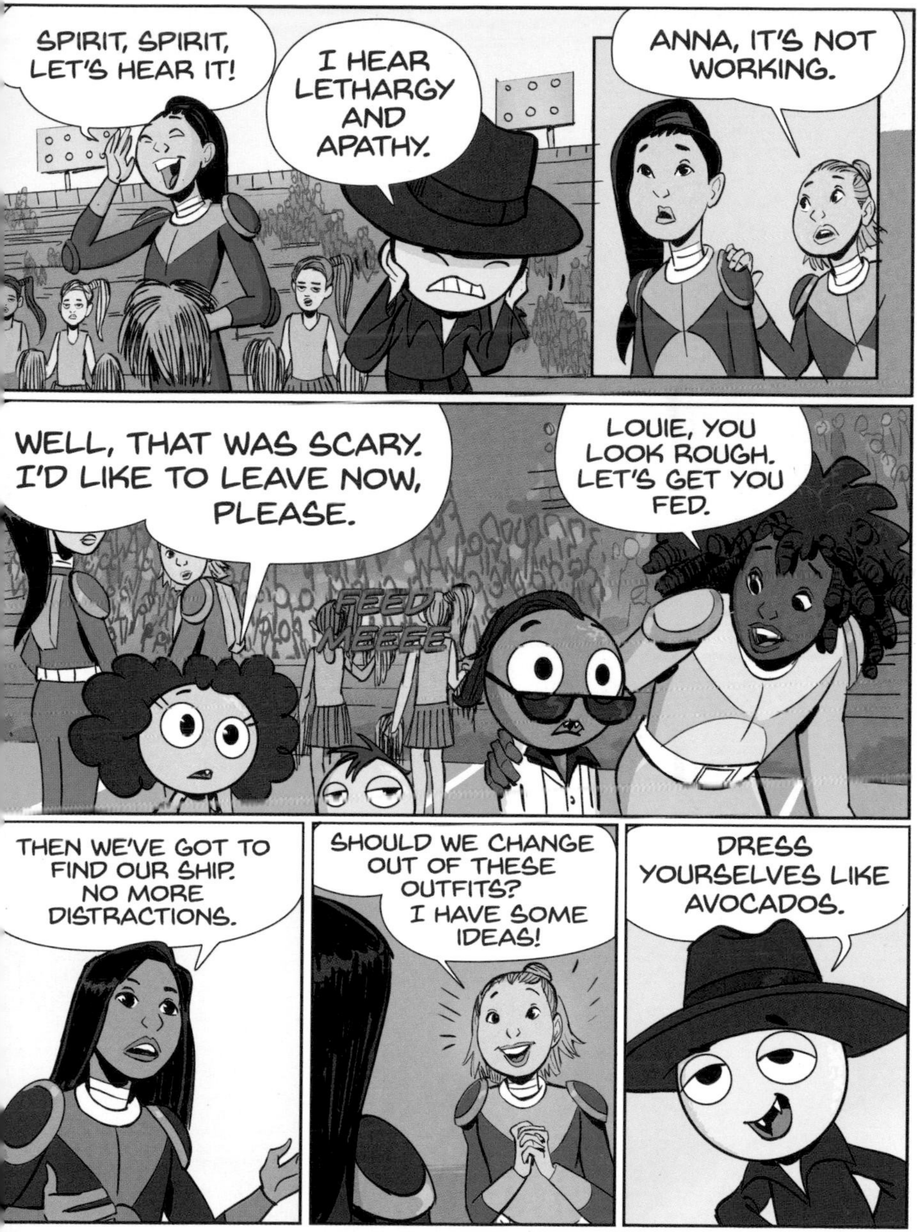
SPIRIT, SPIRIT, LET'S HEAR IT!
I HEAR LETHARGY AND APATHY.
ANNA, IT'S NOT WORKING.
WELL, THAT WAS SCARY. I'D LIKE TO LEAVE NOW, PLEASE.
LOUIE, YOU LOOK ROUGH. LET'S GET YOU FED.
FEED MEEEE
THEN WE'VE GOT TO FIND OUR SHIP. NO MORE DISTRACTIONS.
SHOULD WE CHANGE OUT OF THESE OUTFITS? I HAVE SOME IDEAS!
DRESS YOURSELVES LIKE AVOCADOS.

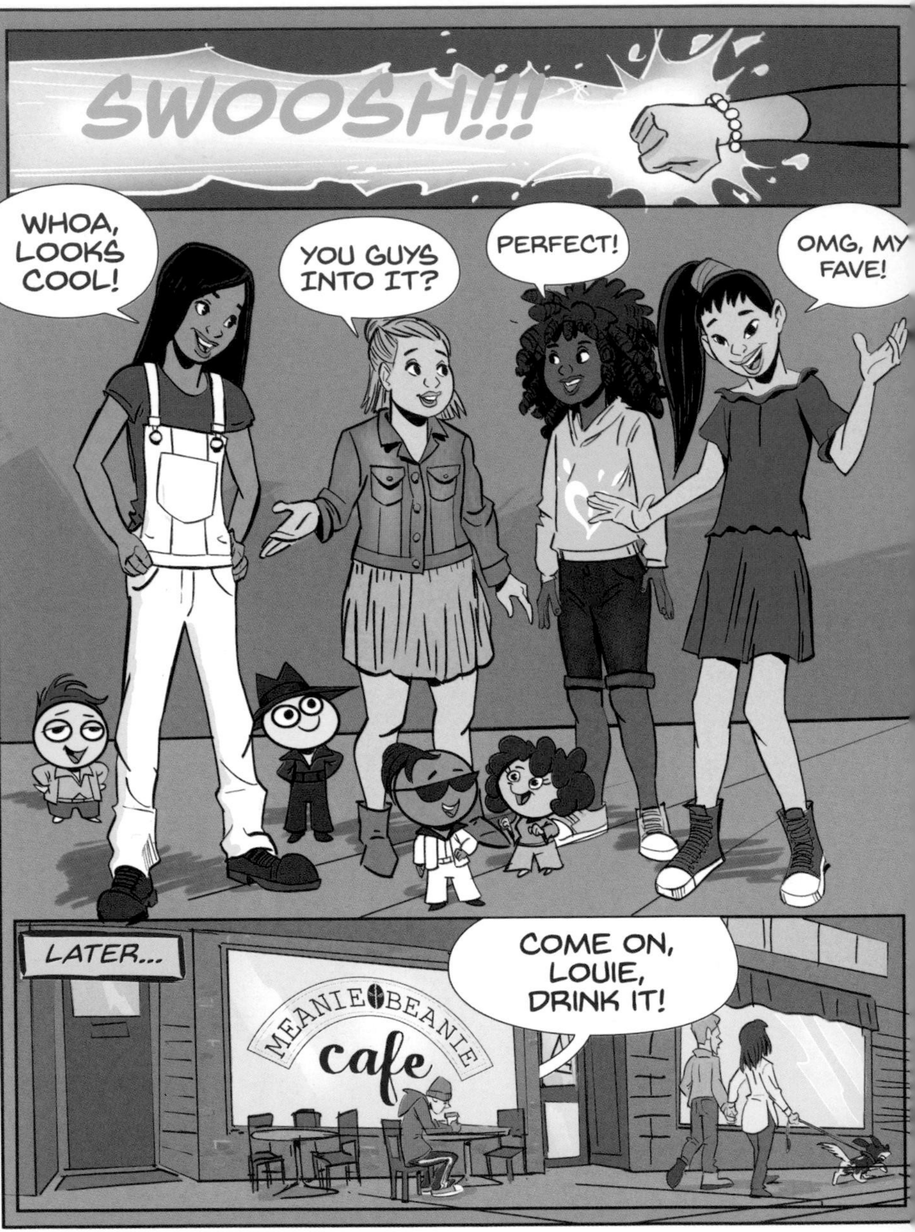
SWOOSH!!!
WHOA, LOOKS COOL!
YOU GUYS INTO IT?
PERFECT!
OMG, MY FAVE!
LATER...
MEANIE BEANIE cafe
COME ON, LOUIE, DRINK IT!

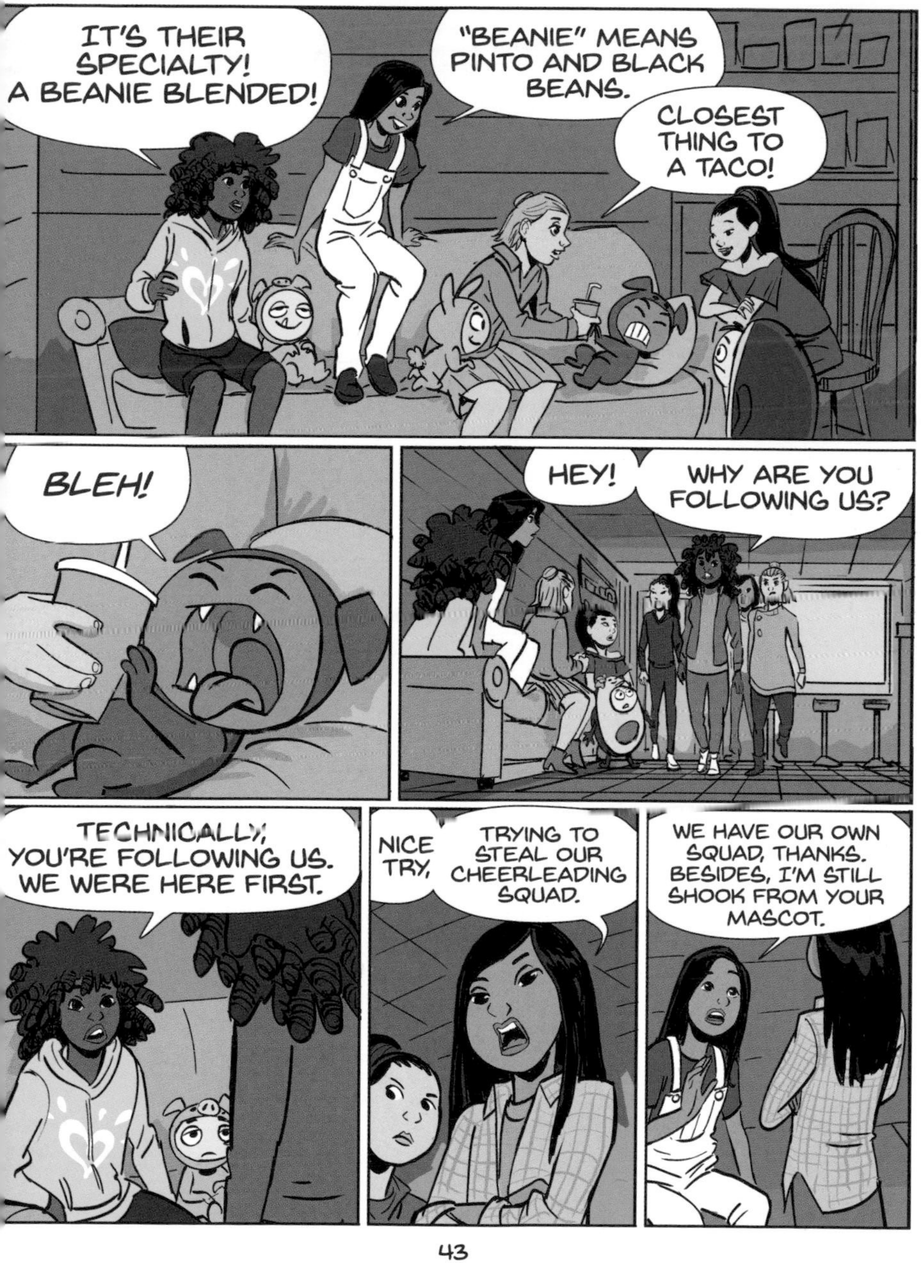
IT'S THEIR SPECIALTY! A BEANIE BLENDED!
"BEANIE" MEANS PINTO AND BLACK BEANS.
CLOSEST THING TO A TACO!
BLEH!
HEY!
WHY ARE YOU FOLLOWING US?
TECHNICALLY, YOU'RE FOLLOWING US. WE WERE HERE FIRST.
NICE TRY,
TRYING TO STEAL OUR CHEERLEADING SQUAD.
WE HAVE OUR OWN SQUAD, THANKS. BESIDES, I'M STILL SHOOK FROM YOUR MASCOT.

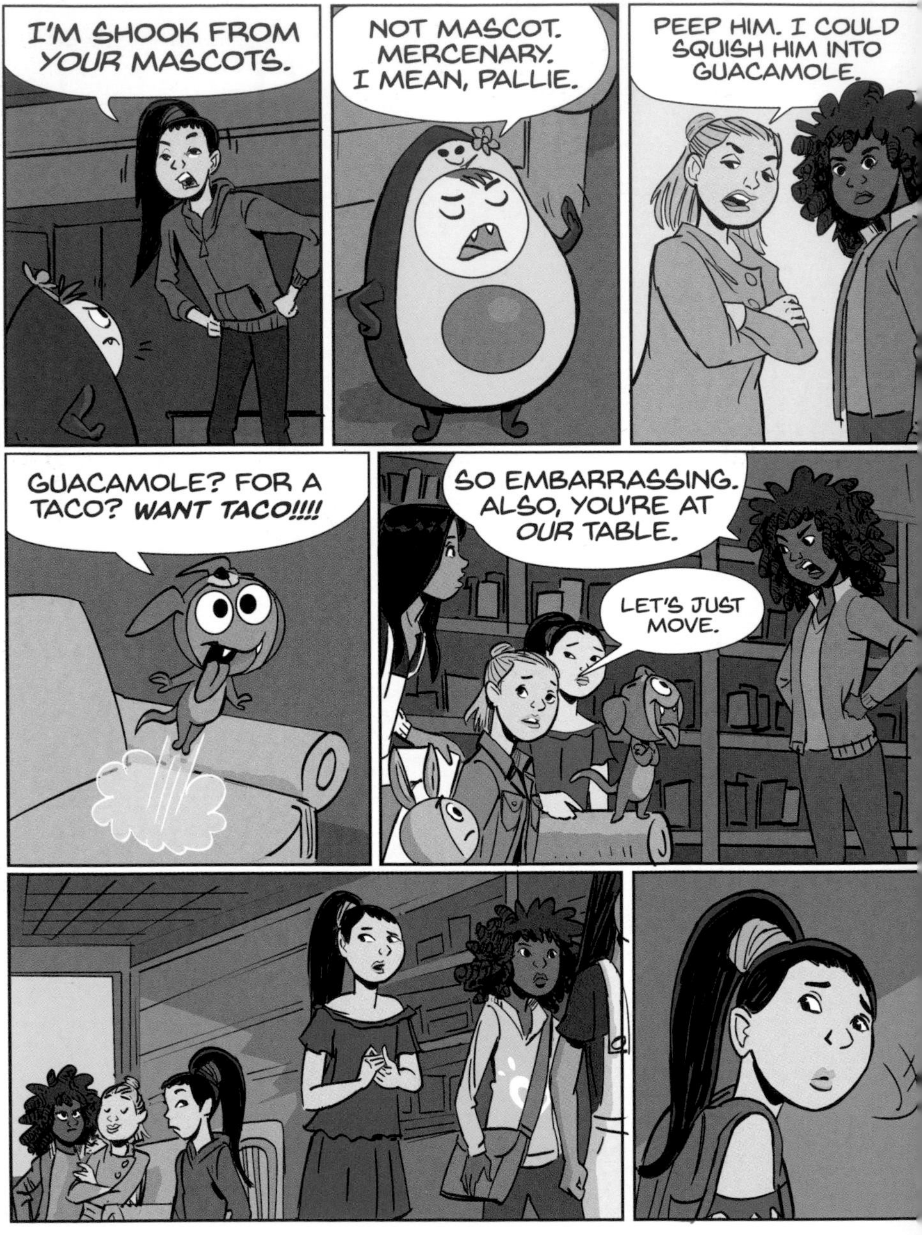

I'M SHOOK FROM YOUR MASCOTS.
NOT MASCOT. MERCENARY. I MEAN, PALLIE.
PEEP HIM. I COULD SQUISH HIM INTO GUACAMOLE.
GUACAMOLE? FOR A TACO? *WANT TACO!!!!*
SO EMBARRASSING. ALSO, YOU'RE AT *OUR* TABLE.
LET'S JUST MOVE.

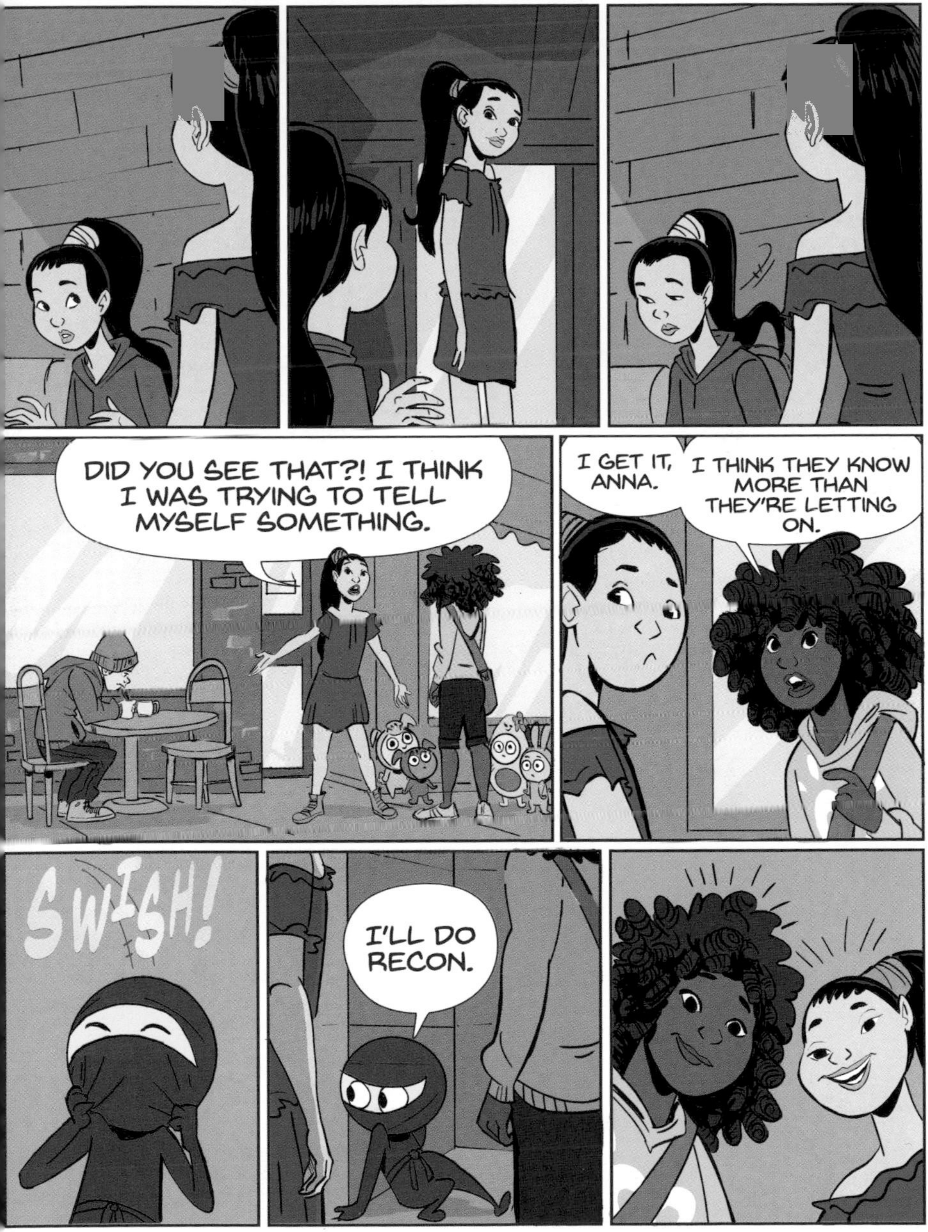
DID YOU SEE THAT?! I THINK I WAS TRYING TO TELL MYSELF SOMETHING.
I GET IT, ANNA.
I THINK THEY KNOW MORE THAN THEY'RE LETTING ON.
SWISH!
I'LL DO RECON.

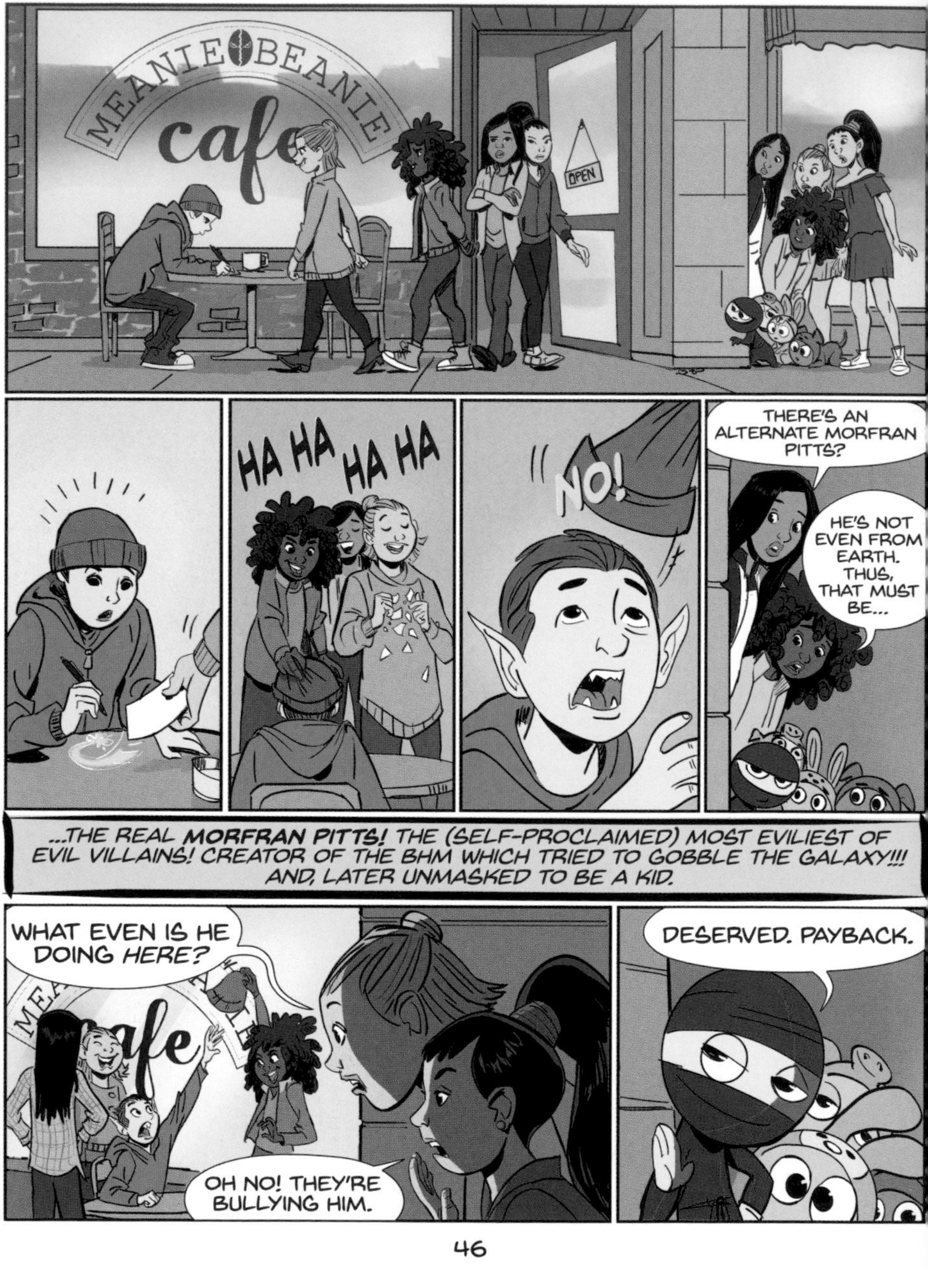
MEANIE BEANIE
cafe
OPEN
HA HA HA HA
NO!
THERE'S AN ALTERNATE MORFRAN PITTS?
HE'S NOT EVEN FROM EARTH. THUS, THAT MUST BE...
...THE REAL **MORFRAN PITTS!** THE (SELF-PROCLAIMED) MOST EVILIEST OF EVIL VILLAINS! CREATOR OF THE BHM WHICH TRIED TO GOBBLE THE GALAXY!!! AND, LATER UNMASKED TO BE A KID.
WHAT EVEN IS HE DOING *HERE?*
OH NO! THEY'RE BULLYING HIM.
DESERVED. PAYBACK.

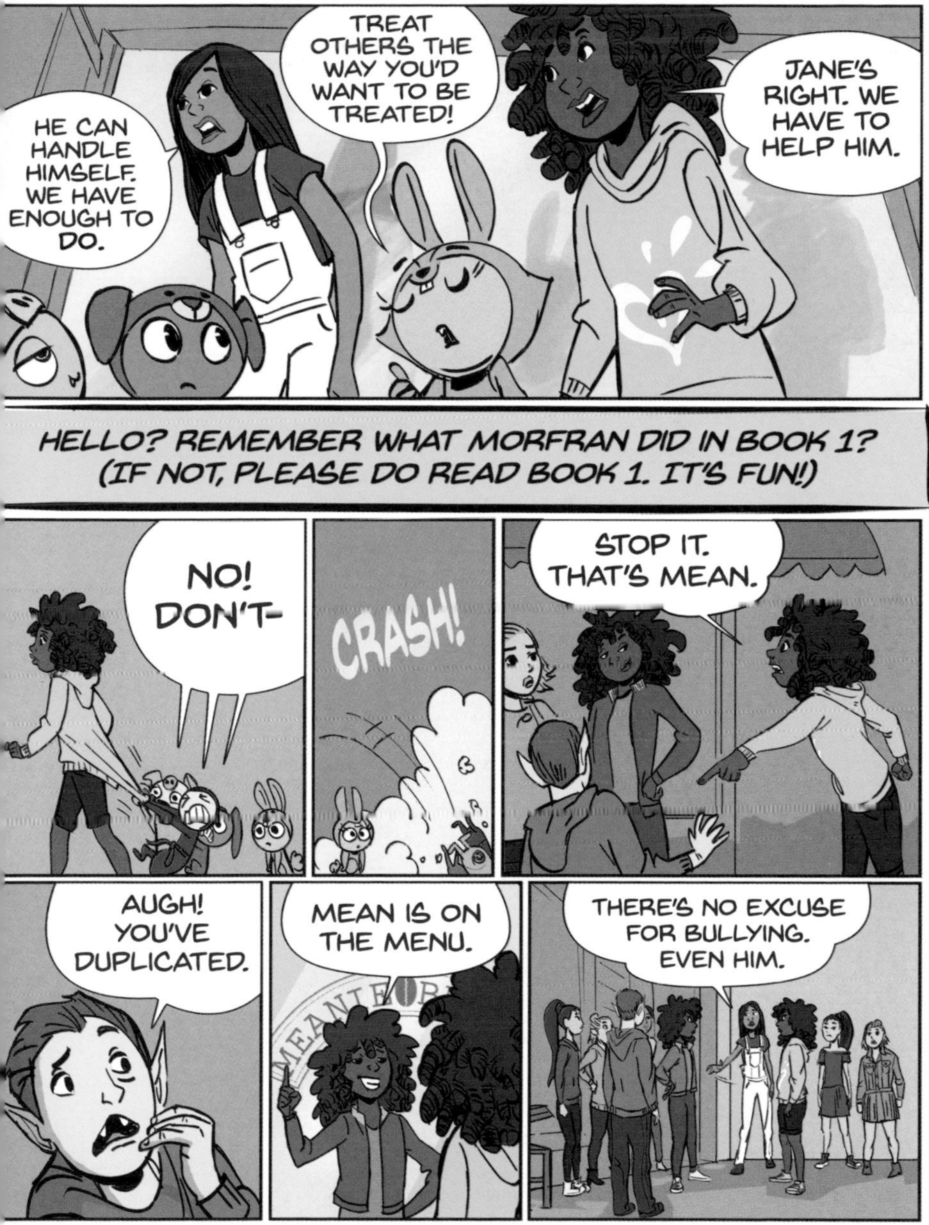

HE CAN HANDLE HIMSELF. WE HAVE ENOUGH TO DO.
TREAT OTHERS THE WAY YOU'D WANT TO BE TREATED!
JANE'S RIGHT. WE HAVE TO HELP HIM.
HELLO? REMEMBER WHAT MORFRAN DID IN BOOK 1? (IF NOT, PLEASE DO READ BOOK 1. IT'S FUN!)
NO! DON'T-
CRASH!
STOP IT. THAT'S MEAN.
AUGH! YOU'VE DUPLICATED.
MEAN IS ON THE MENU.
THERE'S NO EXCUSE FOR BULLYING. EVEN HIM.

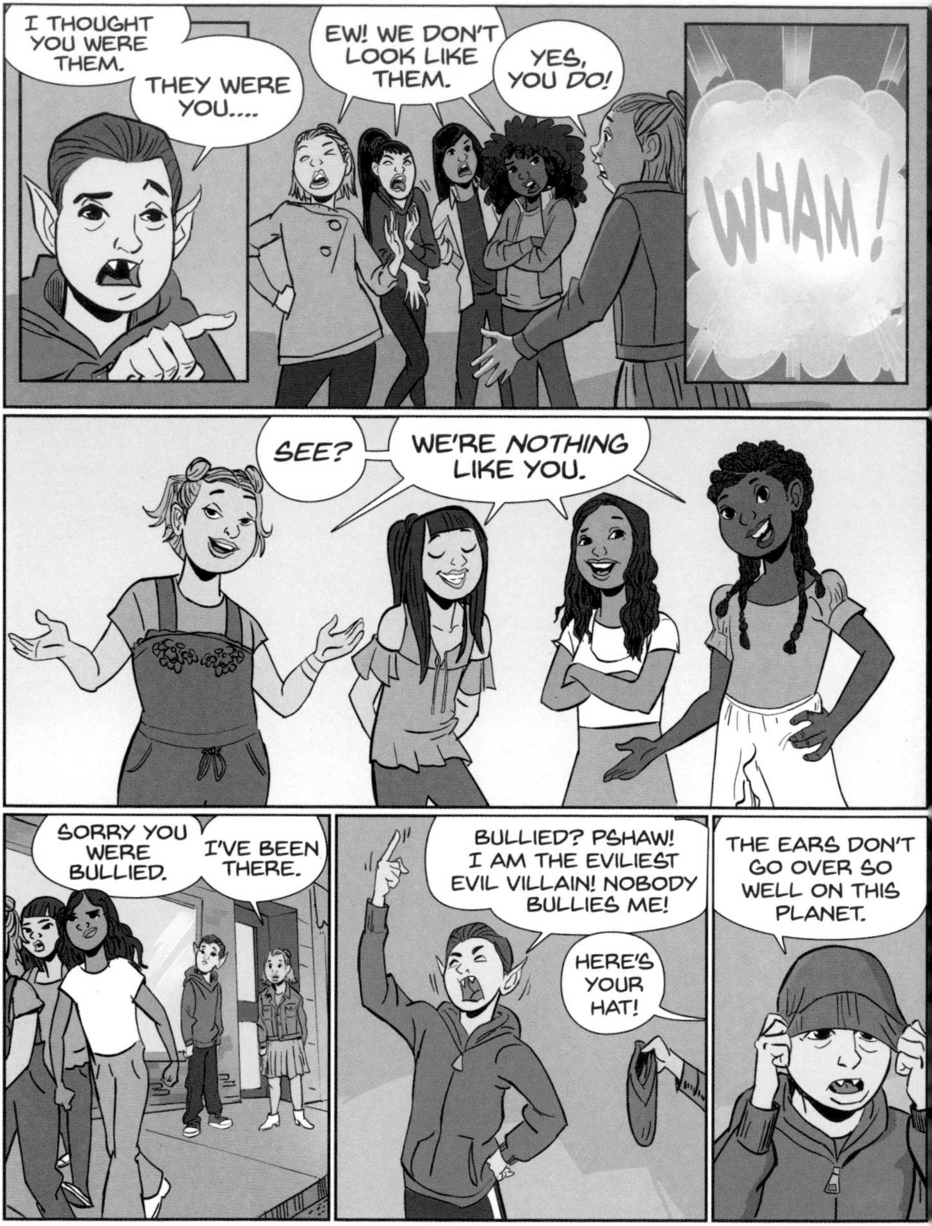
I THOUGHT YOU WERE THEM.
THEY WERE YOU....
EW! WE DON'T LOOK LIKE THEM.
YES, YOU DO!
WHAM!
SEE?
WE'RE NOTHING LIKE YOU.
SORRY YOU WERE BULLIED.
I'VE BEEN THERE.
BULLIED? PSHAW! I AM THE EVILIEST EVIL VILLAIN! NOBODY BULLIES ME!
HERE'S YOUR HAT!
THE EARS DON'T GO OVER SO WELL ON THIS PLANET.

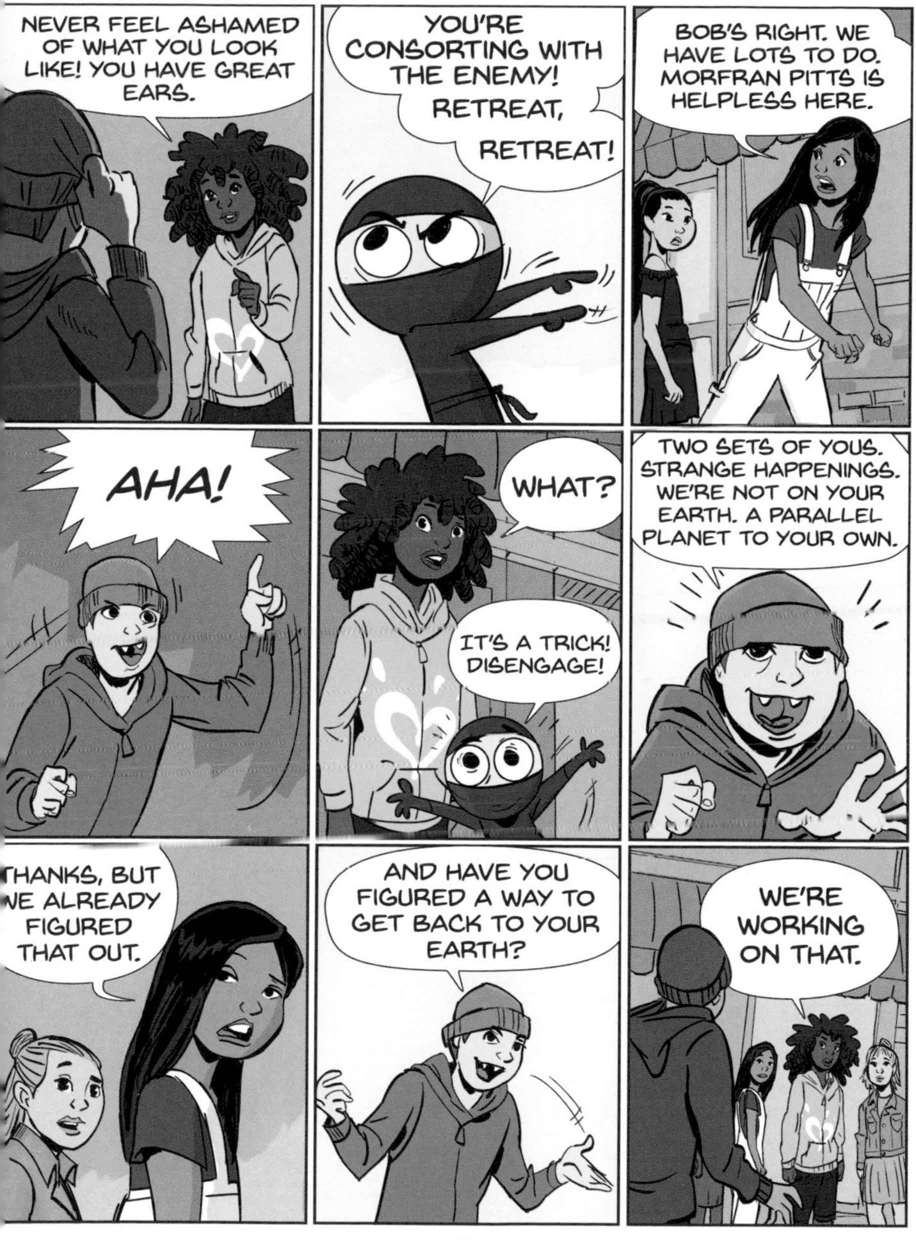
NEVER FEEL ASHAMED OF WHAT YOU LOOK LIKE! YOU HAVE GREAT EARS.
YOU'RE CONSORTING WITH THE ENEMY!
RETREAT,
RETREAT!
BOB'S RIGHT. WE HAVE LOTS TO DO. MORFRAN PITTS IS HELPLESS HERE.
AHA!
WHAT?
IT'S A TRICK! DISENGAGE!
TWO SETS OF YOUS. STRANGE HAPPENINGS. WE'RE NOT ON YOUR EARTH. A PARALLEL PLANET TO YOUR OWN.
THANKS, BUT WE ALREADY FIGURED THAT OUT.
AND HAVE YOU FIGURED A WAY TO GET BACK TO YOUR EARTH?
WE'RE WORKING ON THAT.

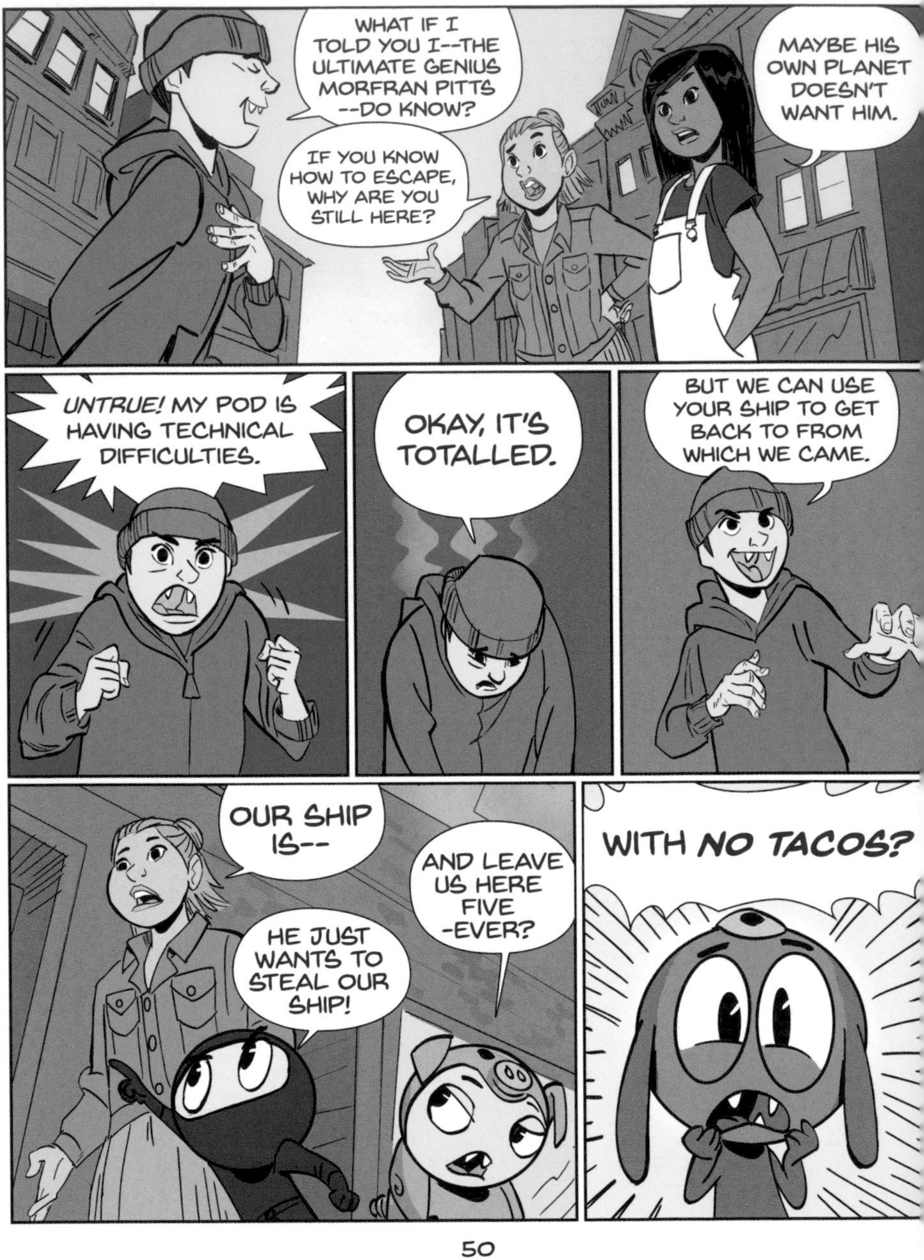
WHAT IF I TOLD YOU I--THE ULTIMATE GENIUS MORFRAN PITTS --DO KNOW?
IF YOU KNOW HOW TO ESCAPE, WHY ARE YOU STILL HERE?
MAYBE HIS OWN PLANET DOESN'T WANT HIM.
UNTRUE! MY POD IS HAVING TECHNICAL DIFFICULTIES.
OKAY, IT'S TOTALLED.
BUT WE CAN USE YOUR SHIP TO GET BACK TO FROM WHICH WE CAME.
OUR SHIP IS--
HE JUST WANTS TO STEAL OUR SHIP!
AND LEAVE US HERE FIVE -EVER?
WITH ***NO TACOS?***

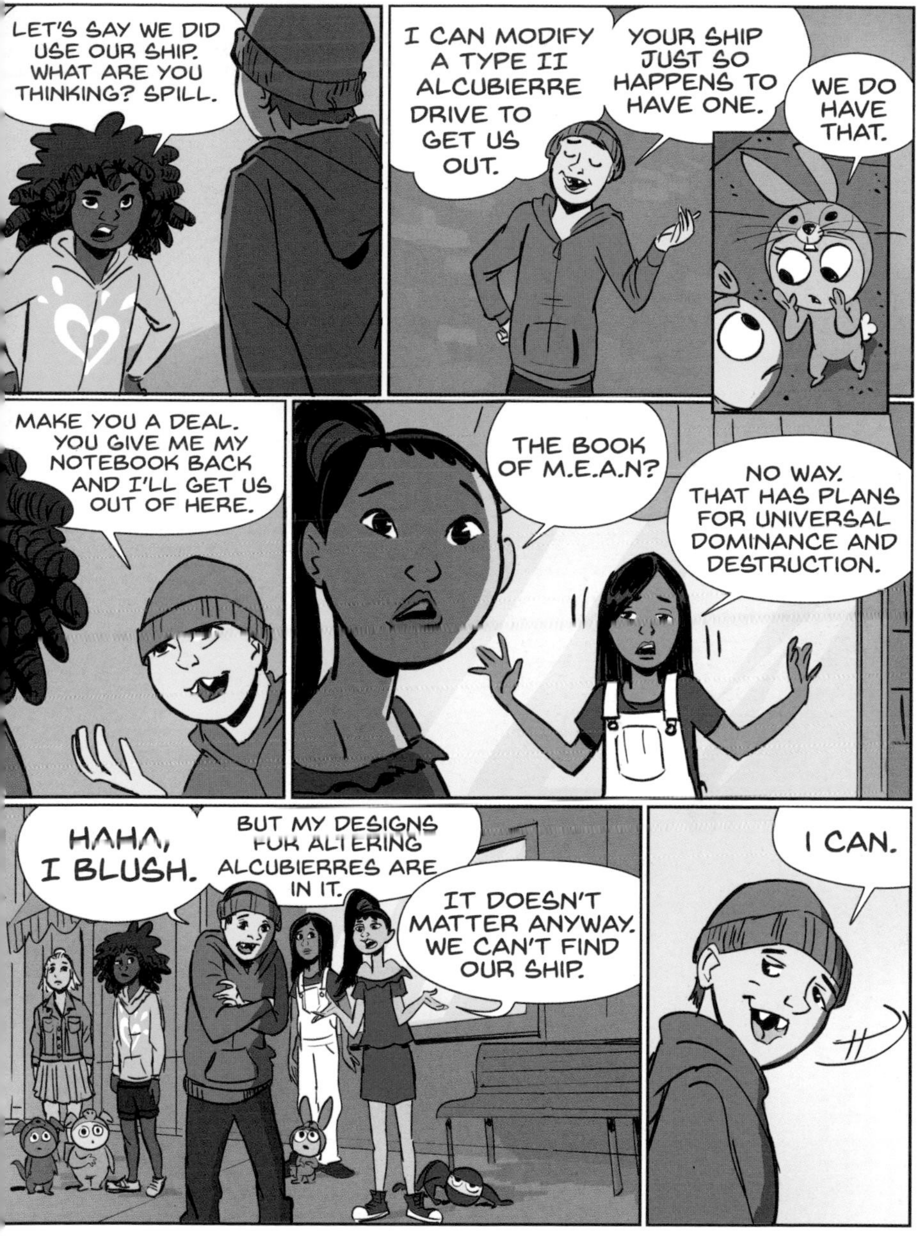

LET'S SAY WE DID USE OUR SHIP. WHAT ARE YOU THINKING? SPILL.
I CAN MODIFY A TYPE II ALCUBIERRE DRIVE TO GET US OUT.
YOUR SHIP JUST SO HAPPENS TO HAVE ONE.
WE DO HAVE THAT.
MAKE YOU A DEAL. YOU GIVE ME MY NOTEBOOK BACK AND I'LL GET US OUT OF HERE.
THE BOOK OF M.E.A.N?
NO WAY. THAT HAS PLANS FOR UNIVERSAL DOMINANCE AND DESTRUCTION.
HAHA, I BLUSH.
BUT MY DESIGNS FOR ALTERING ALCUBIERRES ARE IN IT.
IT DOESN'T MATTER ANYWAY. WE CAN'T FIND OUR SHIP.
I CAN.

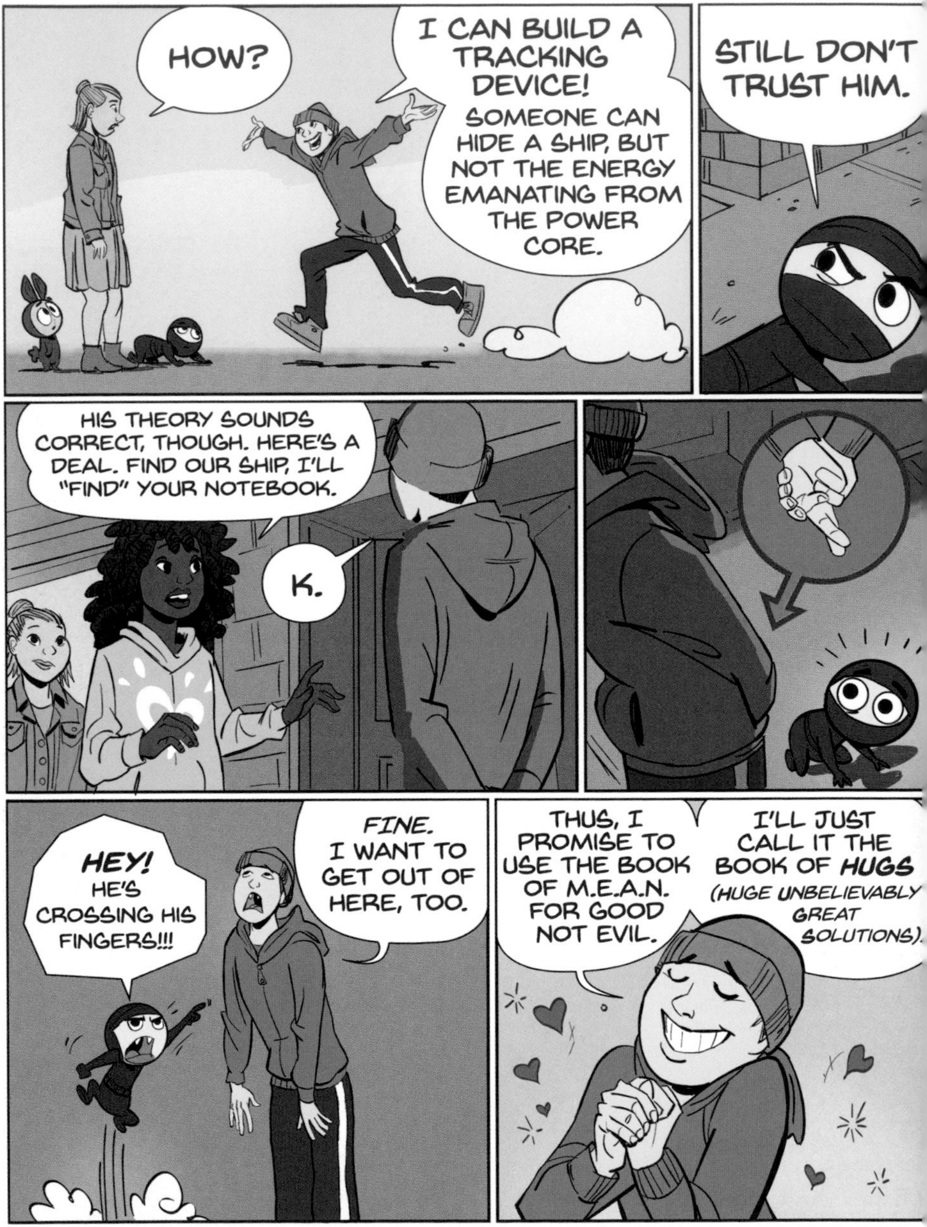
HOW?
I CAN BUILD A TRACKING DEVICE!
SOMEONE CAN HIDE A SHIP, BUT NOT THE ENERGY EMANATING FROM THE POWER CORE.
STILL DON'T TRUST HIM.
HIS THEORY SOUNDS CORRECT, THOUGH. HERE'S A DEAL. FIND OUR SHIP, I'LL "FIND" YOUR NOTEBOOK.
K.
HEY! HE'S CROSSING HIS FINGERS!!!
FINE. I WANT TO GET OUT OF HERE, TOO.
THUS, I PROMISE TO USE THE BOOK OF M.E.A.N. FOR GOOD NOT EVIL.
I'LL JUST CALL IT THE BOOK OF HUGS (HUGE UNBELIEVABLY GREAT SOLUTIONS).

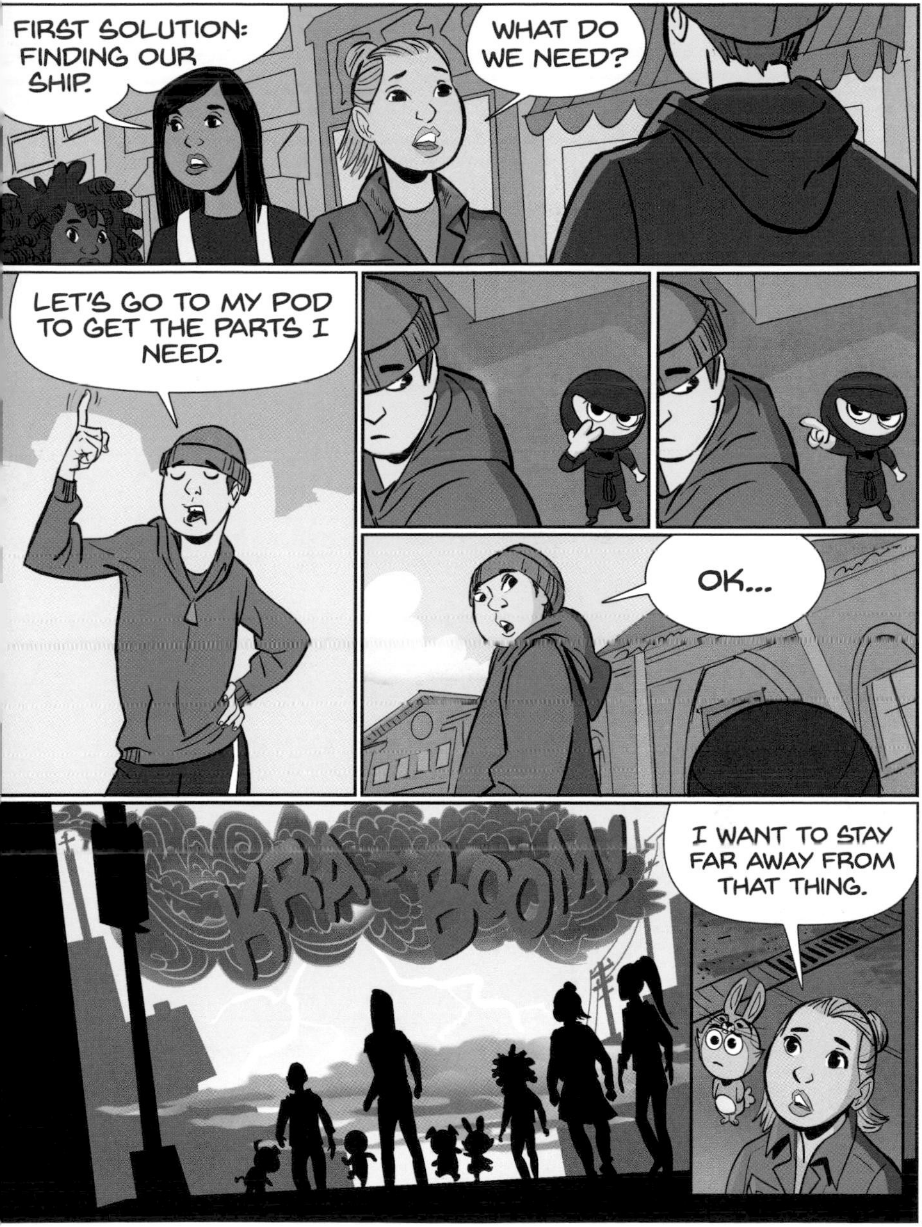
FIRST SOLUTION: FINDING OUR SHIP.
WHAT DO WE NEED?
LET'S GO TO MY POD TO GET THE PARTS I NEED.
OK...
KRA-BOOM!
I WANT TO STAY FAR AWAY FROM THAT THING.

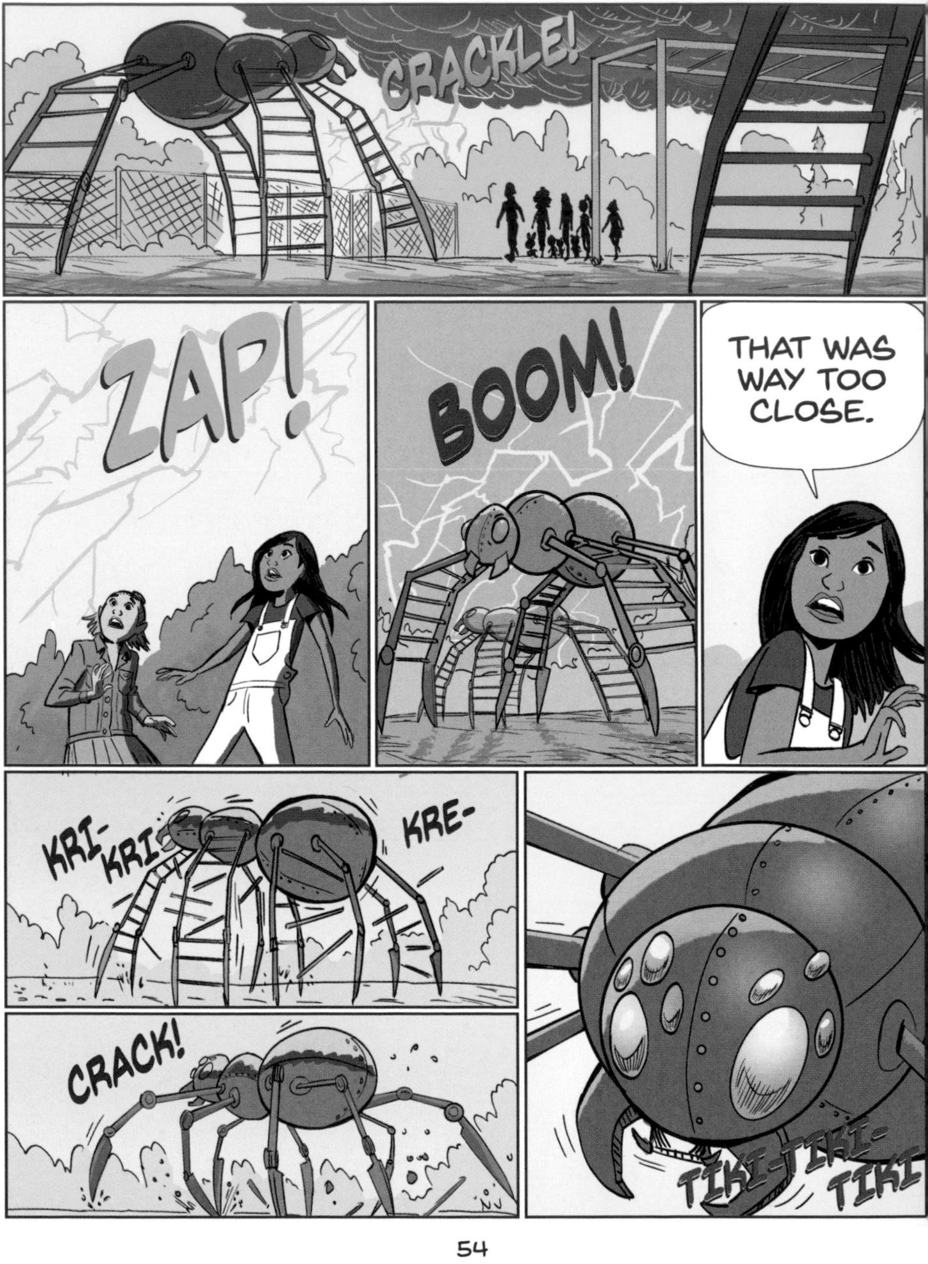
CRACKLE!
ZAP!
BOOM!
THAT WAS WAY TOO CLOSE.
KRI-KRI-
KRE-
CRACK!
TIKI-TIKI-TIKI

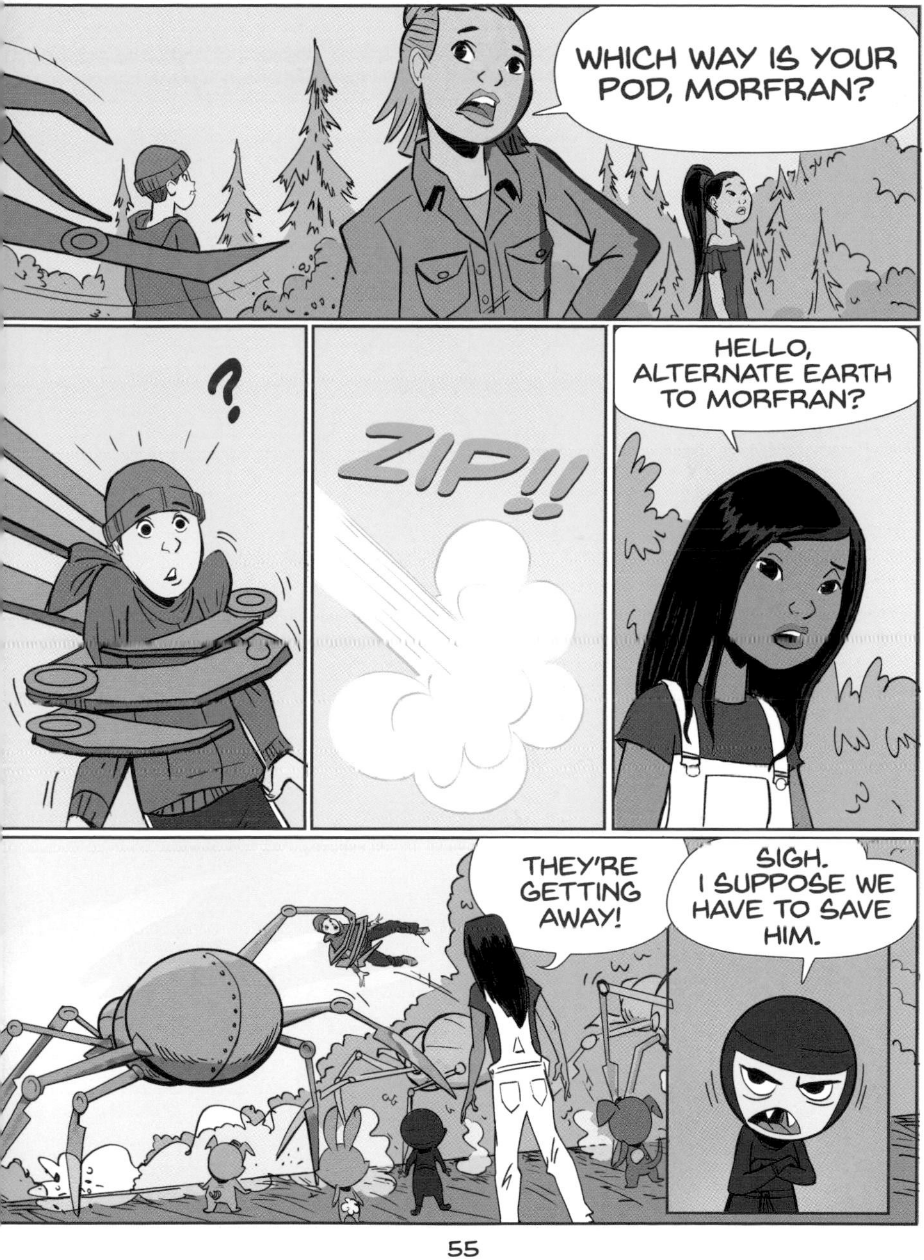
WHICH WAY IS YOUR POD, MORFRAN?
?
ZIP!!
HELLO, ALTERNATE EARTH TO MORFRAN?
THEY'RE GETTING AWAY!
SIGH. I SUPPOSE WE HAVE TO SAVE HIM.

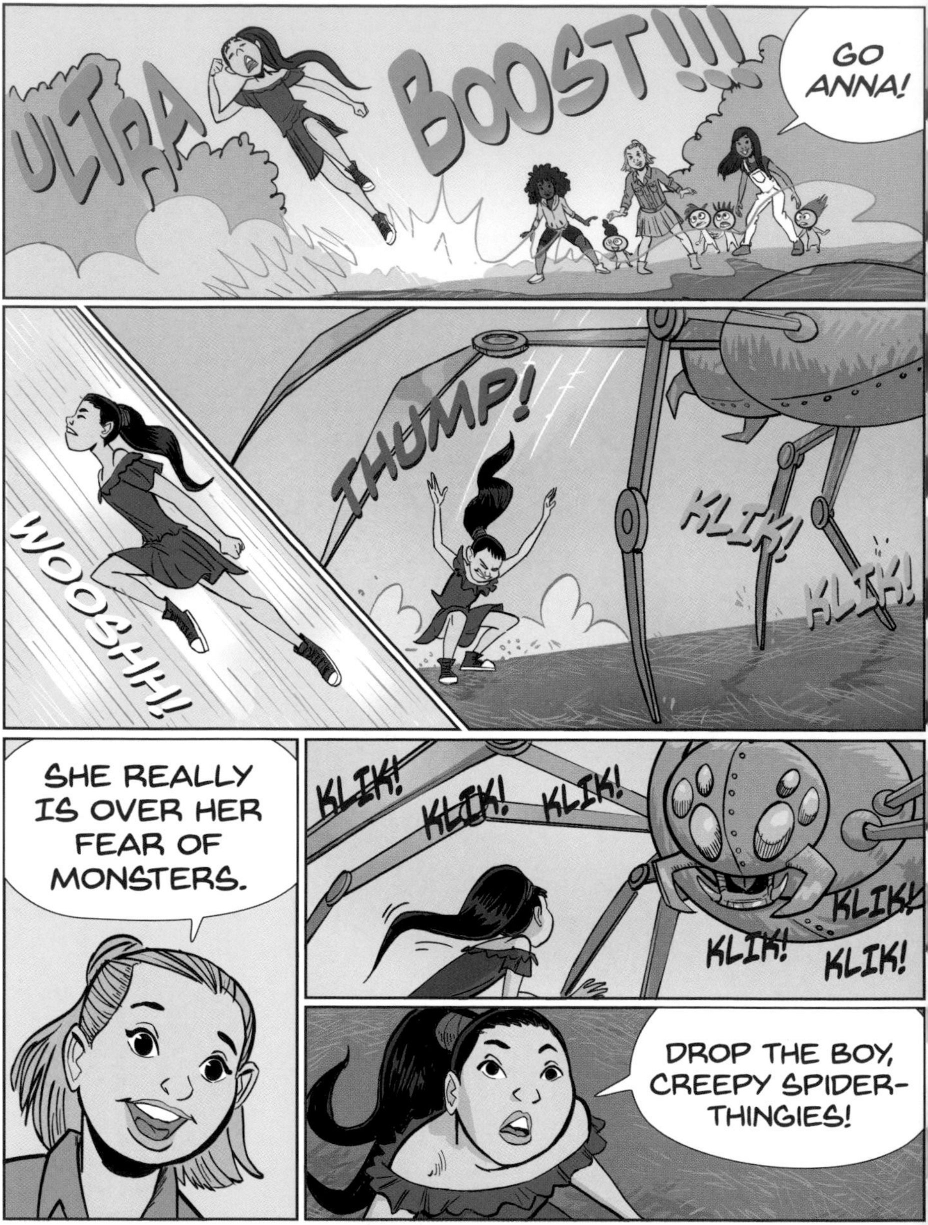
ULTRA BOOST!!!
GO ANNA!
WOOSHH!!
THUMP!
KLIK!
KLIK!
SHE REALLY IS OVER HER FEAR OF MONSTERS.
KLIK!
KLIK!
KLIK!
KLIK!
KLIK!
KLIK!
DROP THE BOY, CREEPY SPIDER-THINGIES!

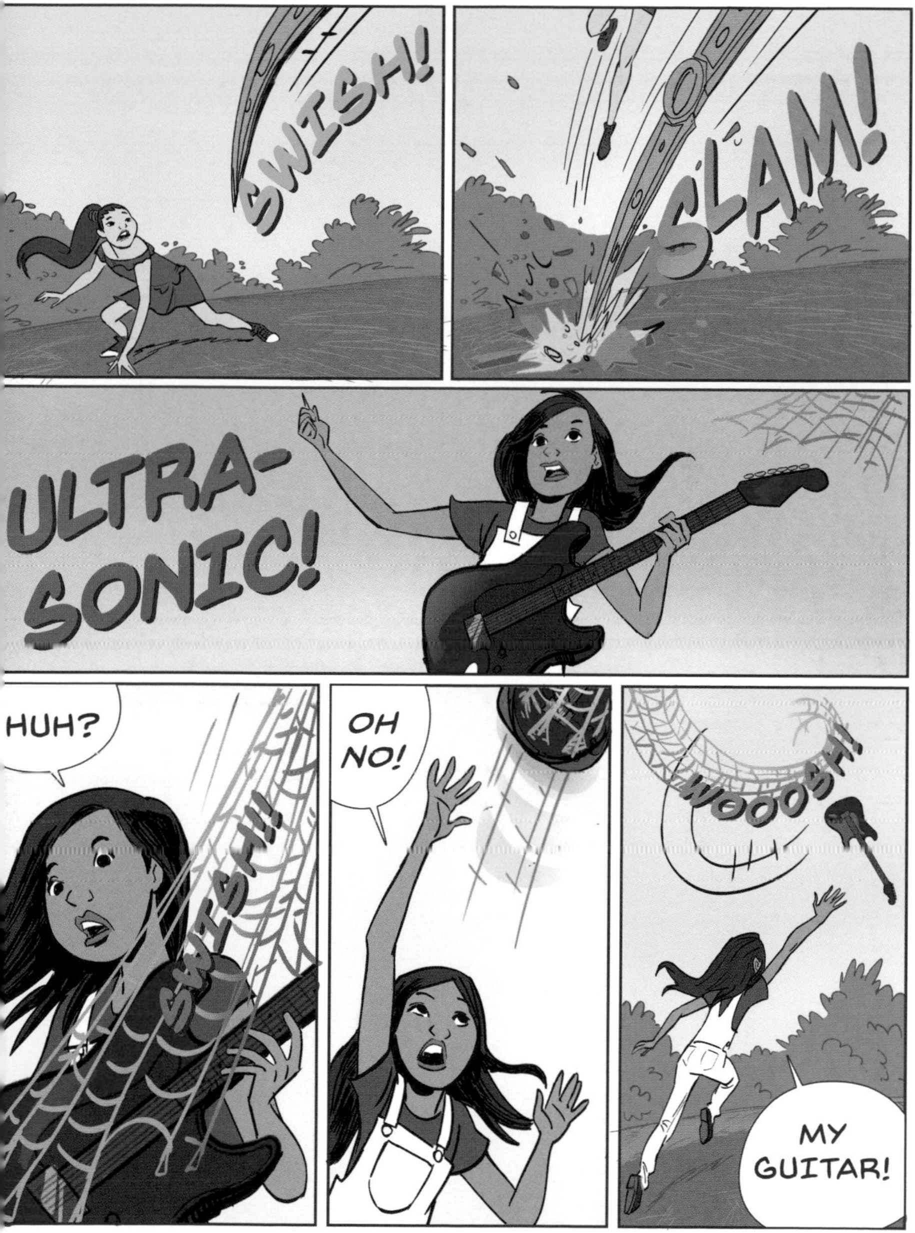
SWISH!
SLAM!
ULTRA-
SONIC!
HUH?
SWISH!!
OH
NO!
WOOOSH!
MY
GUITAR!

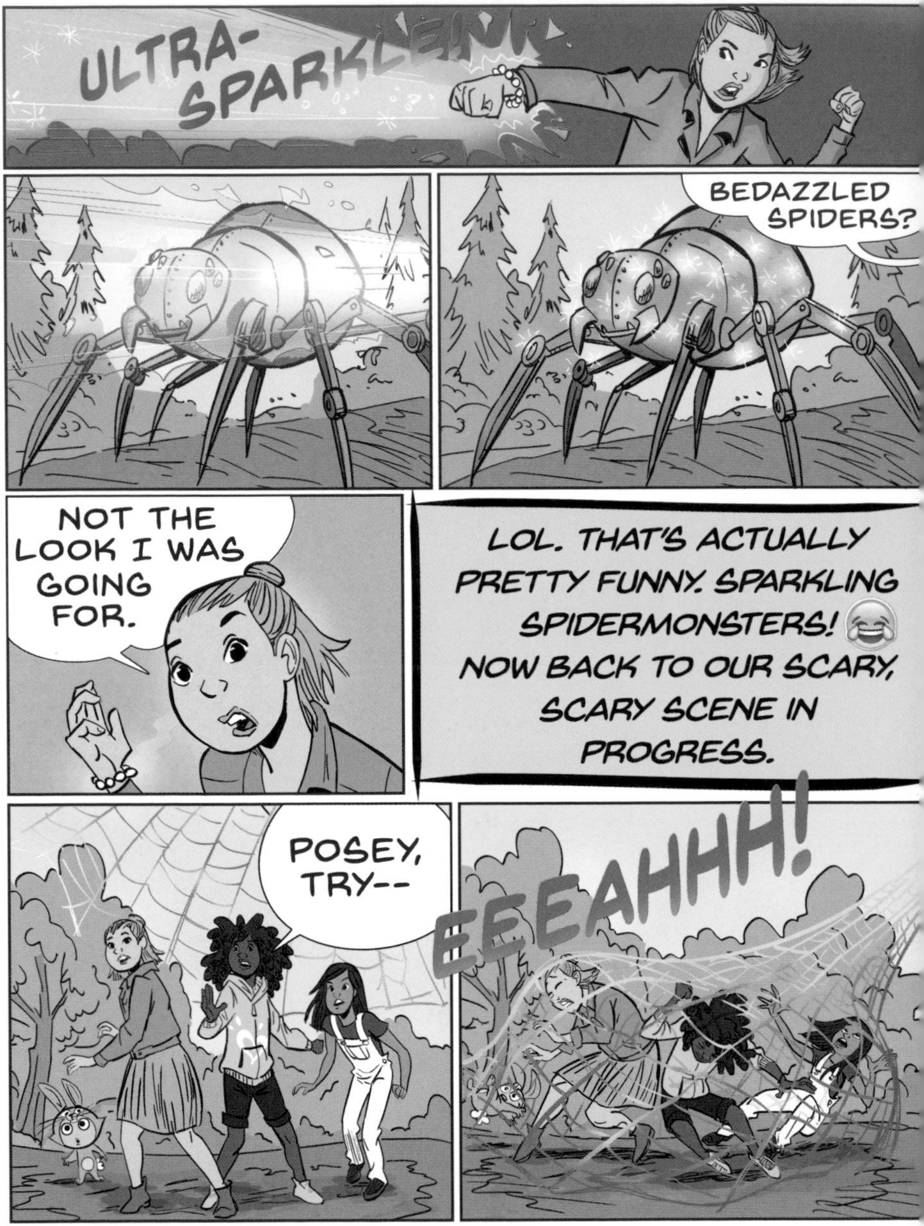
ULTRA-SPARKLE!NK!
BEDAZZLED SPIDERS?
NOT THE LOOK I WAS GOING FOR.
LOL. THAT'S ACTUALLY PRETTY FUNNY. SPARKLING SPIDERMONSTERS! 😂 NOW BACK TO OUR SCARY, SCARY SCENE IN PROGRESS.
POSEY, TRY--
EEEAHHH!

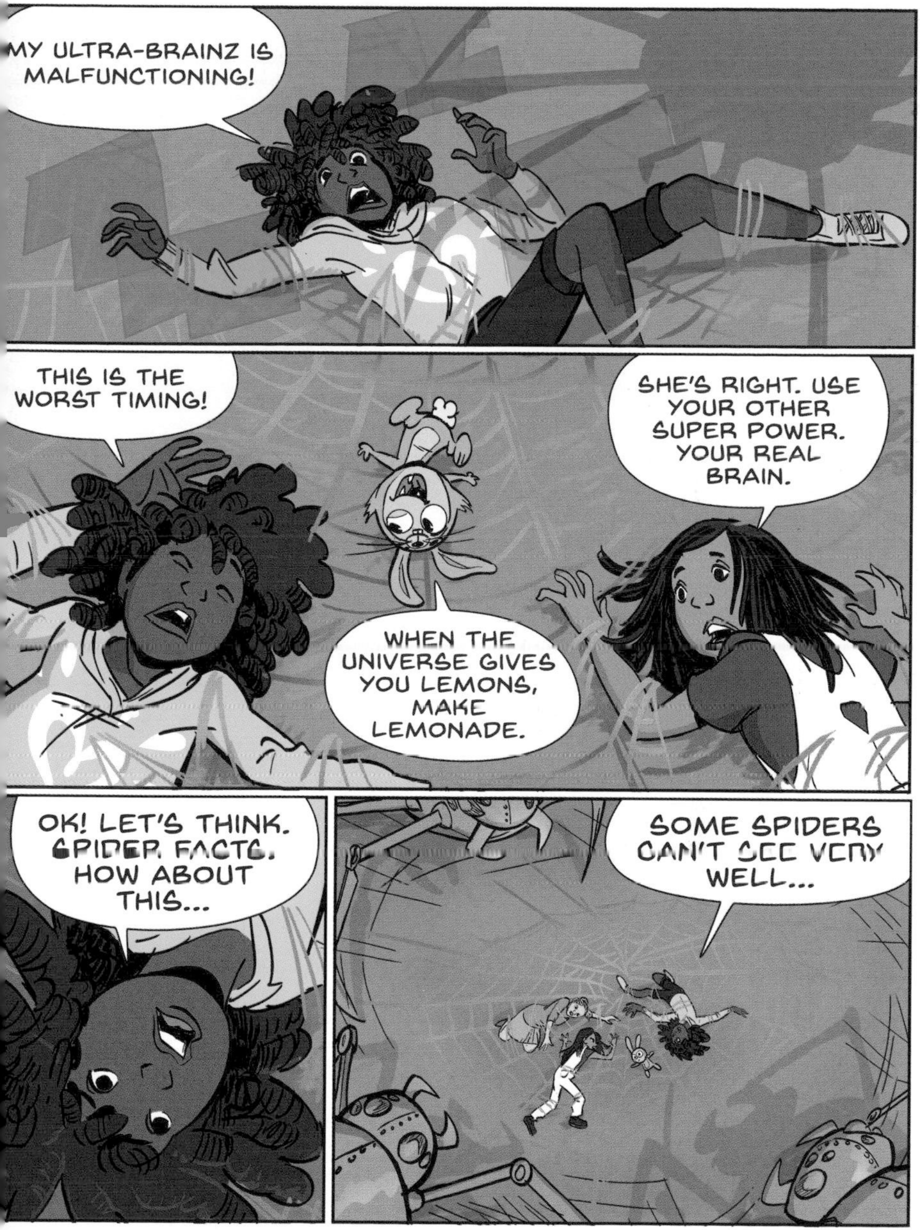
MY ULTRA-BRAINZ IS MALFUNCTIONING!
THIS IS THE WORST TIMING!
SHE'S RIGHT. USE YOUR OTHER SUPER POWER. YOUR REAL BRAIN.
WHEN THE UNIVERSE GIVES YOU LEMONS, MAKE LEMONADE.
OK! LET'S THINK. SPIDER FACTS. HOW ABOUT THIS...
SOME SPIDERS CAN'T SEE VERY WELL...

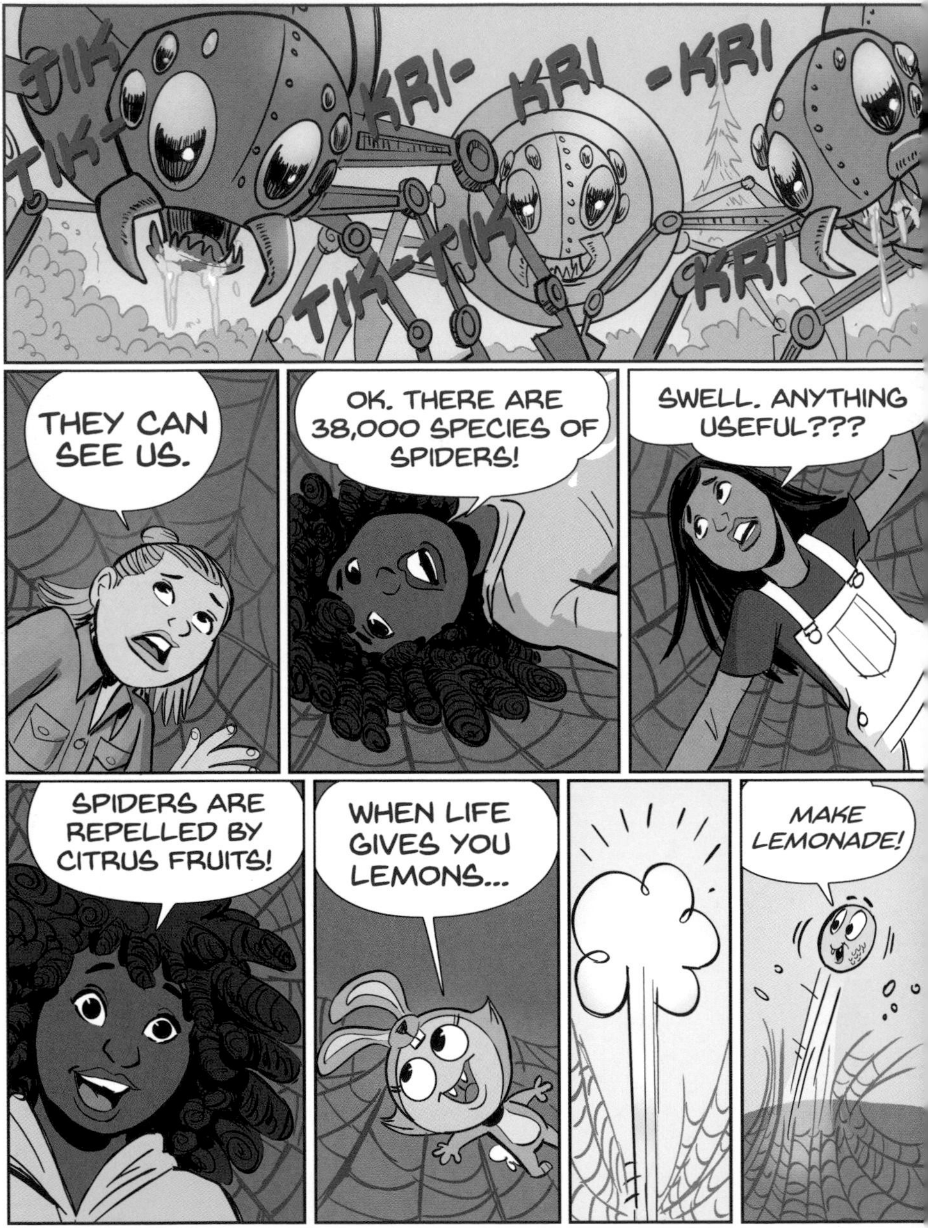
TIK
TIK-
KRI-
KRI
-KRI
TIK-TIK
KRI
THEY CAN SEE US.
OK. THERE ARE 38,000 SPECIES OF SPIDERS!
SWELL. ANYTHING USEFUL???
SPIDERS ARE REPELLED BY CITRUS FRUITS!
WHEN LIFE GIVES YOU LEMONS...
MAKE LEMONADE!

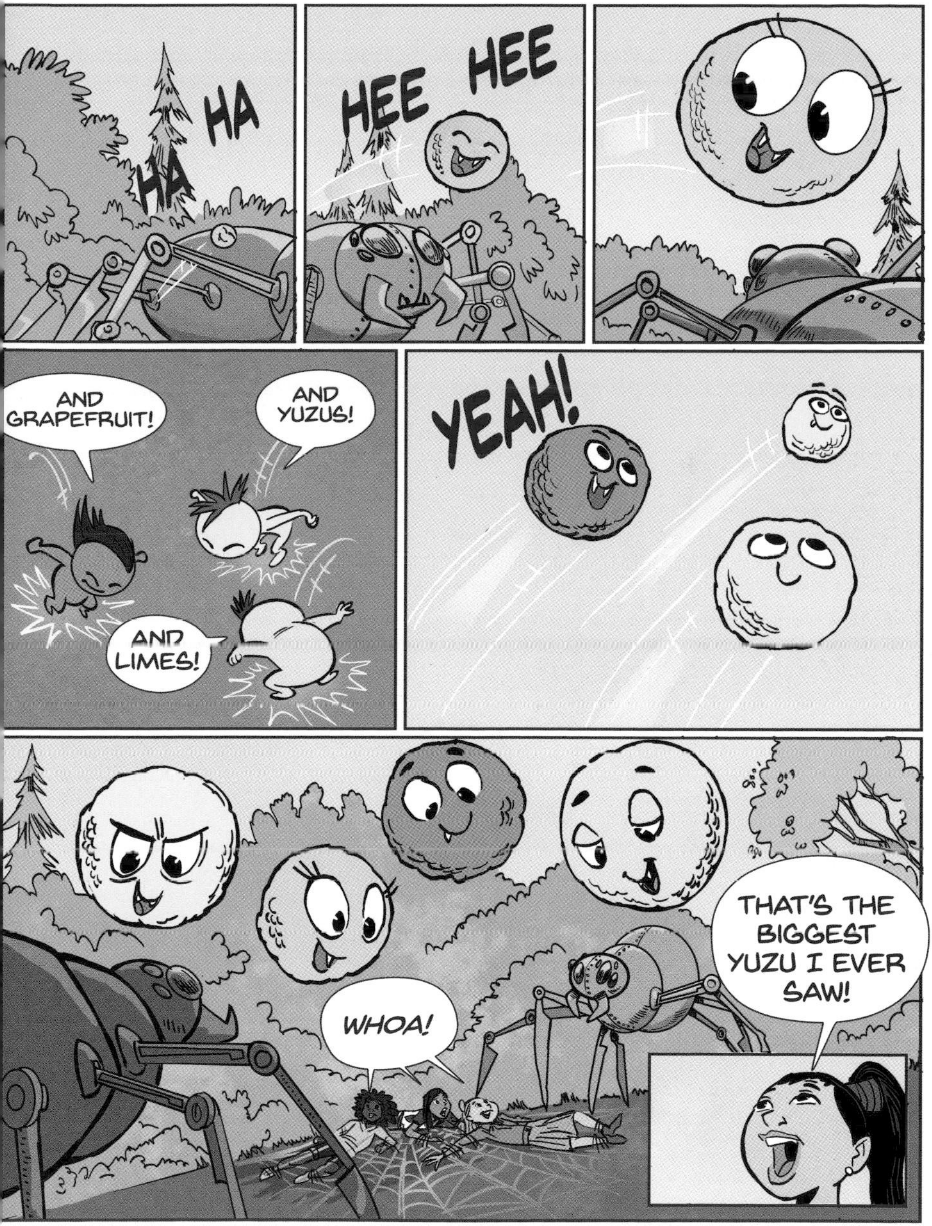

HA HA HA
HEE HEE
AND GRAPEFRUIT!
AND YUZUS!
AND LIMES!
YEAH!
THAT'S THE BIGGEST YUZU I EVER SAW!
WHOA!

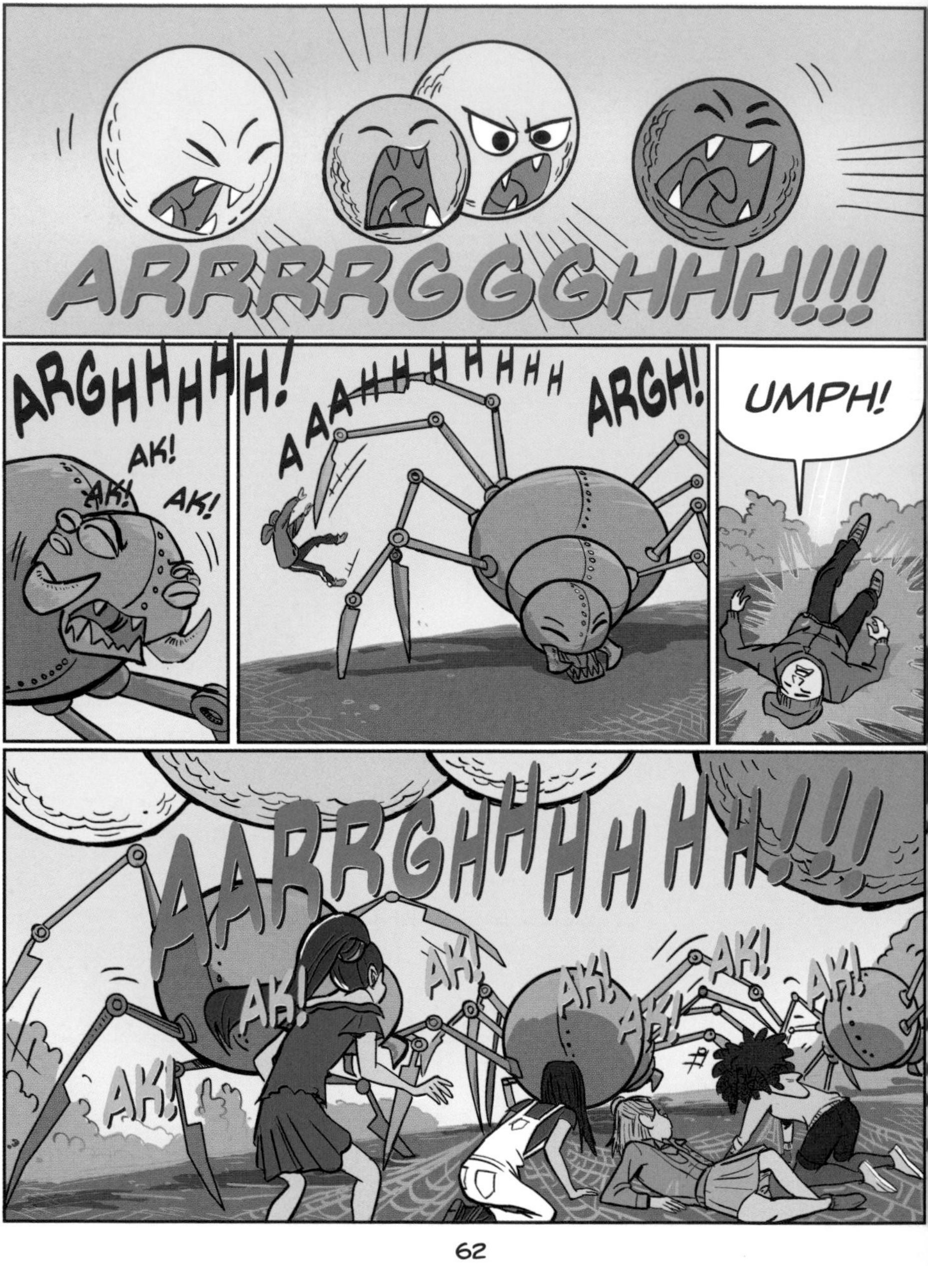
ARRRRGGGHHH!!!
ARGHHHHHH!
AK!
AK!
AK!
AAAHHHHHHHHH
ARGH!
UMPH!
AARRGHHHHHHH!!!
AK!
AK!
AK!
AK!
AK!
AK!
AK!

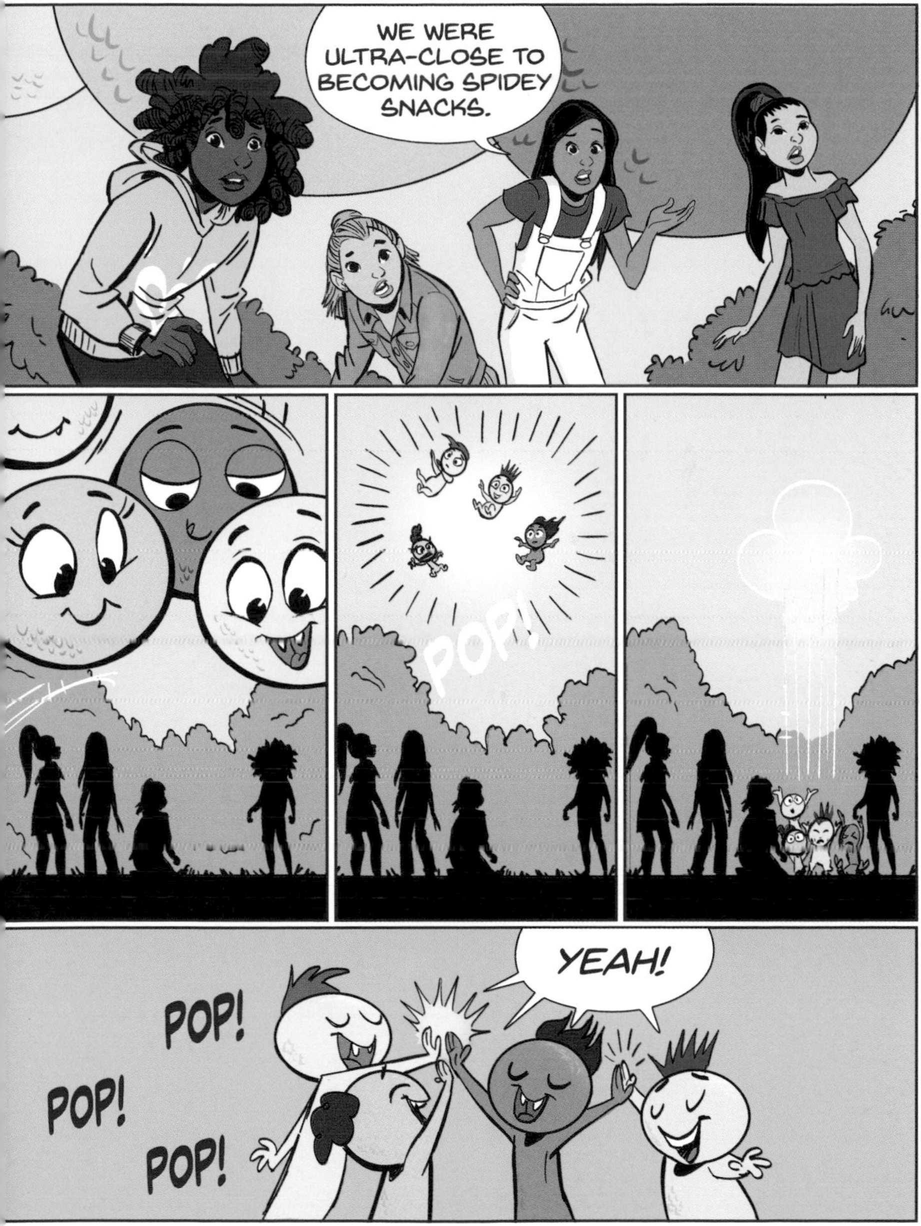
WE WERE ULTRA-CLOSE TO BECOMING SPIDEY SNACKS.
POP!
YEAH!
POP!
POP!
POP!

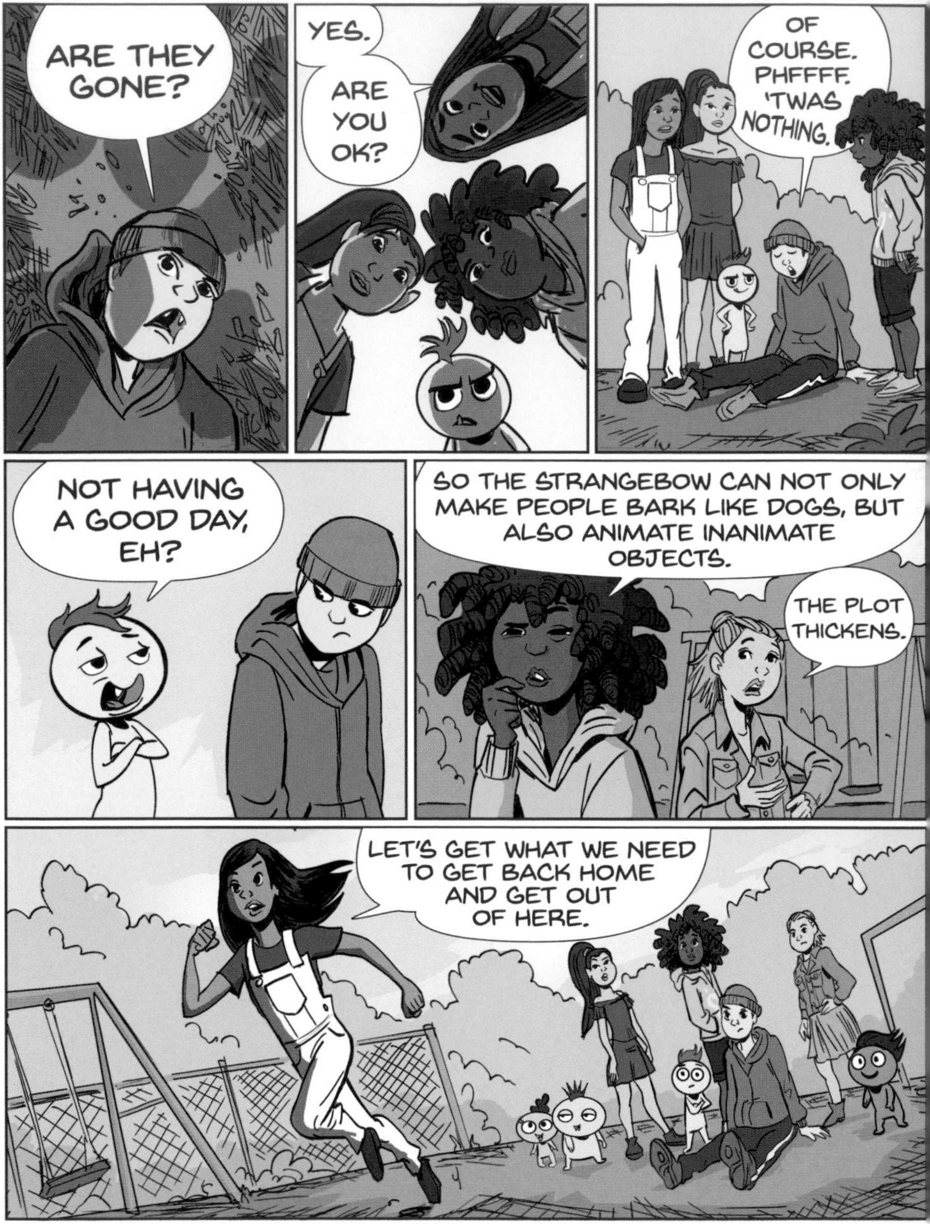

ARE THEY GONE?
YES.
ARE YOU OK?
OF COURSE. PHFFFF. 'TWAS NOTHING.
NOT HAVING A GOOD DAY, EH?
SO THE STRANGEBOW CAN NOT ONLY MAKE PEOPLE BARK LIKE DOGS, BUT ALSO ANIMATE INANIMATE OBJECTS.
THE PLOT THICKENS.
LET'S GET WHAT WE NEED TO GET BACK HOME AND GET OUT OF HERE.

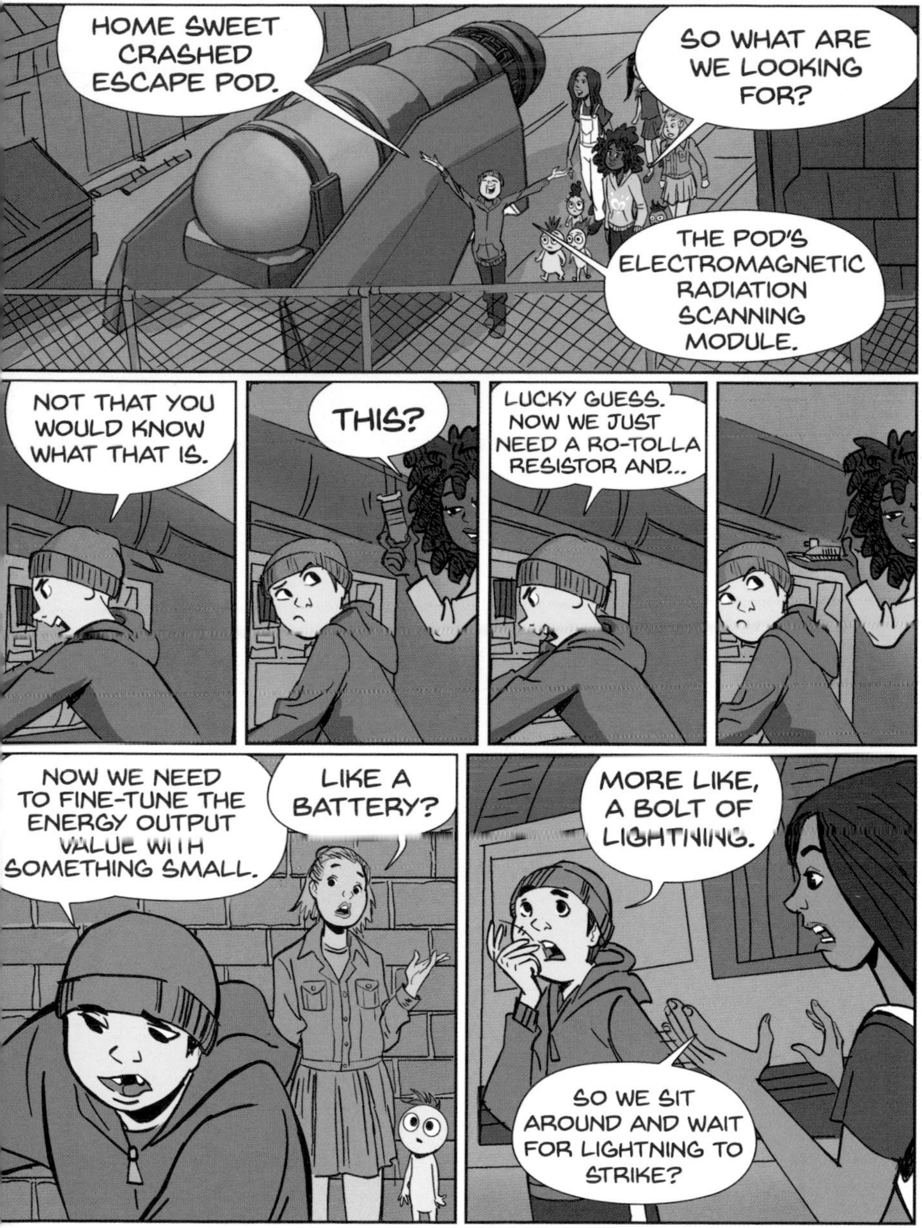
HOME SWEET CRASHED ESCAPE POD.
SO WHAT ARE WE LOOKING FOR?
THE POD'S ELECTROMAGNETIC RADIATION SCANNING MODULE.
NOT THAT YOU WOULD KNOW WHAT THAT IS.
THIS?
LUCKY GUESS. NOW WE JUST NEED A RO-TOLLA RESISTOR AND...
NOW WE NEED TO FINE-TUNE THE ENERGY OUTPUT VALUE WITH SOMETHING SMALL.
LIKE A BATTERY?
MORE LIKE, A BOLT OF LIGHTNING.
SO WE SIT AROUND AND WAIT FOR LIGHTNING TO STRIKE?

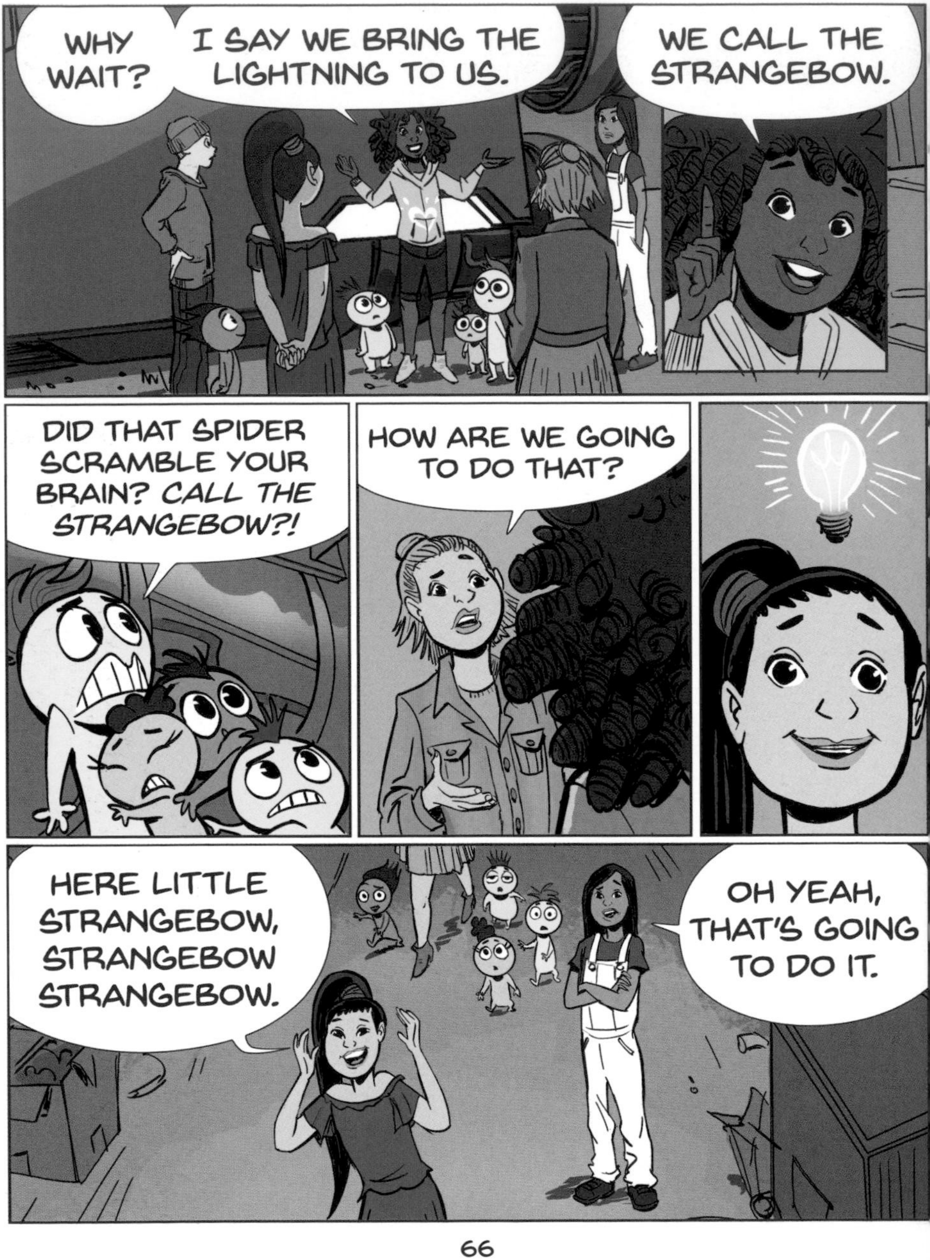
WHY WAIT?
I SAY WE BRING THE LIGHTNING TO US.
WE CALL THE STRANGEBOW.
DID THAT SPIDER SCRAMBLE YOUR BRAIN? CALL THE STRANGEBOW?!
HOW ARE WE GOING TO DO THAT?
HERE LITTLE STRANGEBOW, STRANGEBOW STRANGEBOW.
OH YEAH, THAT'S GOING TO DO IT.

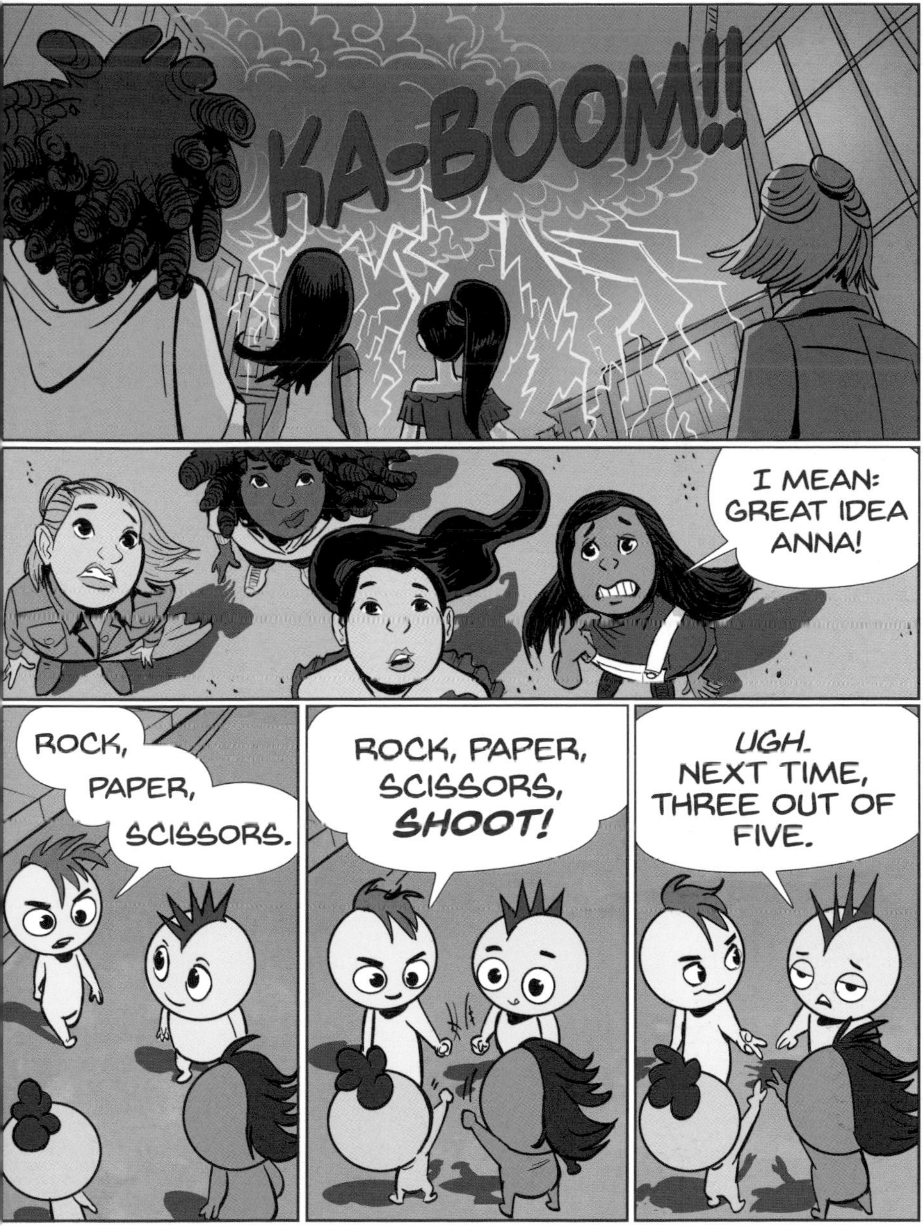
KA-BOOM!!
I MEAN: GREAT IDEA ANNA!
ROCK, PAPER, SCISSORS.
ROCK, PAPER, SCISSORS, *SHOOT!*
UGH. NEXT TIME, THREE OUT OF FIVE.

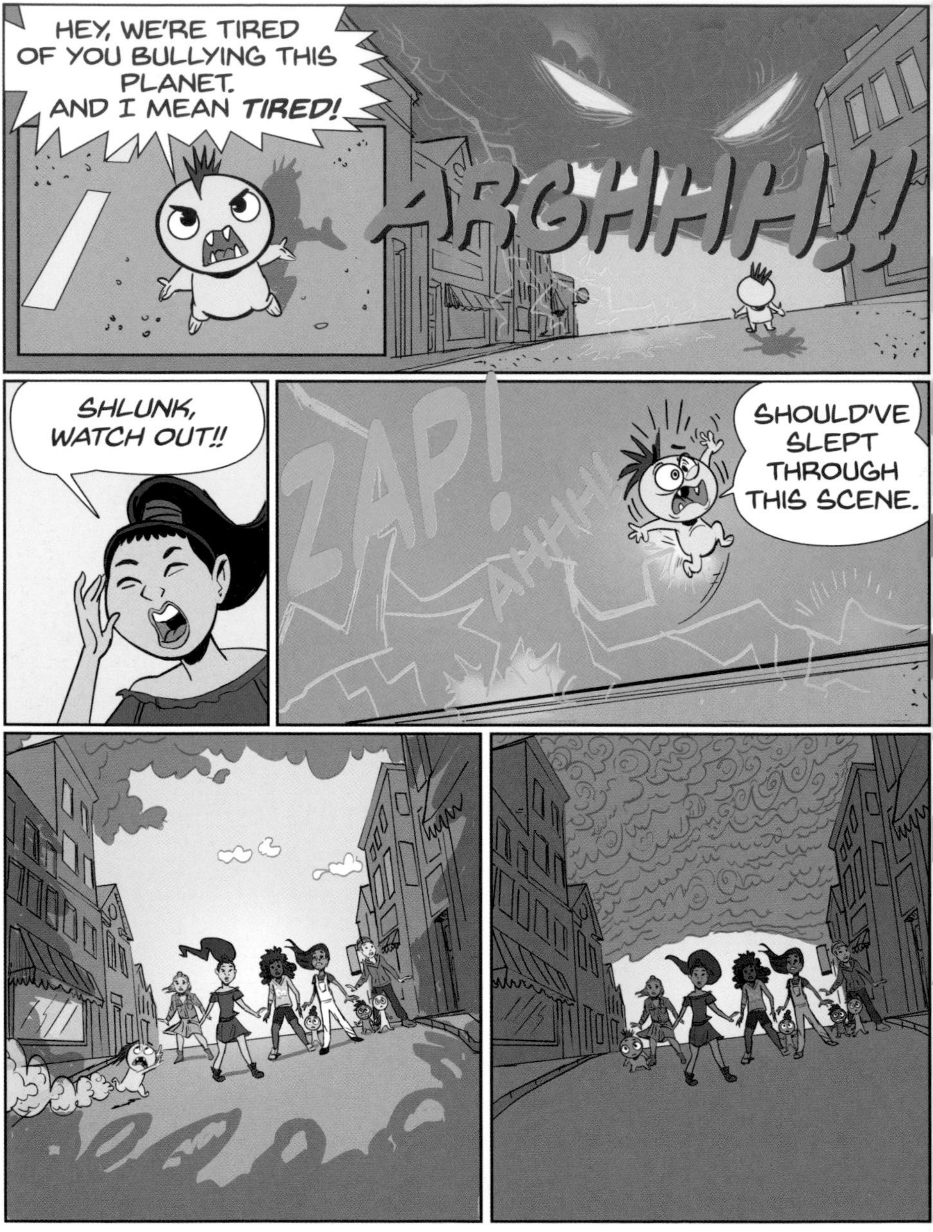
HEY, WE'RE TIRED OF YOU BULLYING THIS PLANET. AND I MEAN TIRED!
ARGHHH!!
SHLUNK, WATCH OUT!!
ZAP!
AHHH!
SHOULD'VE SLEPT THROUGH THIS SCENE.

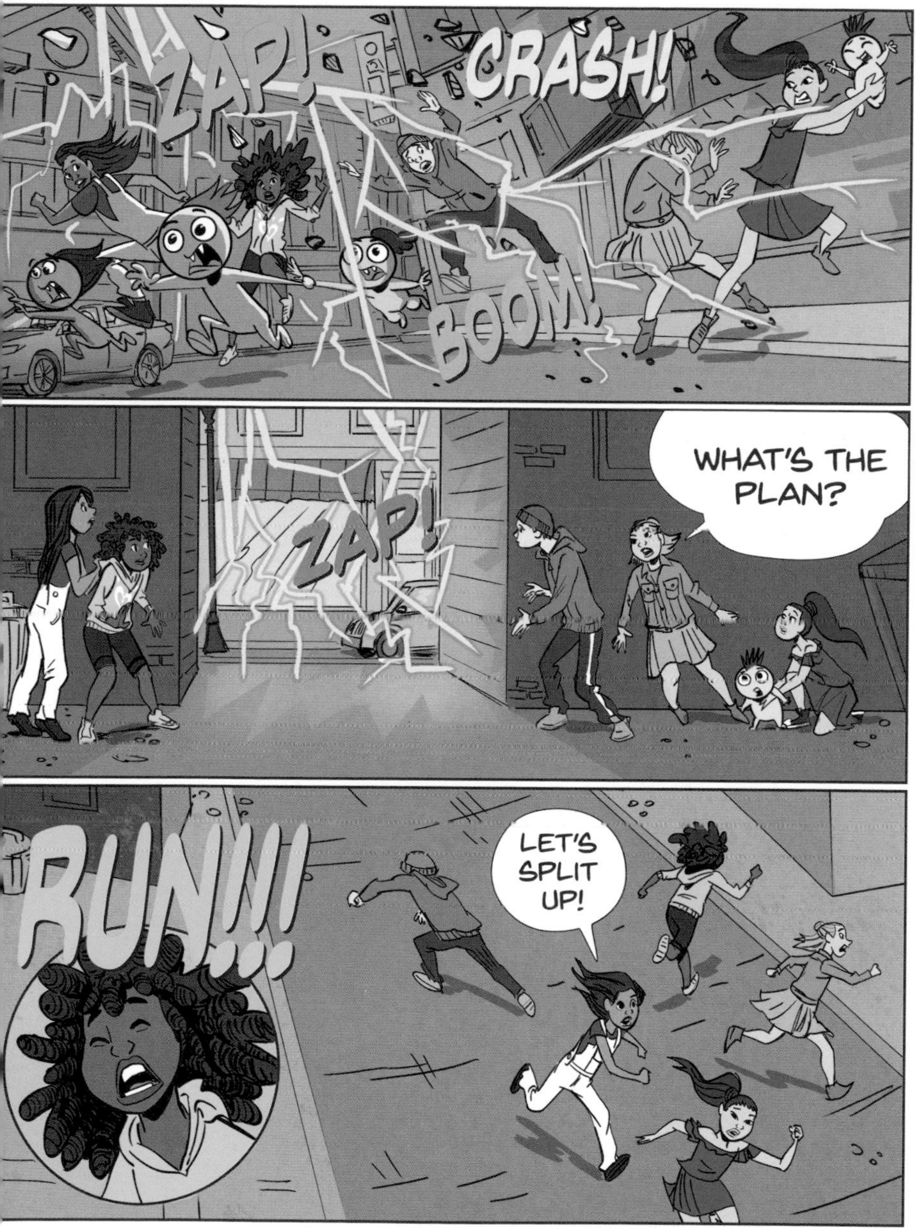
ZAP!
CRASH!
BOOM!
ZAP!
WHAT'S THE PLAN?
RUN!!!
LET'S SPLIT UP!

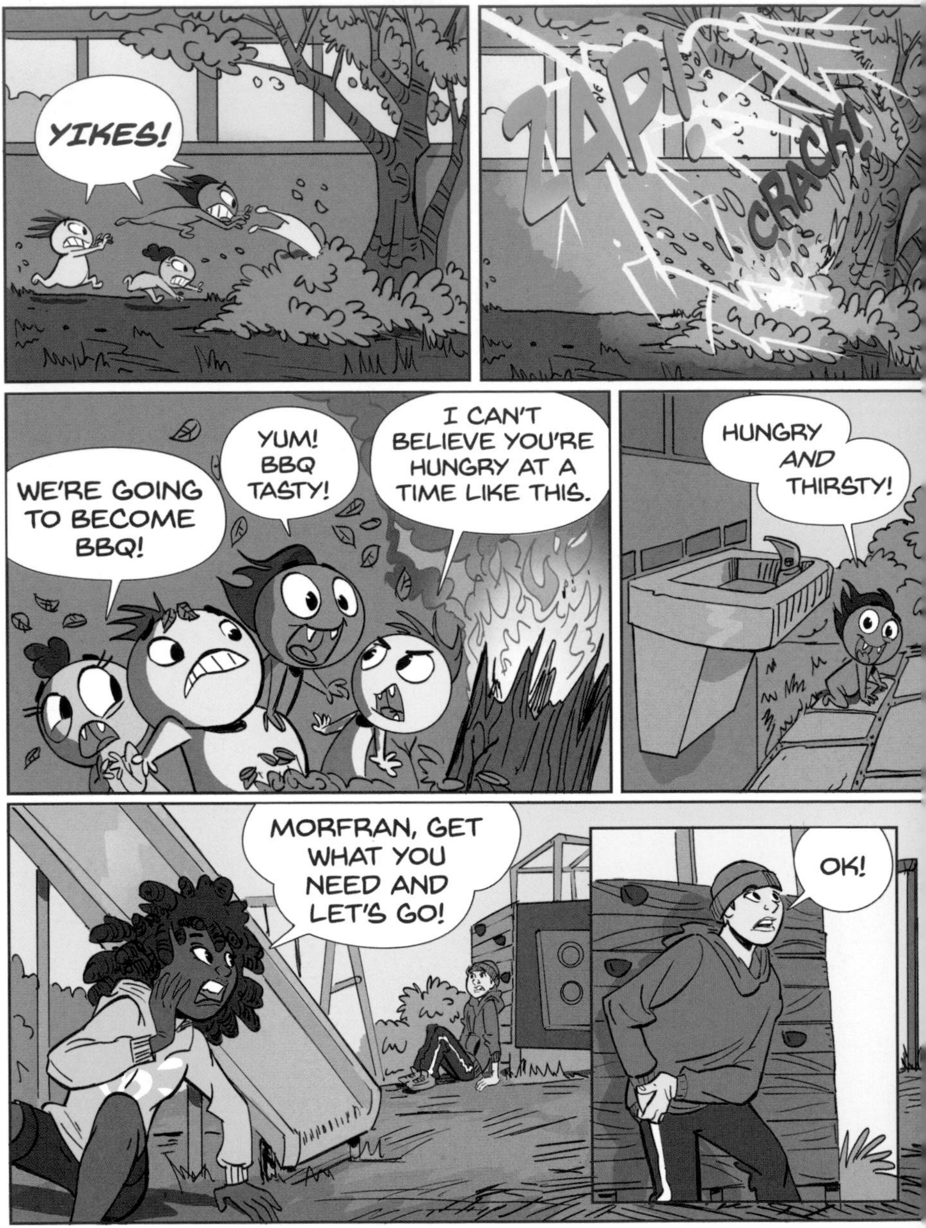
YIKES!
ZAP!
CRACK!
WE'RE GOING TO BECOME BBQ!
YUM! BBQ TASTY!
I CAN'T BELIEVE YOU'RE HUNGRY AT A TIME LIKE THIS.
HUNGRY AND THIRSTY!
MORFRAN, GET WHAT YOU NEED AND LET'S GO!
OK!

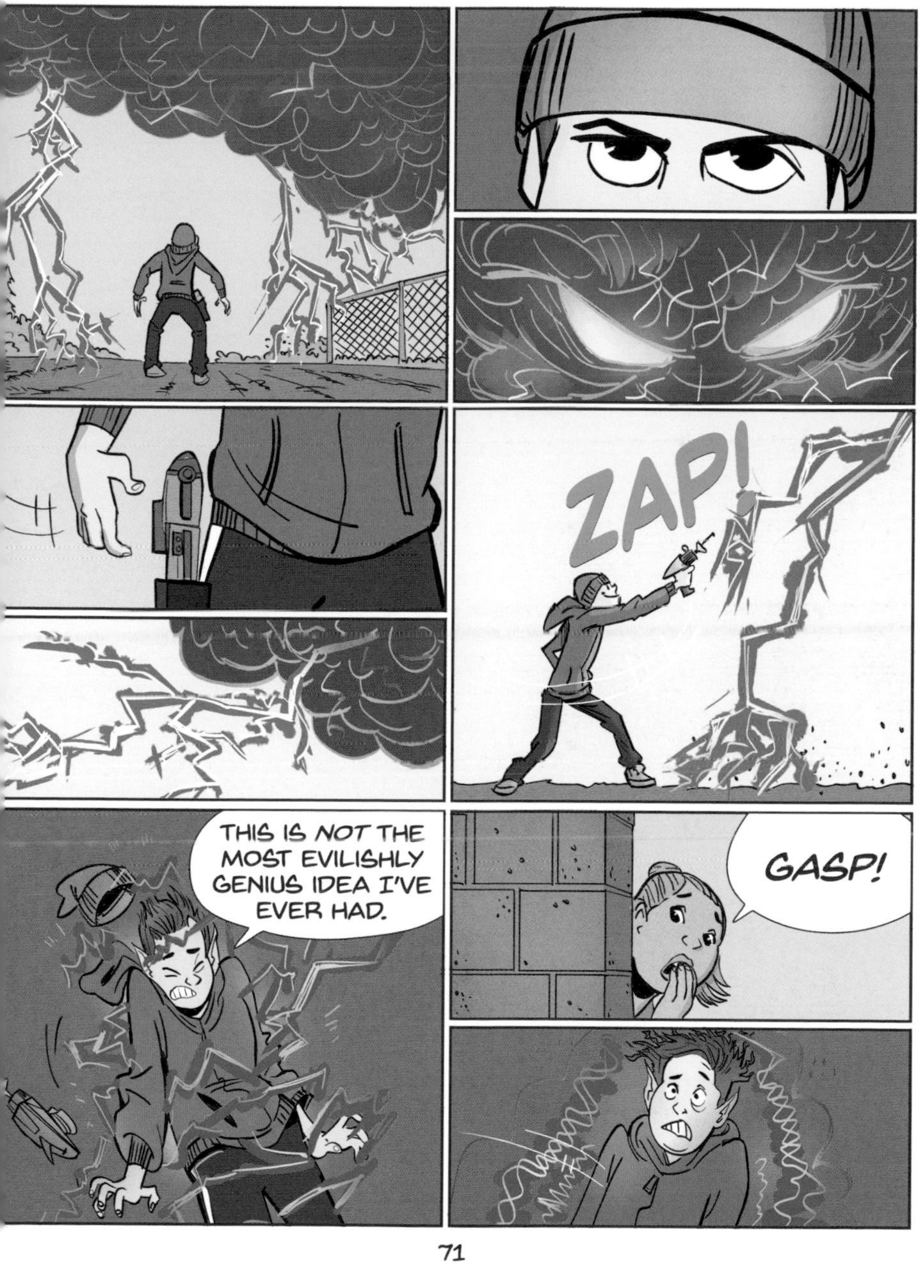
ZAP!
THIS IS NOT THE MOST EVILISHLY GENIUS IDEA I'VE EVER HAD.
GASP!

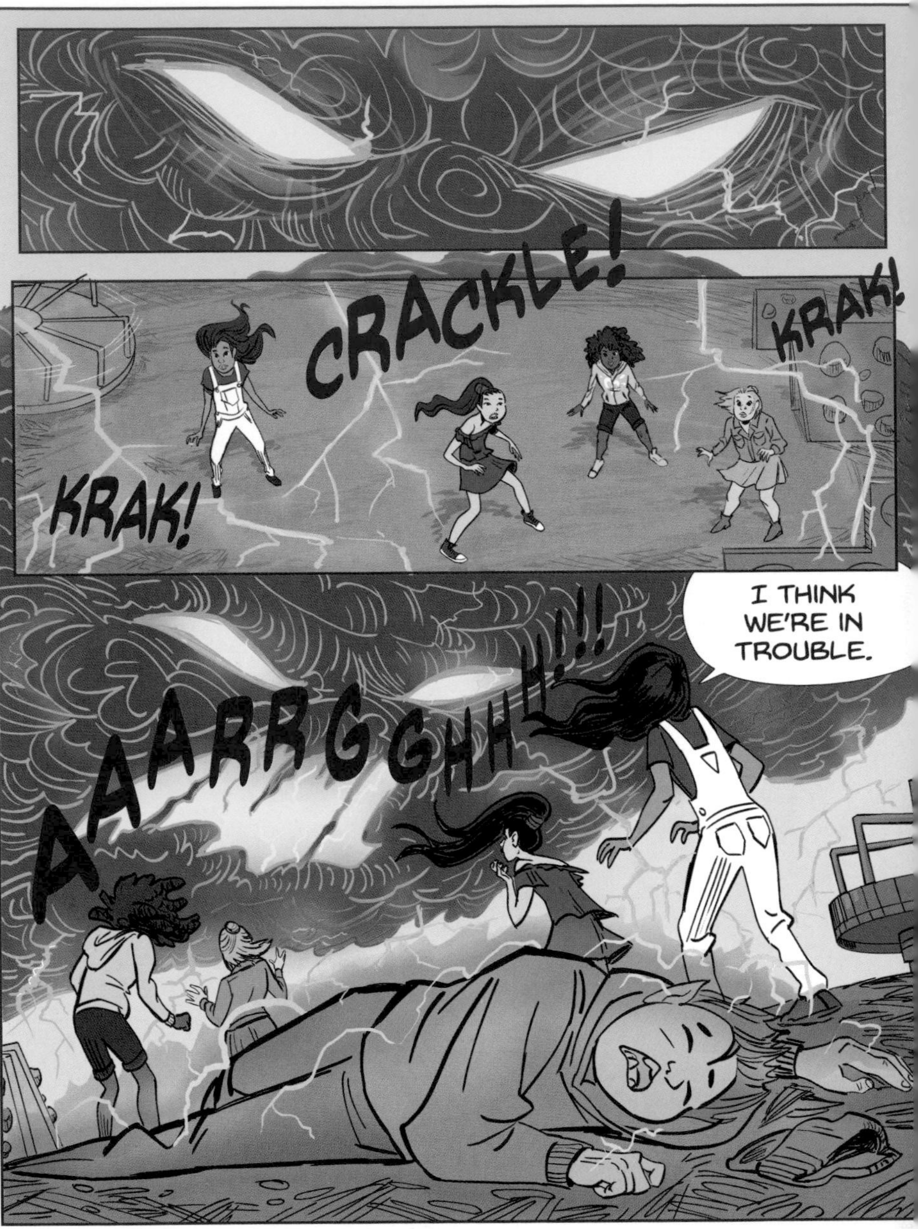
CRACKLE!
KRAK!
KRAK!
AAARRGGHHH!!!
I THINK WE'RE IN TROUBLE.

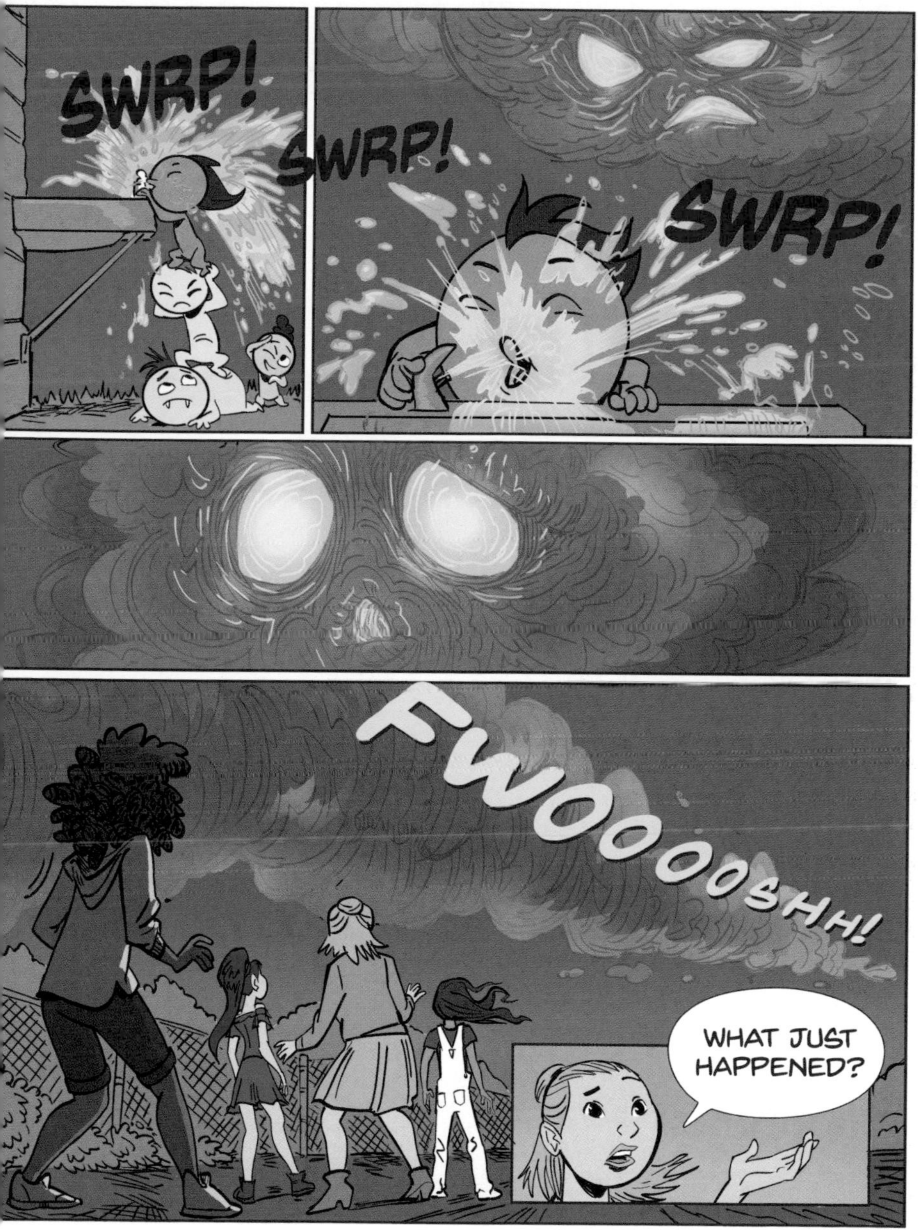
SWRP!
SWRP!
SWRP!
FWOOOOOSHH!
WHAT JUST HAPPENED?

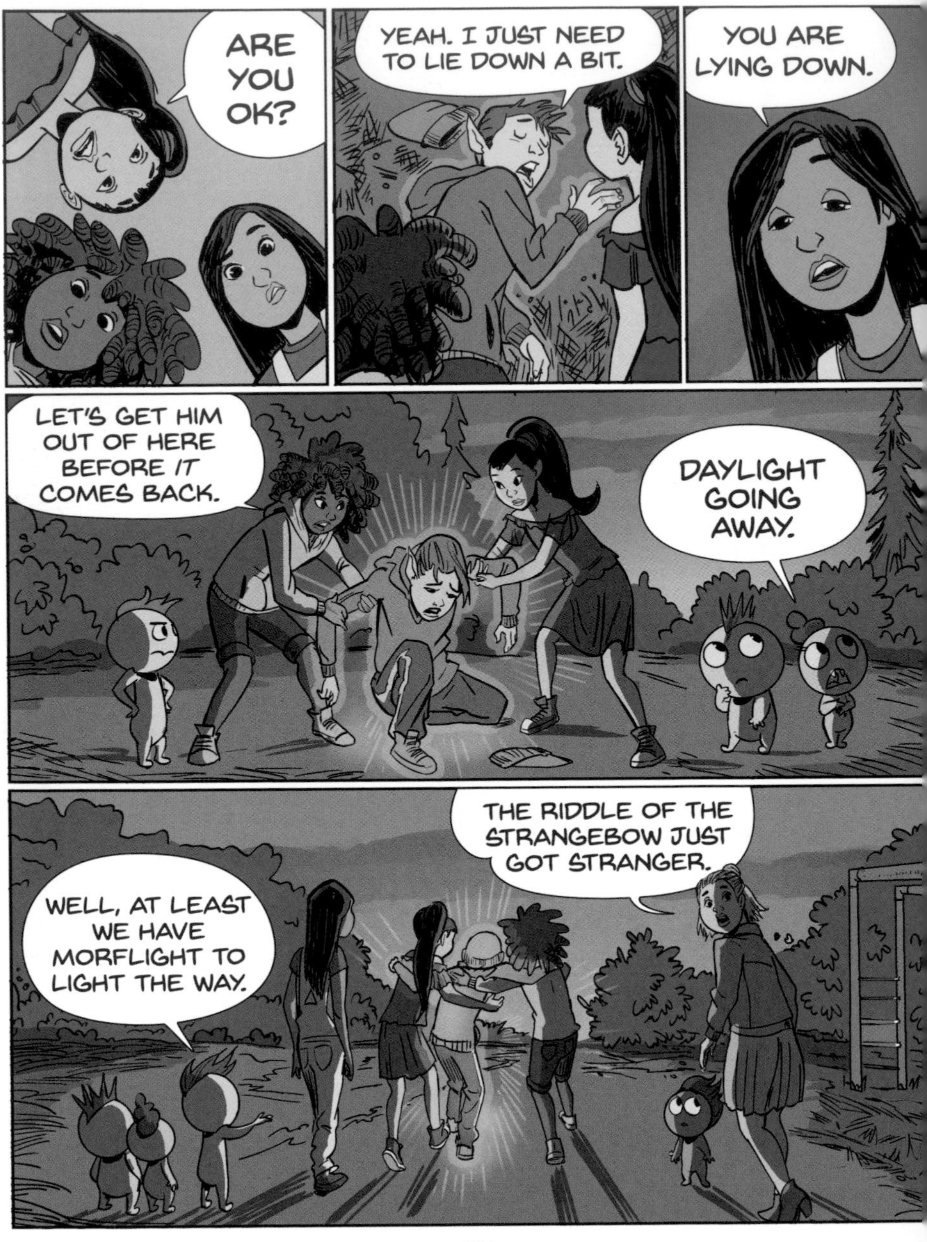
ARE YOU OK?
YEAH. I JUST NEED TO LIE DOWN A BIT.
YOU ARE LYING DOWN.
LET'S GET HIM OUT OF HERE BEFORE *IT* COMES BACK.
DAYLIGHT GOING AWAY.
THE RIDDLE OF THE STRANGEBOW JUST GOT STRANGER.
WELL, AT LEAST WE HAVE MORFLIGHT TO LIGHT THE WAY.

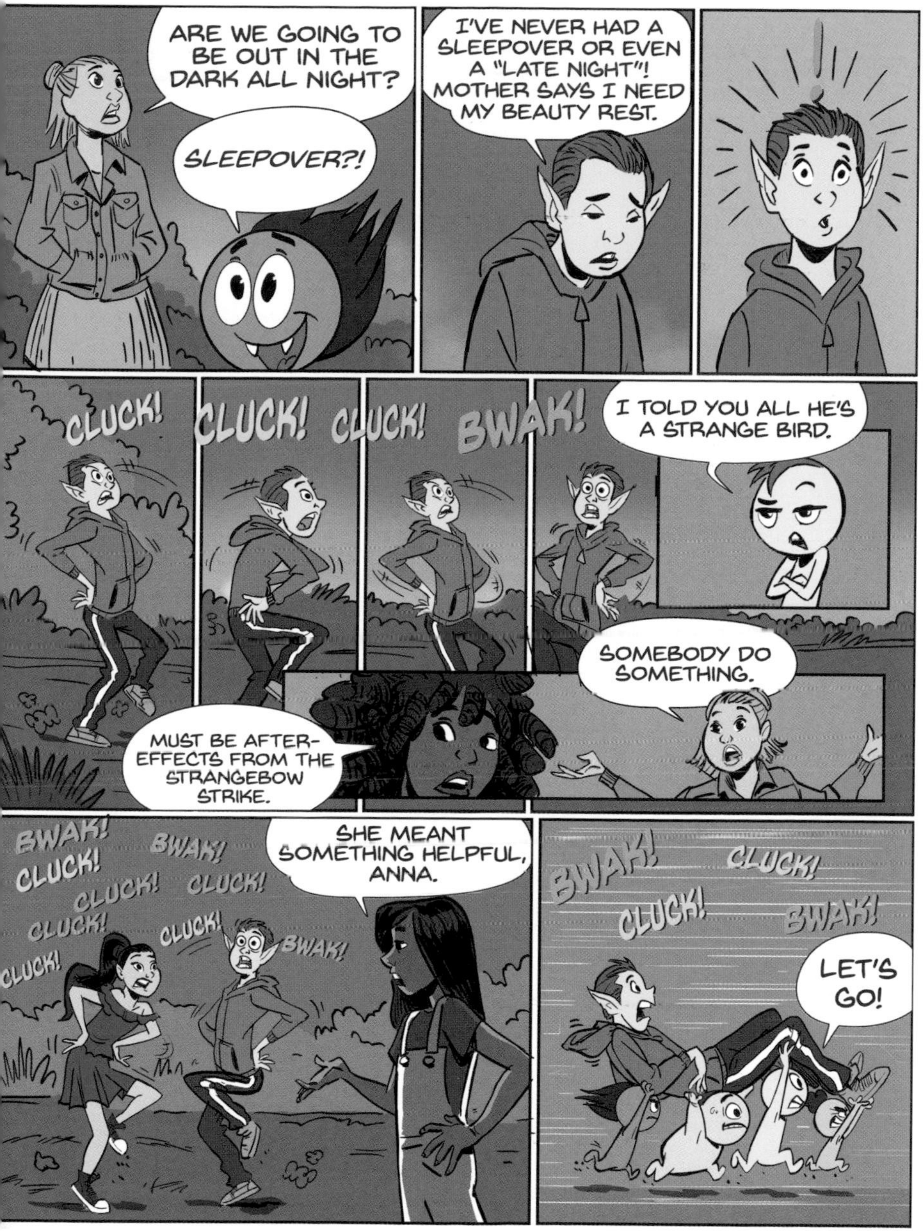
ARE WE GOING TO BE OUT IN THE DARK ALL NIGHT?
SLEEPOVER?!
I'VE NEVER HAD A SLEEPOVER OR EVEN A "LATE NIGHT"! MOTHER SAYS I NEED MY BEAUTY REST.
CLUCK!
CLUCK!
CLUCK!
BWAK!
I TOLD YOU ALL HE'S A STRANGE BIRD.
SOMEBODY DO SOMETHING.
MUST BE AFTER-EFFECTS FROM THE STRANGEBOW STRIKE.
BWAK!
BWAK!
CLUCK!
CLUCK!
CLUCK!
CLUCK!
CLUCK!
CLUCK!
BWAK!
SHE MEANT SOMETHING HELPFUL, ANNA.
BWAK!
CLUCK!
CLUCK!
BWAK!
LET'S GO!

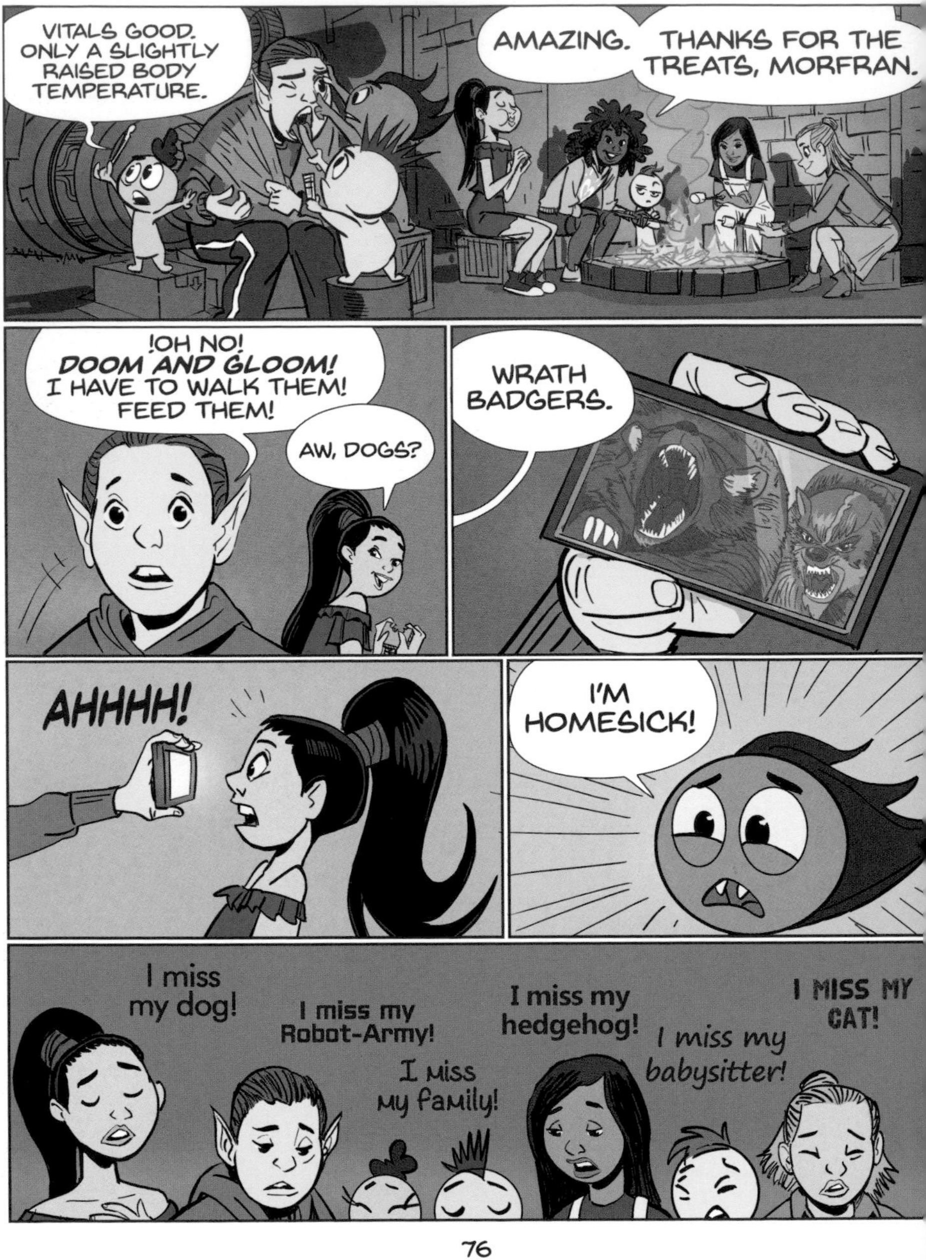
VITALS GOOD. ONLY A SLIGHTLY RAISED BODY TEMPERATURE.
AMAZING.
THANKS FOR THE TREATS, MORFRAN.
!OH NO! DOOM AND GLOOM! I HAVE TO WALK THEM! FEED THEM!
AW, DOGS?
WRATH BADGERS.
AHHHH!
I'M HOMESICK!
I miss my dog!
I miss my Robot-Army!
I Miss my family!
I miss my hedgehog!
I miss my babysitter!
I MISS MY CAT!

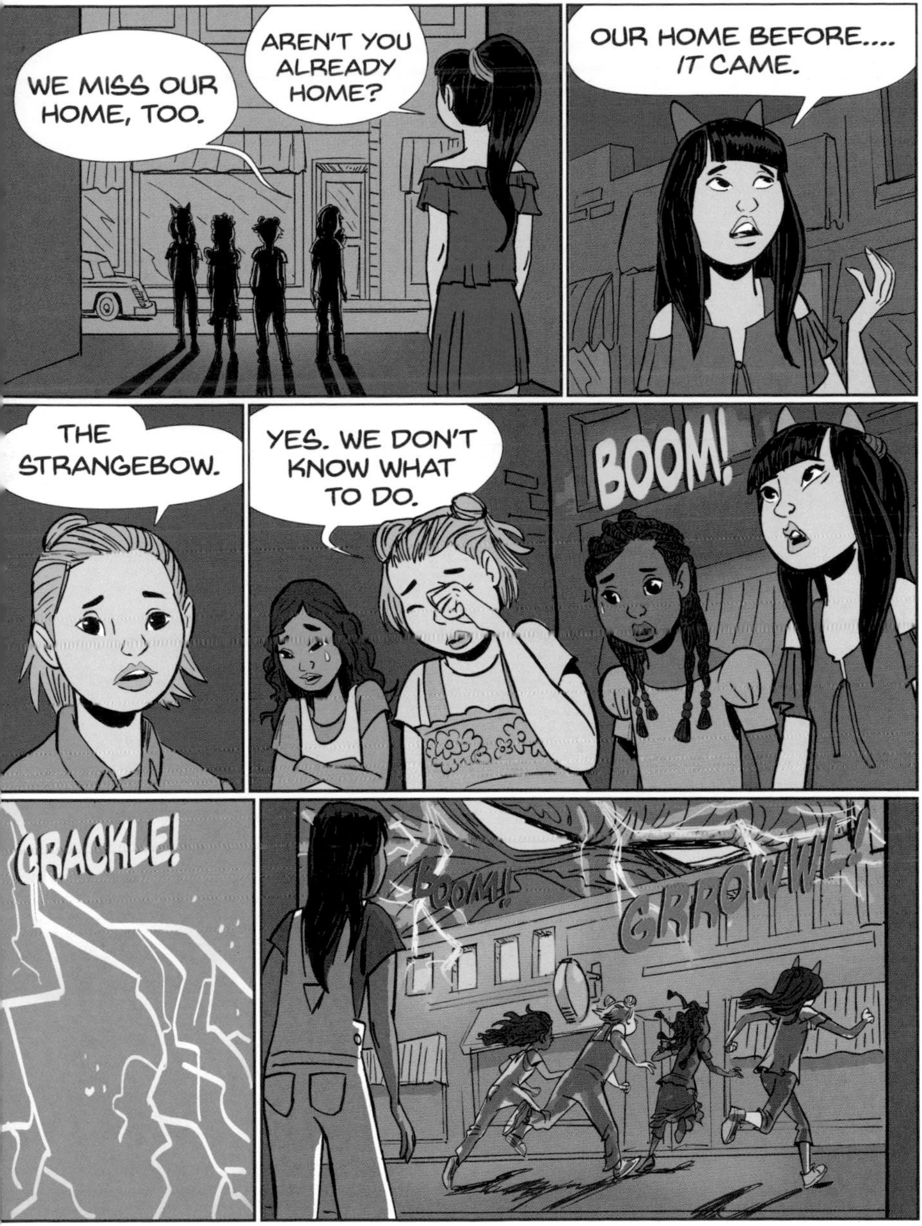
WE MISS OUR HOME, TOO.
AREN'T YOU ALREADY HOME?
OUR HOME BEFORE.... IT CAME.
THE STRANGEBOW.
YES. WE DON'T KNOW WHAT TO DO.
BOOM!
CRACKLE!
BOOM!
GRROWWL!

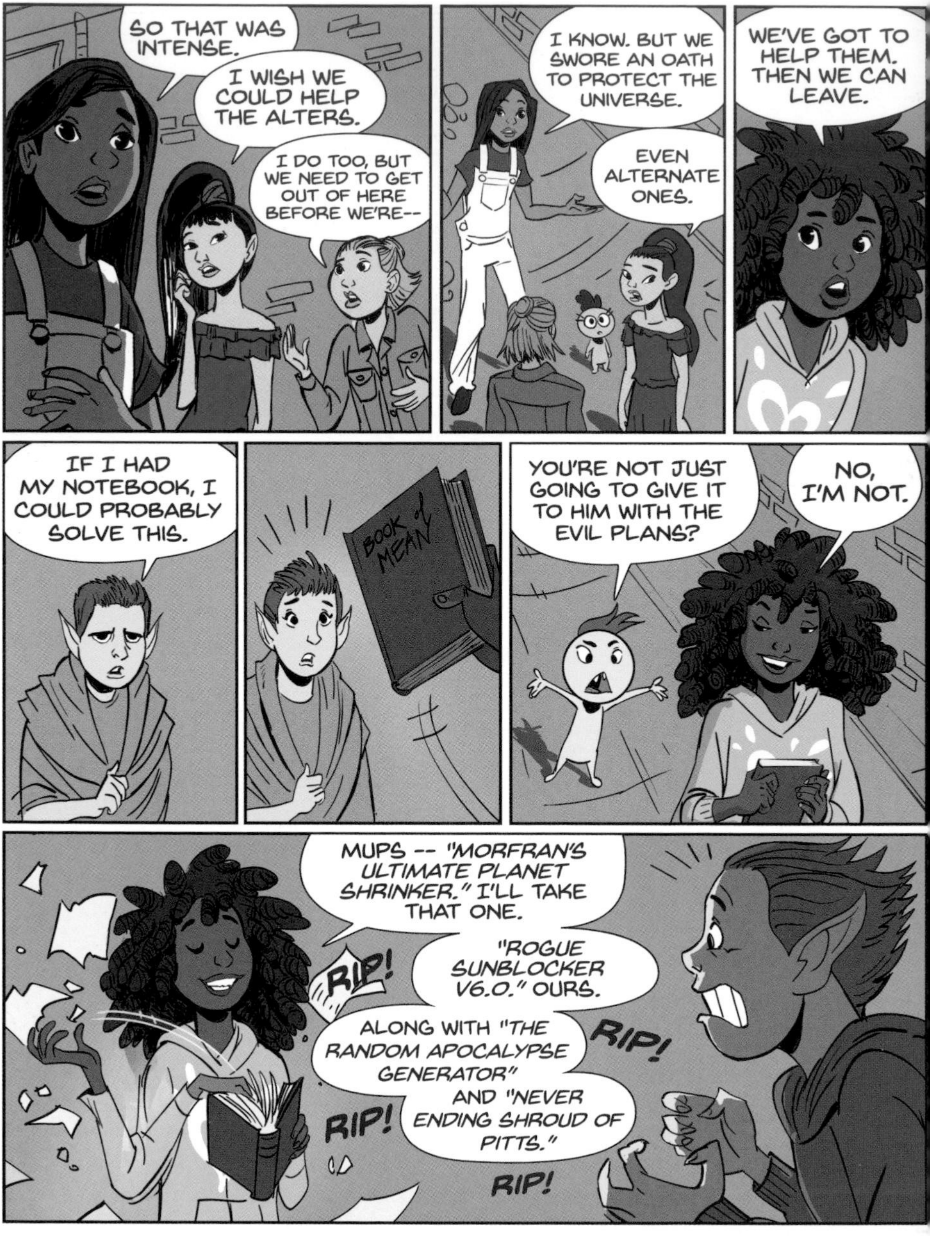
SO THAT WAS INTENSE.
I WISH WE COULD HELP THE ALTERS.
I DO TOO, BUT WE NEED TO GET OUT OF HERE BEFORE WE'RE--
I KNOW. BUT WE SWORE AN OATH TO PROTECT THE UNIVERSE.
EVEN ALTERNATE ONES.
WE'VE GOT TO HELP THEM. THEN WE CAN LEAVE.
IF I HAD MY NOTEBOOK, I COULD PROBABLY SOLVE THIS.
BOOK of MEAN
YOU'RE NOT JUST GOING TO GIVE IT TO HIM WITH THE EVIL PLANS?
NO, I'M NOT.
MUPS -- "MORFRAN'S ULTIMATE PLANET SHRINKER." I'LL TAKE THAT ONE.
RIP!
"ROGUE SUNBLOCKER V6.0." OURS.
RIP!
ALONG WITH "THE RANDOM APOCALYPSE GENERATOR"
AND "NEVER ENDING SHROUD OF PITTS."
RIP!
RIP!

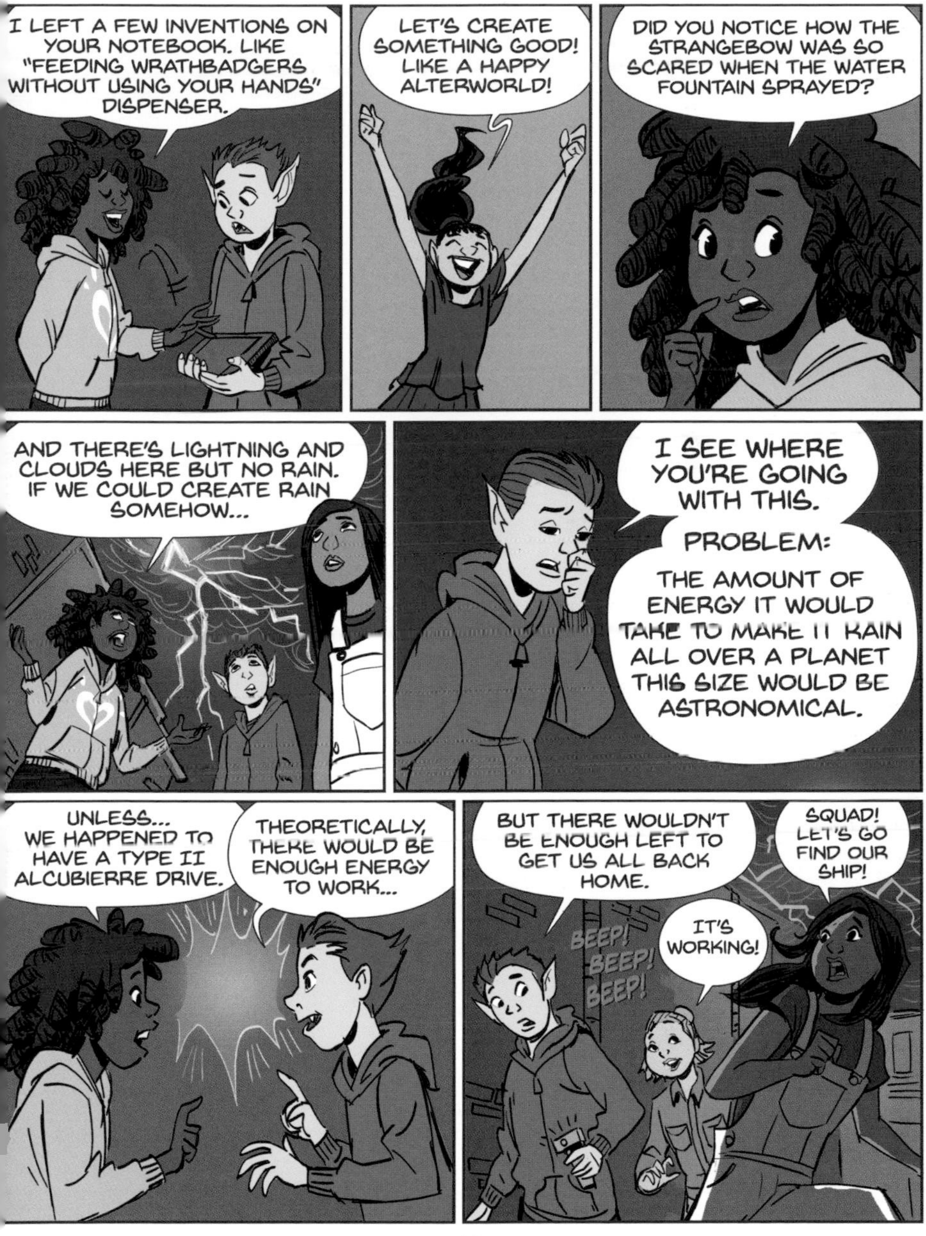
I LEFT A FEW INVENTIONS ON YOUR NOTEBOOK. LIKE "FEEDING WRATHBADGERS WITHOUT USING YOUR HANDS" DISPENSER.
LET'S CREATE SOMETHING GOOD! LIKE A HAPPY ALTERWORLD!
DID YOU NOTICE HOW THE STRANGEBOW WAS SO SCARED WHEN THE WATER FOUNTAIN SPRAYED?
AND THERE'S LIGHTNING AND CLOUDS HERE BUT NO RAIN. IF WE COULD CREATE RAIN SOMEHOW...
I SEE WHERE YOU'RE GOING WITH THIS.
PROBLEM:
THE AMOUNT OF ENERGY IT WOULD TAKE TO MAKE IT RAIN ALL OVER A PLANET THIS SIZE WOULD BE ASTRONOMICAL.
UNLESS... WE HAPPENED TO HAVE A TYPE II ALCUBIERRE DRIVE.
THEORETICALLY, THERE WOULD BE ENOUGH ENERGY TO WORK...
BUT THERE WOULDN'T BE ENOUGH LEFT TO GET US ALL BACK HOME.
SQUAD! LET'S GO FIND OUR SHIP!
BEEP! BEEP! BEEP!
IT'S WORKING!

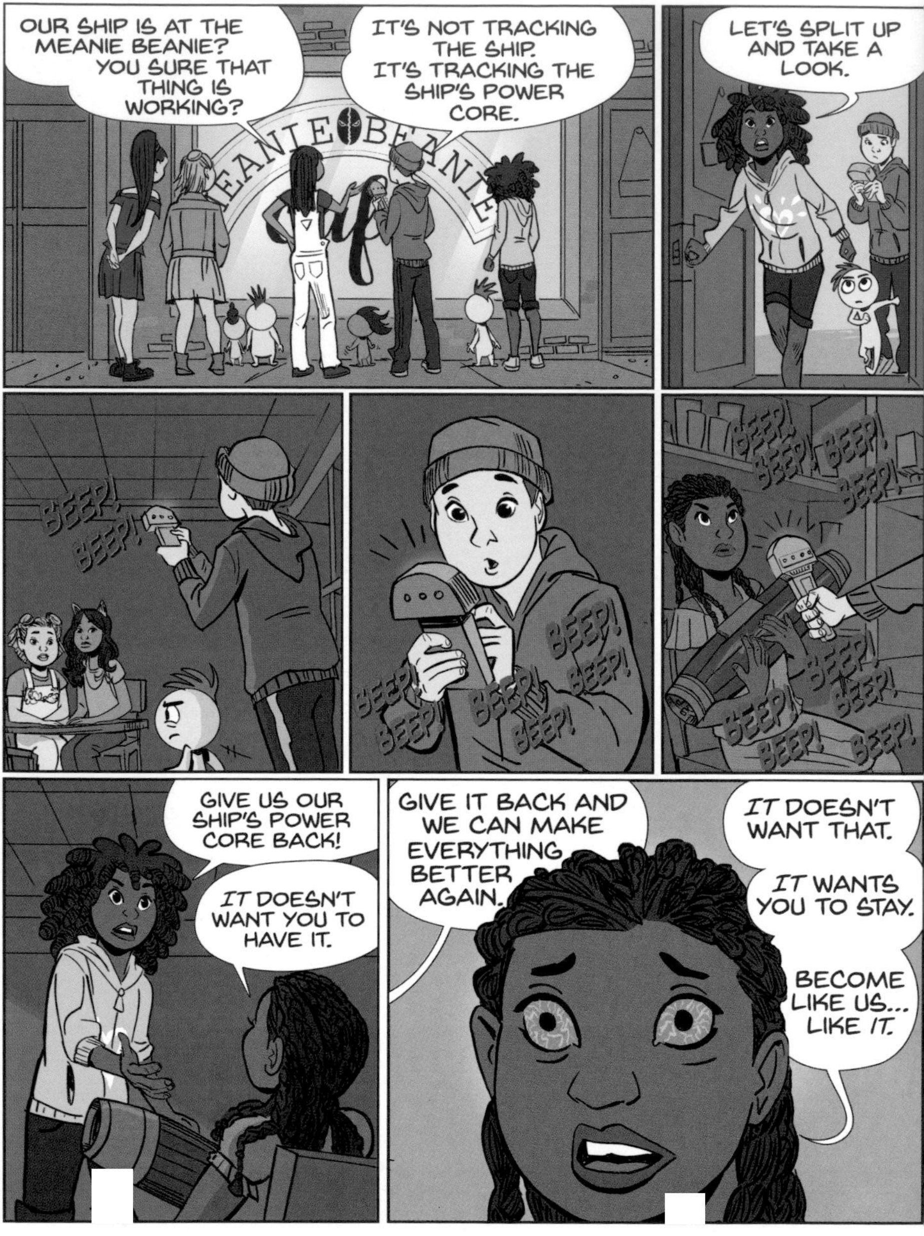
OUR SHIP IS AT THE MEANIE BEANIE? YOU SURE THAT THING IS WORKING?
IT'S NOT TRACKING THE SHIP. IT'S TRACKING THE SHIP'S POWER CORE.
MEANIE BEANIE
LET'S SPLIT UP AND TAKE A LOOK.
BEEP! BEEP!
BEEP! BEEP! BEEP! BEEP! BEEP! BEEP!
BEEP! BEEP! BEEP! BEEP! BEEP! BEEP! BEEP! BEEP! BEEP! BEEP!
GIVE US OUR SHIP'S POWER CORE BACK!
IT DOESN'T WANT YOU TO HAVE IT.
GIVE IT BACK AND WE CAN MAKE EVERYTHING BETTER AGAIN.
IT DOESN'T WANT THAT.
IT WANTS YOU TO STAY.
BECOME LIKE US... LIKE *IT*.

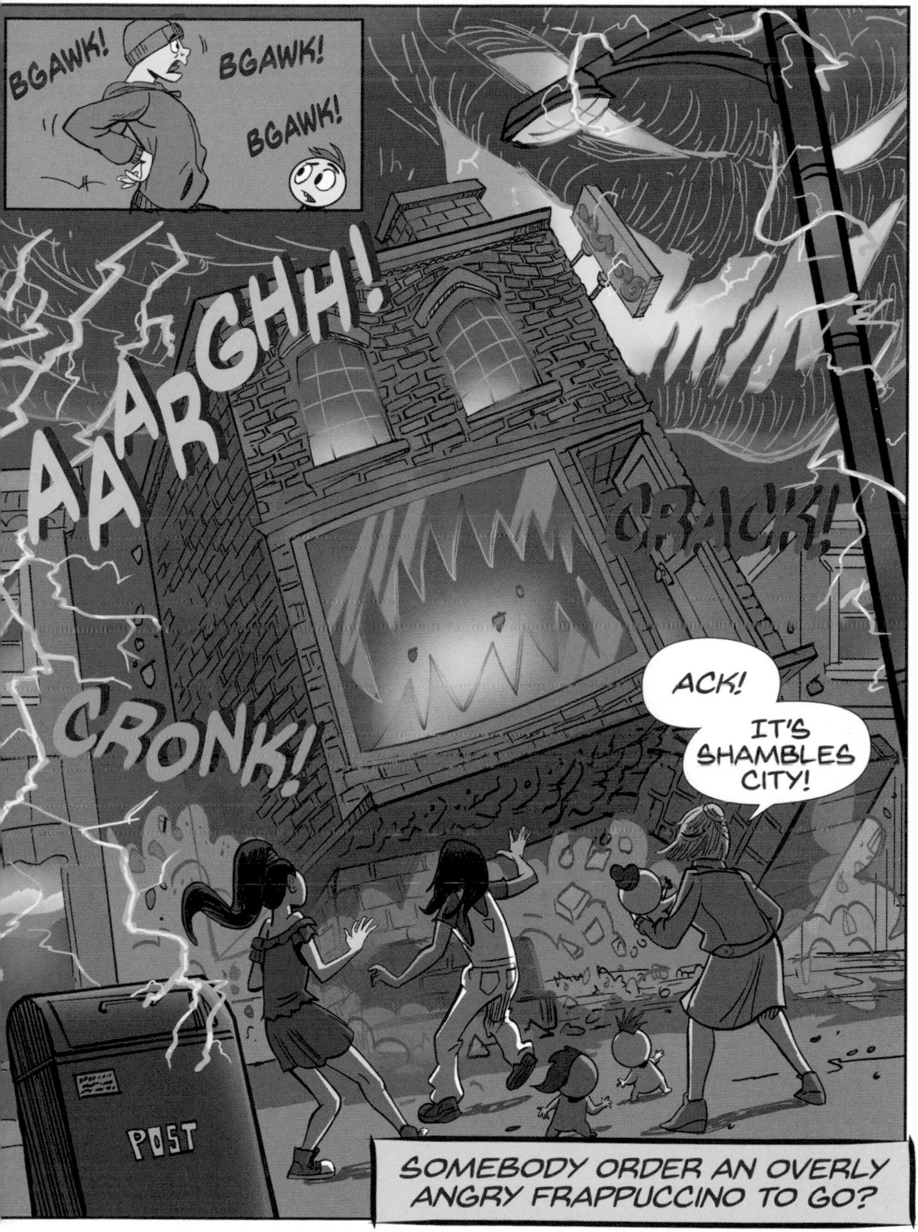
BGAWK!
BGAWK!
BGAWK!
AAARGHH!
CRACK!
CRONK!
ACK!
IT'S SHAMBLES CITY!
SOMEBODY ORDER AN OVERLY ANGRY FRAPPUCCINO TO GO?
POST

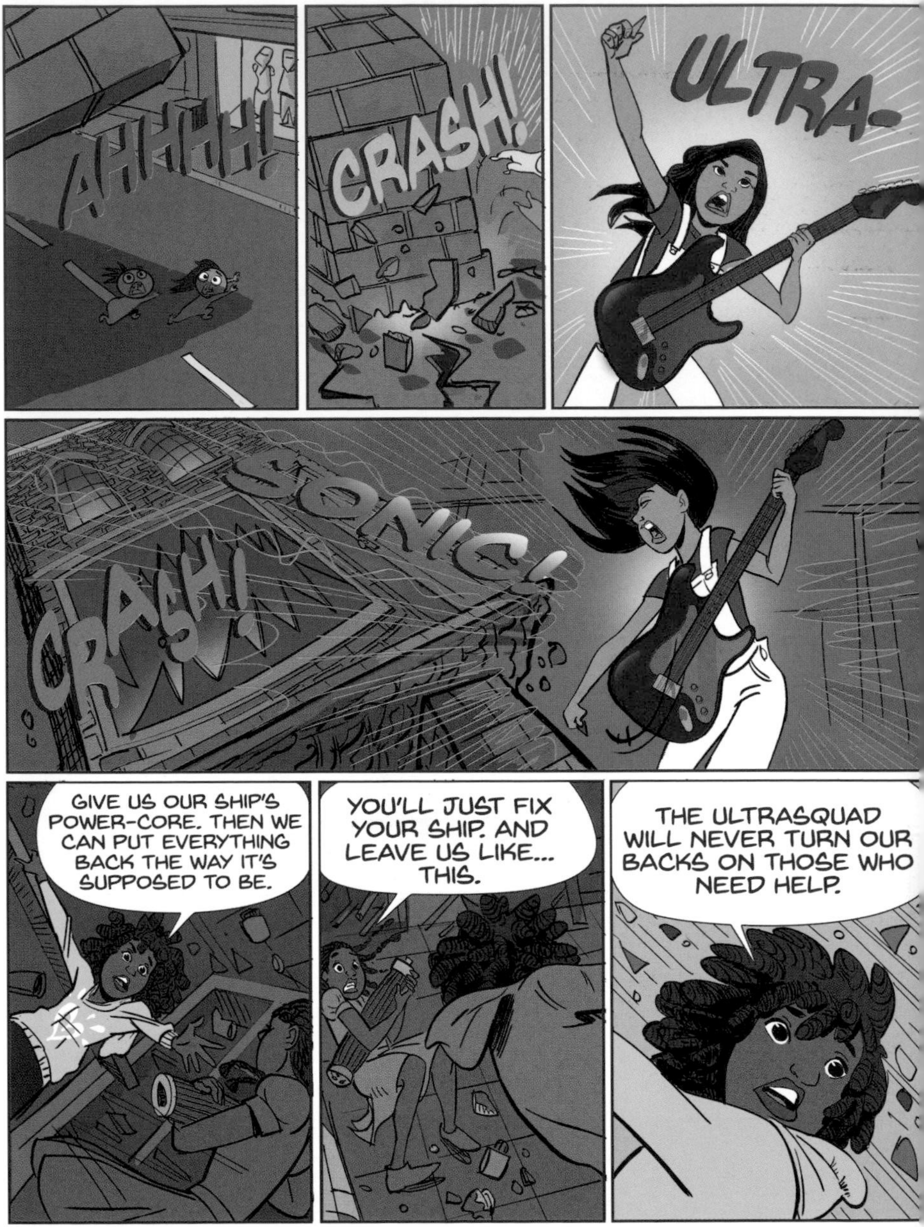
AHHHH!
CRASH!
ULTRA-
SONIC!
CRASH!
GIVE US OUR SHIP'S POWER-CORE. THEN WE CAN PUT EVERYTHING BACK THE WAY IT'S SUPPOSED TO BE.
YOU'LL JUST FIX YOUR SHIP. AND LEAVE US LIKE... THIS.
THE ULTRASQUAD WILL NEVER TURN OUR BACKS ON THOSE WHO NEED HELP.

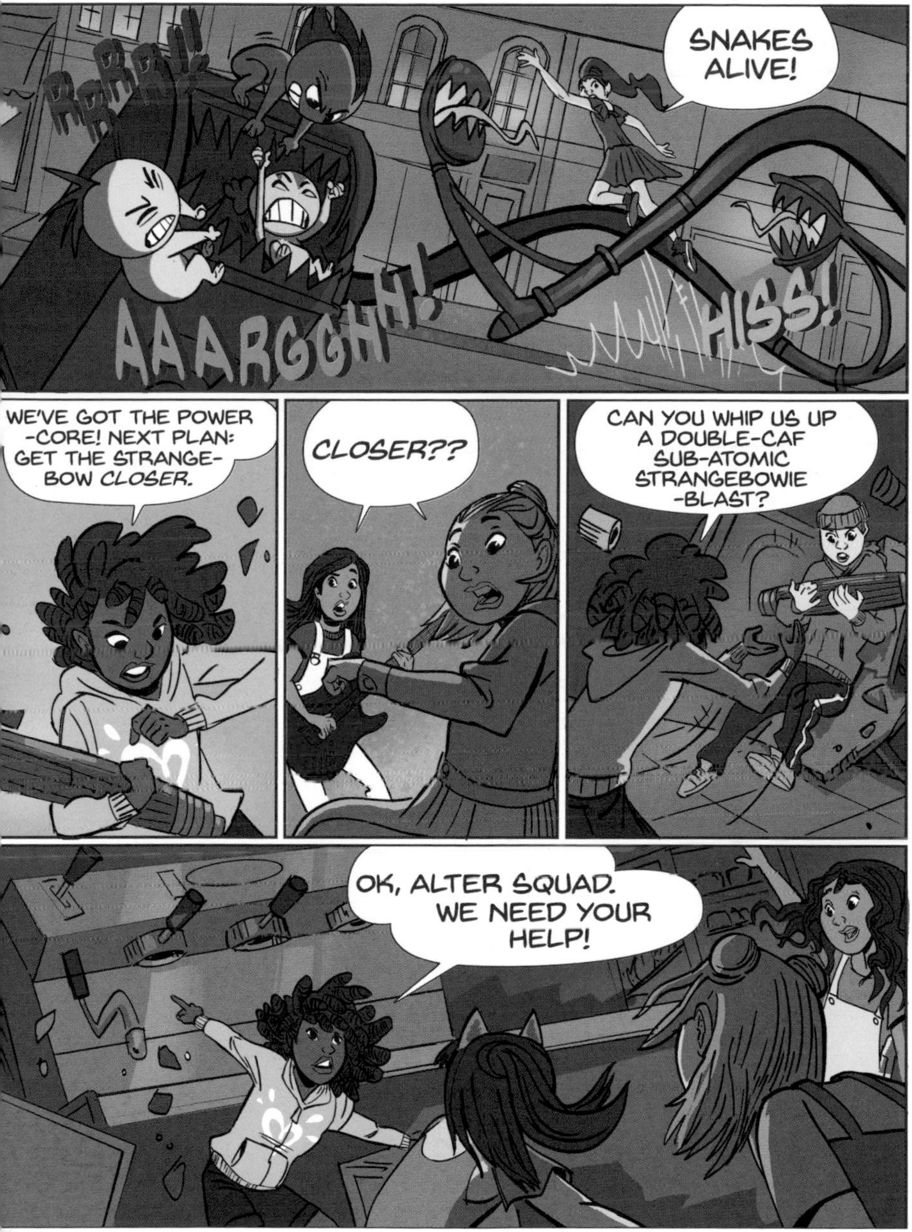
RRRR!!
AAARGGHH!
SNAKES ALIVE!
HISS!!
WE'VE GOT THE POWER-CORE! NEXT PLAN: GET THE STRANGE-BOW *CLOSER.*
CLOSER??
CAN YOU WHIP US UP A DOUBLE-CAF SUB-ATOMIC STRANGEBOWIE-BLAST?
OK, ALTER SQUAD. WE NEED YOUR HELP!

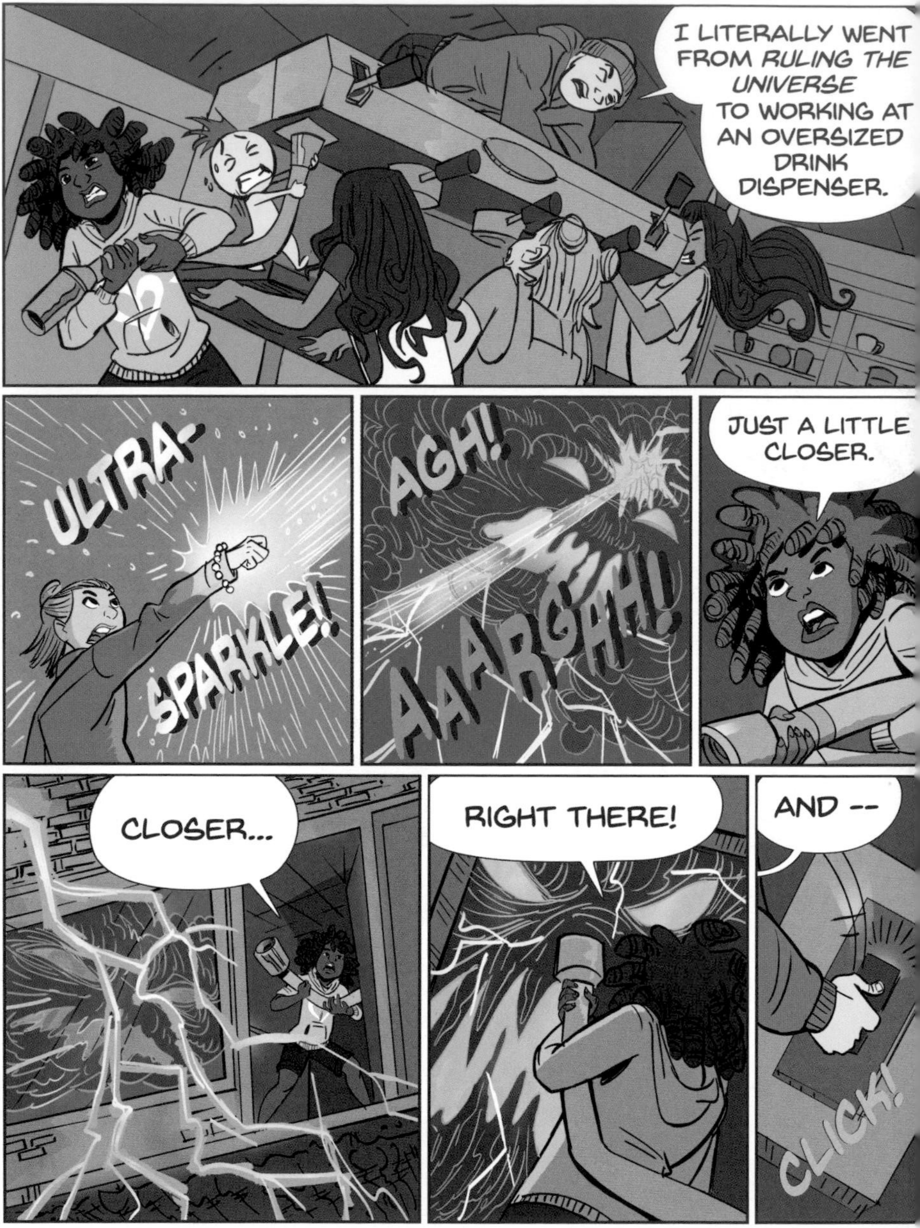
I LITERALLY WENT FROM RULING THE UNIVERSE TO WORKING AT AN OVERSIZED DRINK DISPENSER.
ULTRA-SPARKLE!
AGH!
AAARGHH!
JUST A LITTLE CLOSER.
CLOSER...
RIGHT THERE!
AND --
CLICK!

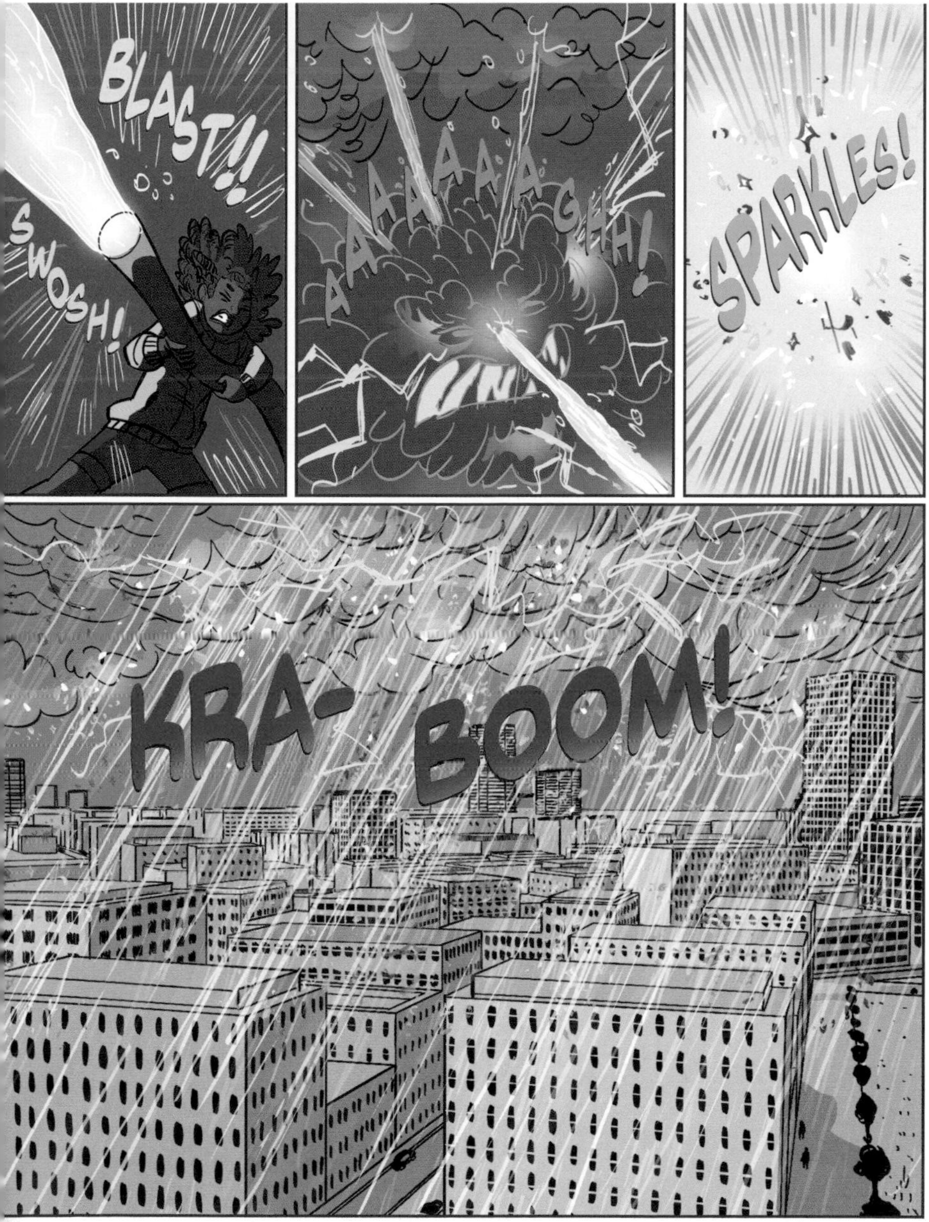
BLAST!!!
SWOSH!
AAAAAAAGHH!
SPARKLES!
KRA-BOOM!

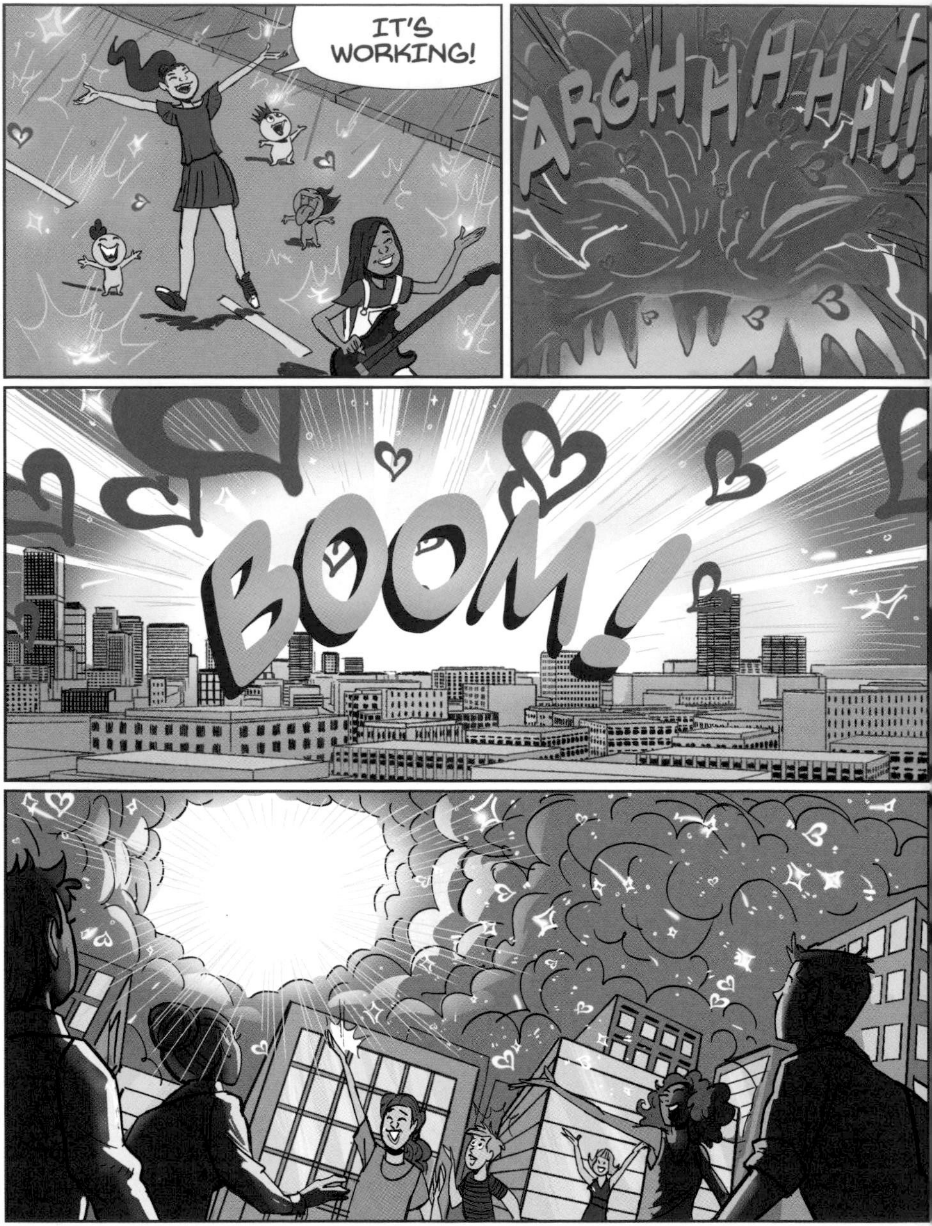
IT'S WORKING!
ARGHHHHH!!
BOOM!

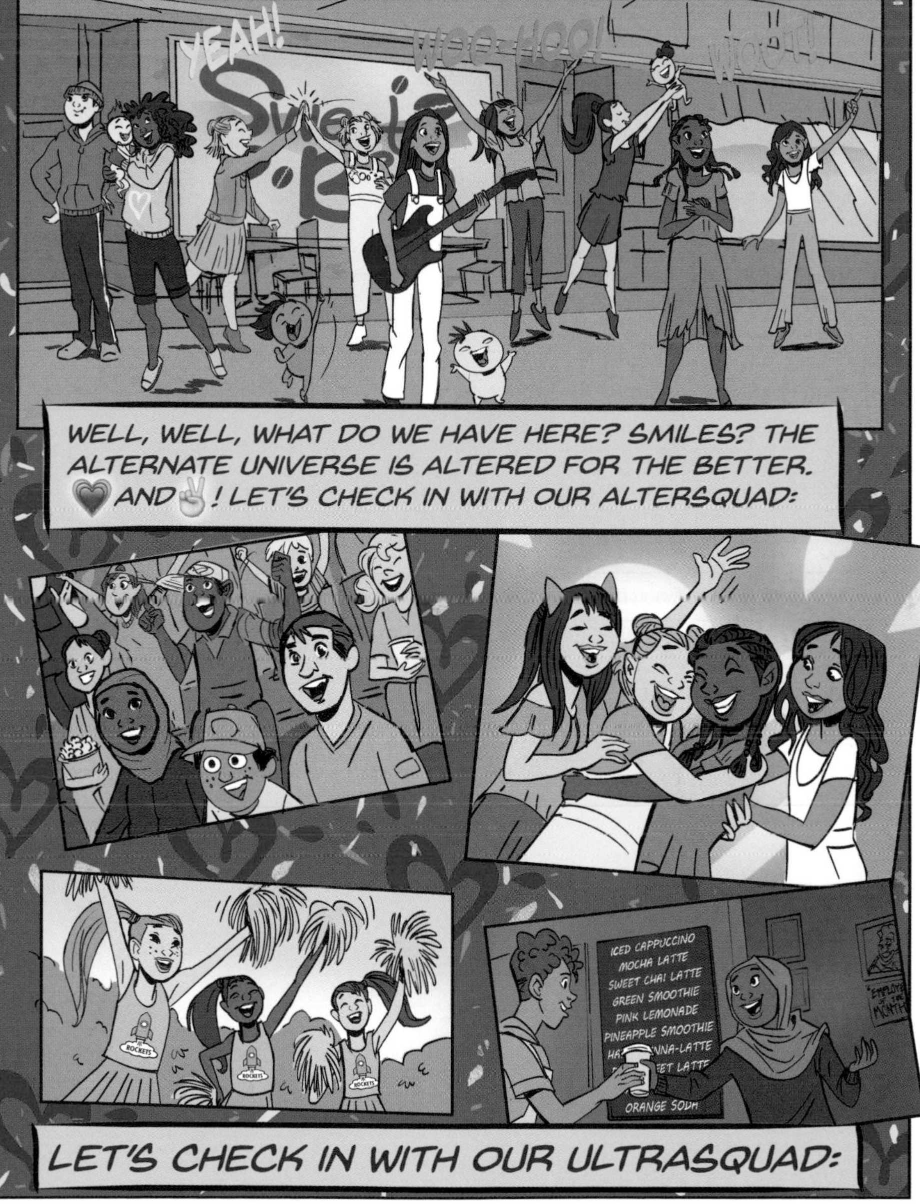
YEAH!
WOO-HOO!
WOOT!!
WELL, WELL, WHAT DO WE HAVE HERE? SMILES? THE ALTERNATE UNIVERSE IS ALTERED FOR THE BETTER. 💙 AND ✌️! LET'S CHECK IN WITH OUR ALTERSQUAD:
ROCKETS
ROCKETS
ROCKETS
ICED CAPPUCCINO
MOCHA LATTE
SWEET CHAI LATTE
GREEN SMOOTHIE
PINK LEMONADE
PINEAPPLE SMOOTHIE
ORANGE SODA
LET'S CHECK IN WITH OUR ULTRASQUAD:

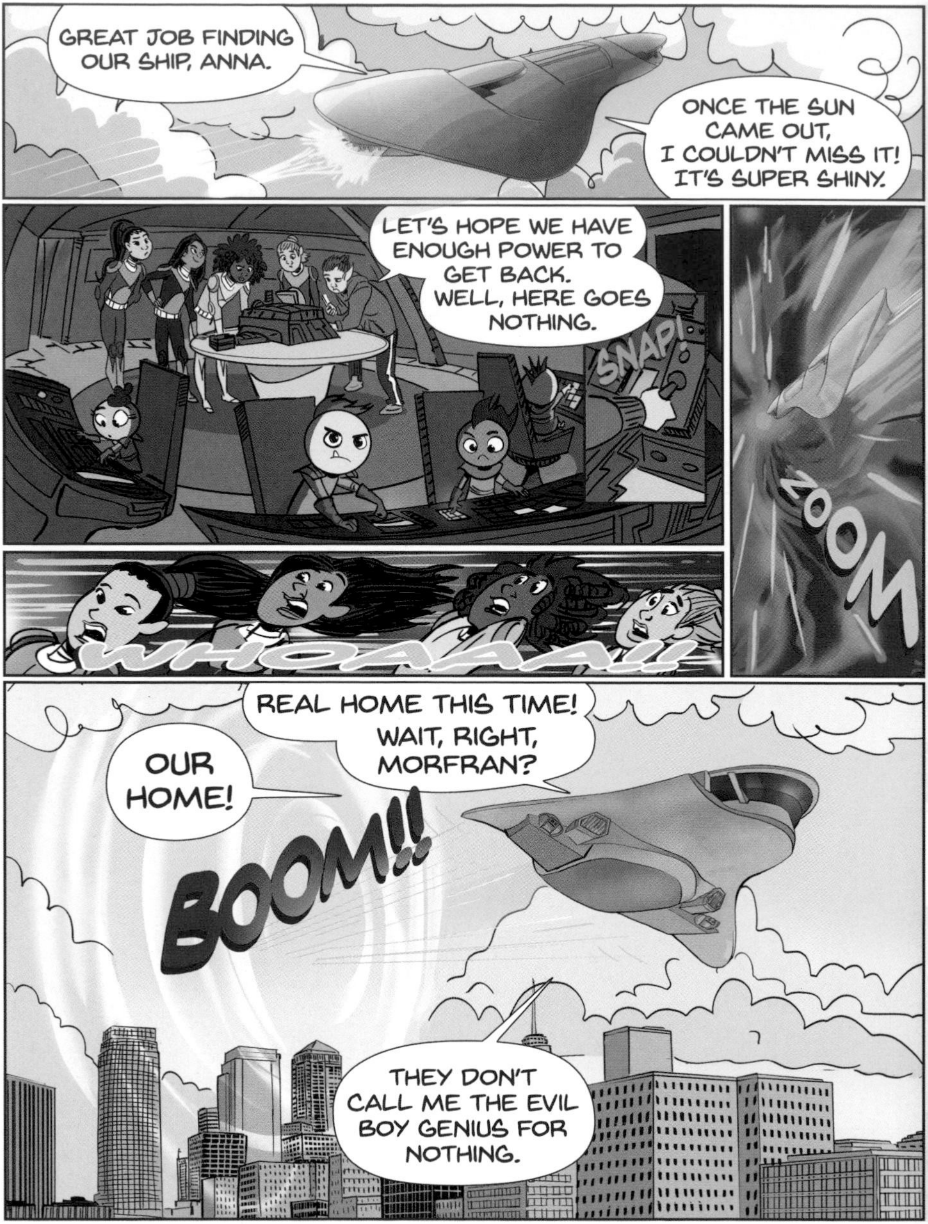
GREAT JOB FINDING OUR SHIP, ANNA.
ONCE THE SUN CAME OUT, I COULDN'T MISS IT! IT'S SUPER SHINY.
LET'S HOPE WE HAVE ENOUGH POWER TO GET BACK. WELL, HERE GOES NOTHING.
SNAP!
ZOOM
WHOAAAA!!
REAL HOME THIS TIME! WAIT, RIGHT, MORFRAN?
OUR HOME!
BOOM!!
THEY DON'T CALL ME THE EVIL BOY GENIUS FOR NOTHING.

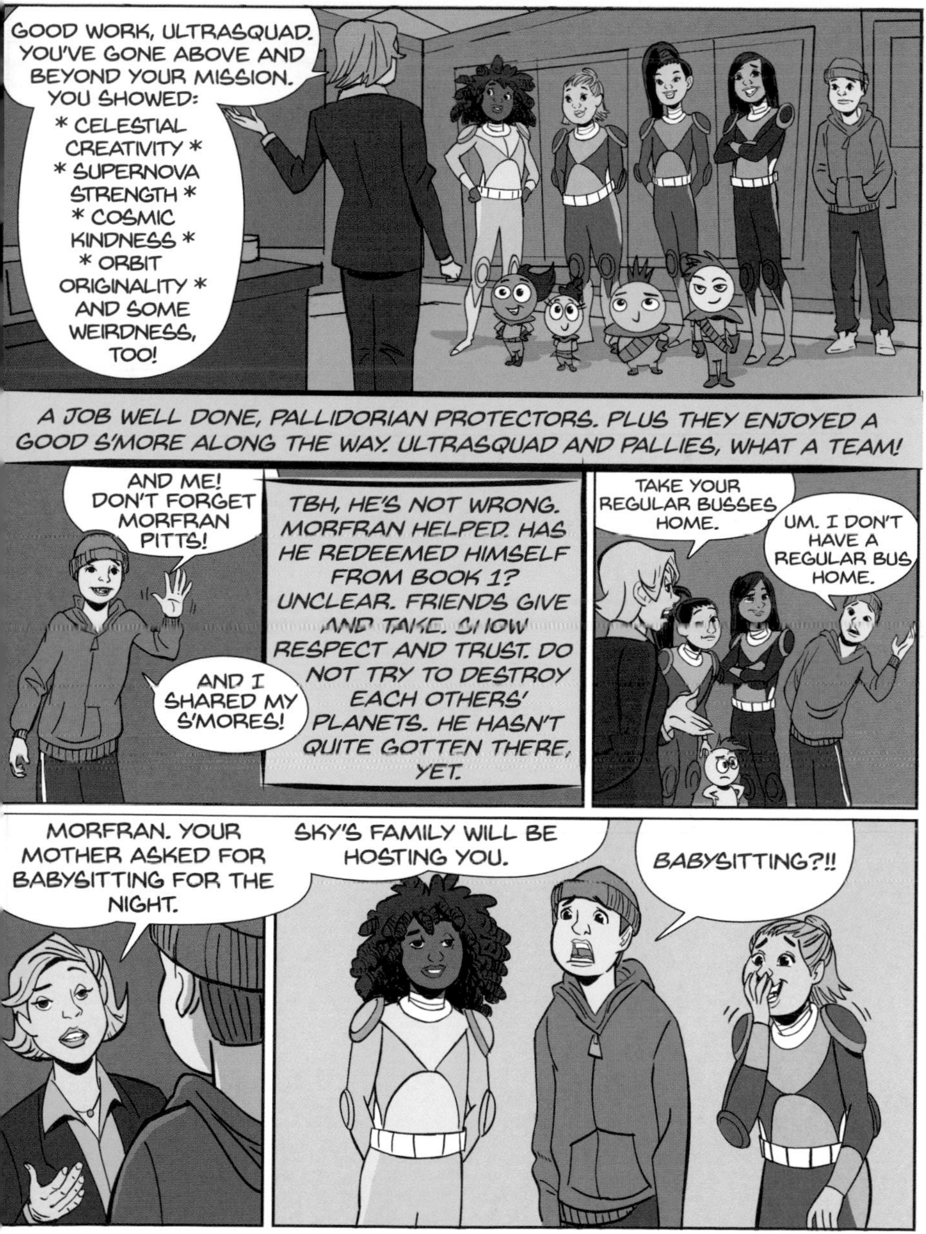

GOOD WORK, ULTRASQUAD. YOU'VE GONE ABOVE AND BEYOND YOUR MISSION. YOU SHOWED: * CELESTIAL CREATIVITY * * SUPERNOVA STRENGTH * * COSMIC KINDNESS * * ORBIT ORIGINALITY * AND SOME WEIRDNESS, TOO!
A JOB WELL DONE, PALLIDORIAN PROTECTORS. PLUS THEY ENJOYED A GOOD S'MORE ALONG THE WAY. ULTRASQUAD AND PALLIES, WHAT A TEAM!
AND ME! DON'T FORGET MORFRAN PITTS!
AND I SHARED MY S'MORES!
TBH, HE'S NOT WRONG. MORFRAN HELPED. HAS HE REDEEMED HIMSELF FROM BOOK 1? UNCLEAR. FRIENDS GIVE AND TAKE. SHOW RESPECT AND TRUST. DO NOT TRY TO DESTROY EACH OTHERS' PLANETS. HE HASN'T QUITE GOTTEN THERE, YET.
TAKE YOUR REGULAR BUSSES HOME.
UM. I DON'T HAVE A REGULAR BUS HOME.
MORFRAN. YOUR MOTHER ASKED FOR BABYSITTING FOR THE NIGHT.
SKY'S FAMILY WILL BE HOSTING YOU.
BABYSITTING?!!

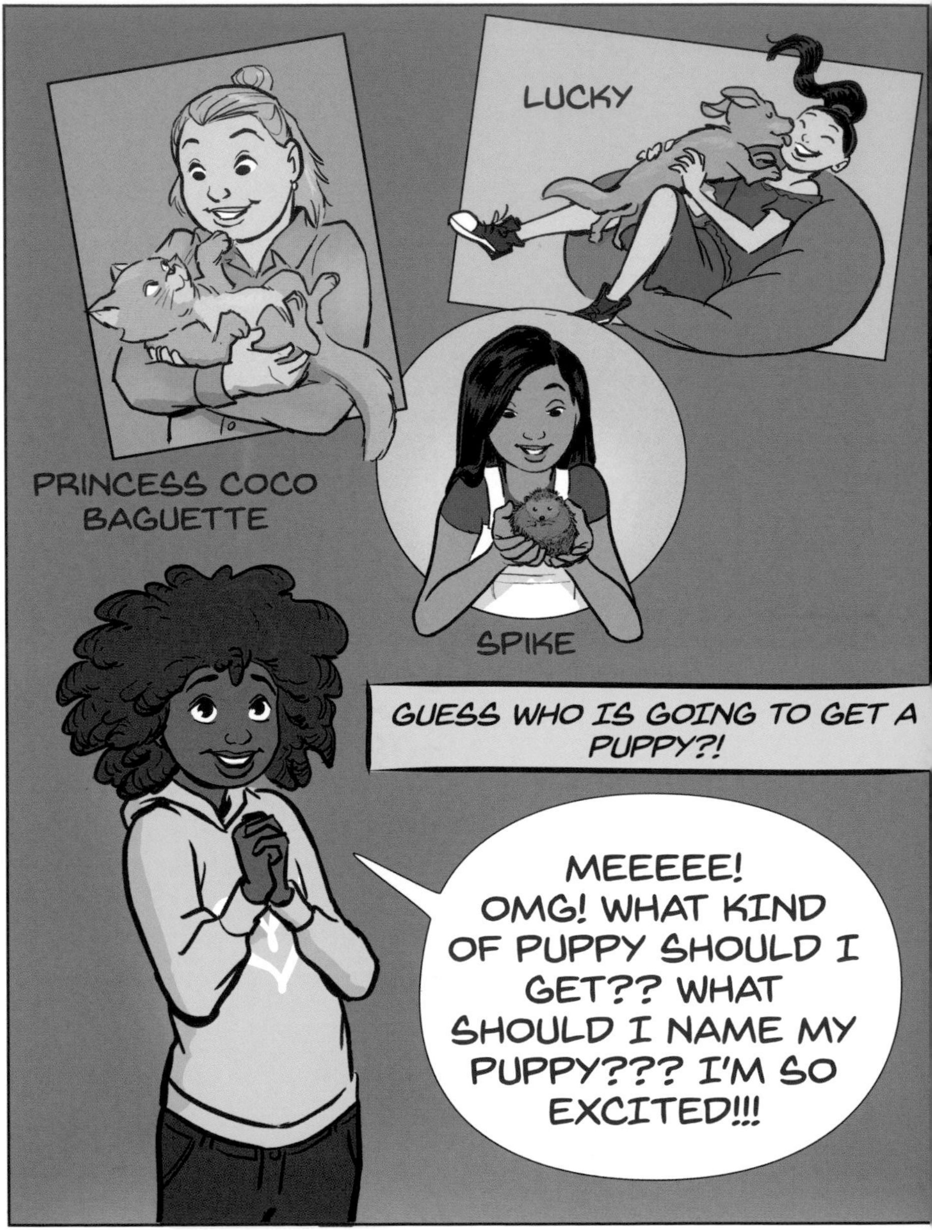
LUCKY
PRINCESS COCO BAGUETTE
SPIKE
GUESS WHO IS GOING TO GET A PUPPY?!
MEEEEEE! OMG! WHAT KIND OF PUPPY SHOULD I GET?? WHAT SHOULD I NAME MY PUPPY??? I'M SO EXCITED!!!

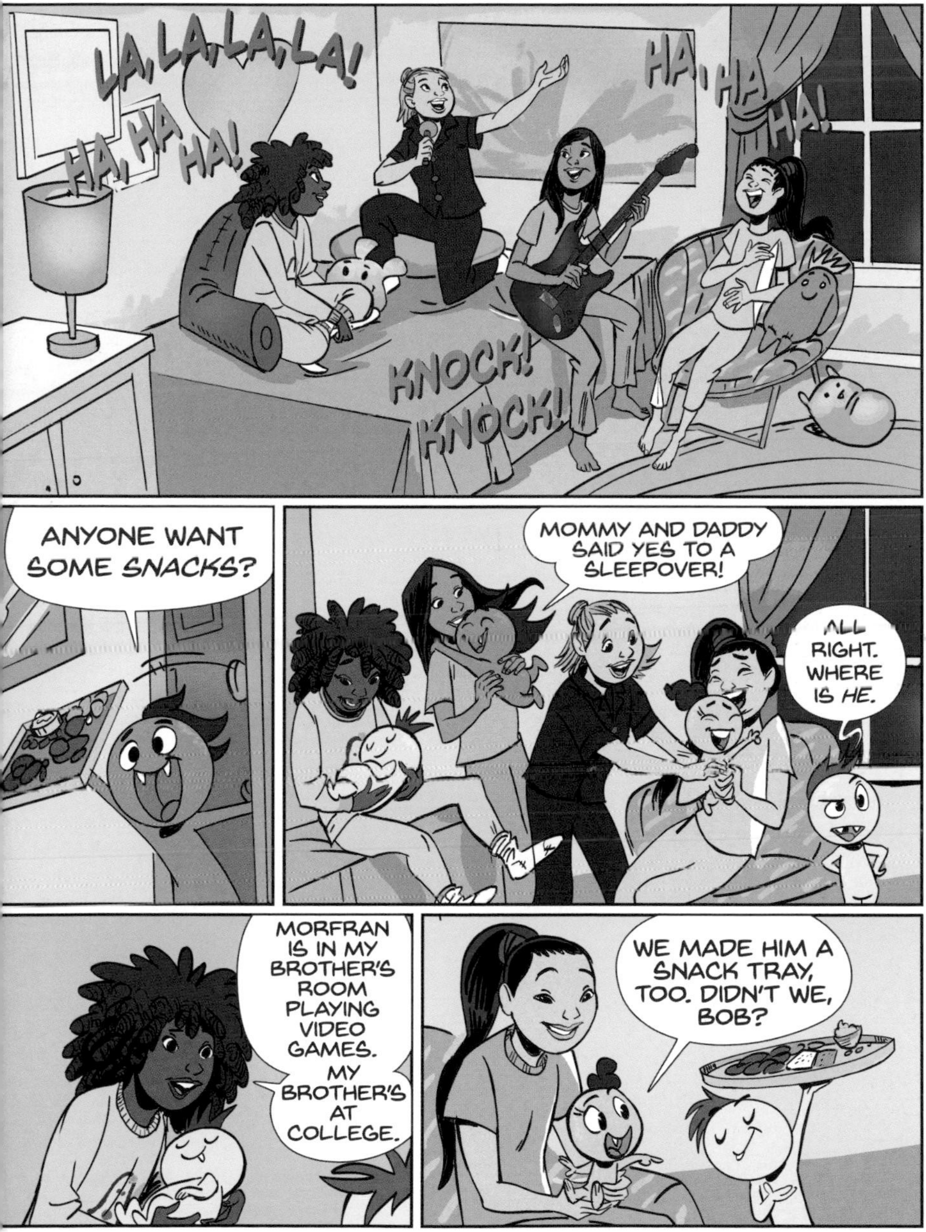
LA, LA, LA, LA!
HA, HA HA!
HA, HA HA!
KNOCK! KNOCK!
ANYONE WANT SOME SNACKS?
MOMMY AND DADDY SAID YES TO A SLEEPOVER!
ALL RIGHT. WHERE IS HE.
MORFRAN IS IN MY BROTHER'S ROOM PLAYING VIDEO GAMES.
MY BROTHER'S AT COLLEGE.
WE MADE HIM A SNACK TRAY, TOO. DIDN'T WE, BOB?

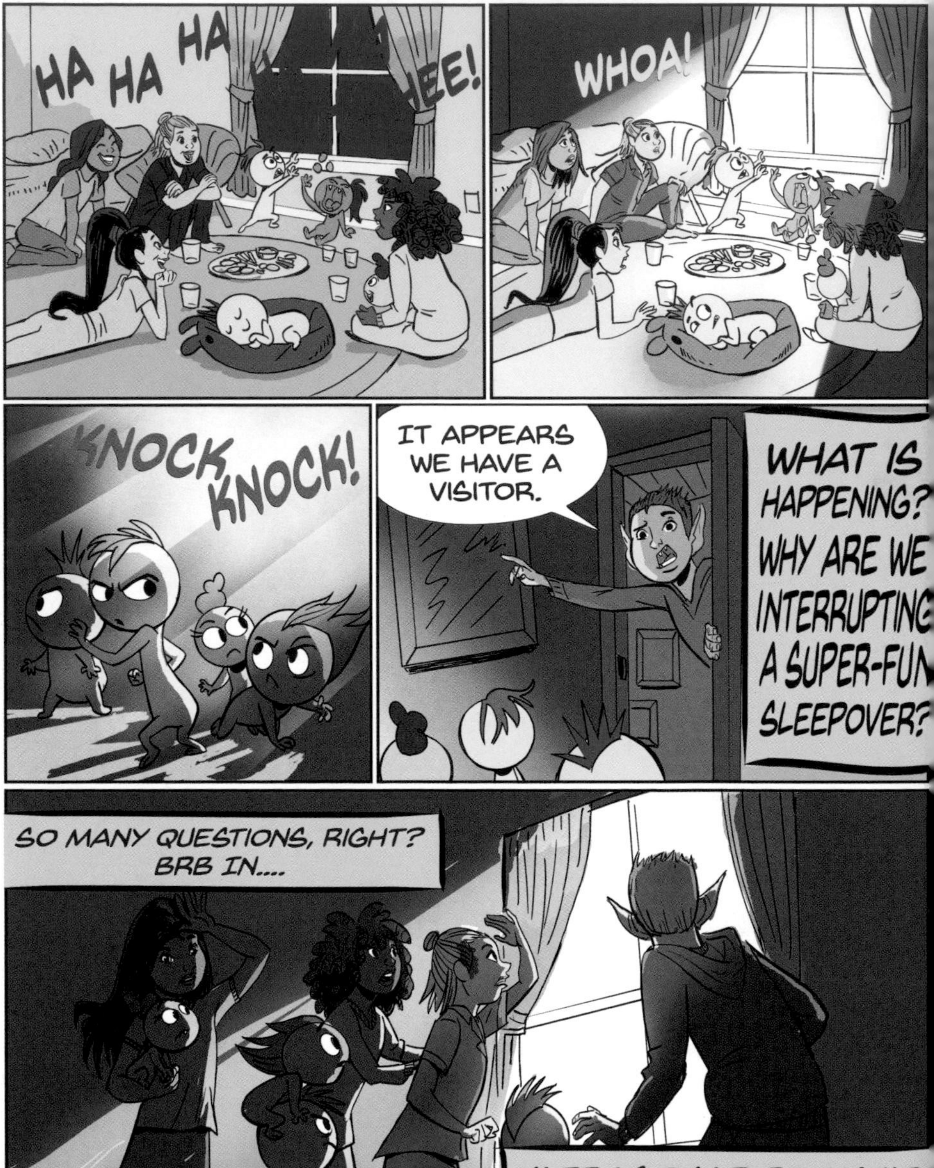
HA HA HA
HEE!
WHOA!
KNOCK KNOCK!
IT APPEARS WE HAVE A VISITOR.
WHAT IS HAPPENING? WHY ARE WE INTERRUPTING A SUPER-FUN SLEEPOVER?
SO MANY QUESTIONS, RIGHT? BRB IN....
ULTRASQUAD BOOK #3!

WHO'S IN YOUR SQUAD?

NAME:_____

Superpower:_____

Zodiac:_____

NAME:_____

Superpower:_____

Zodiac:_____

NAME:_____

Superpower:_____

Zodiac:_____

NAME:_____

Superpower:_____

Zodiac:_____

CONNECT THE CONSTELLATIONS

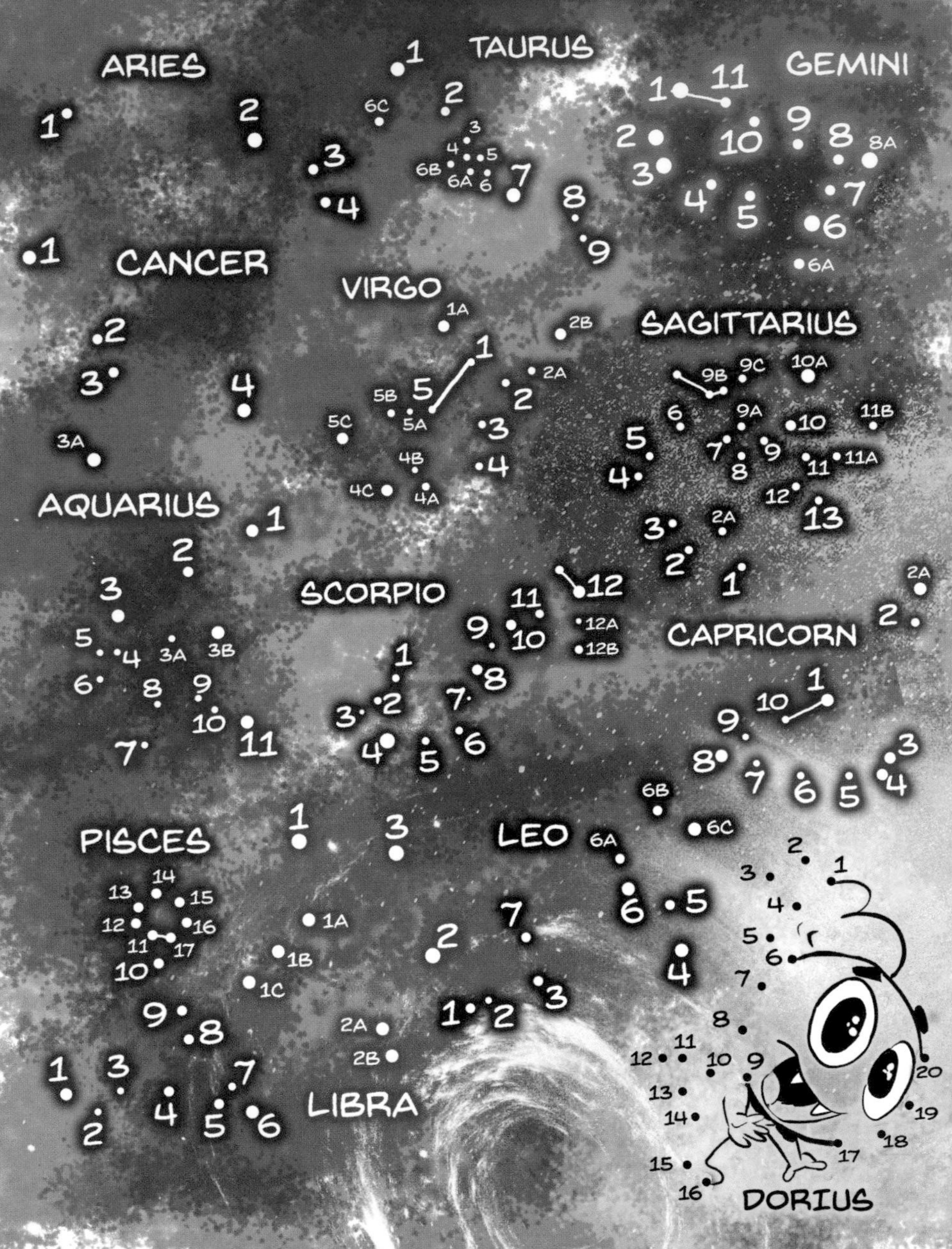

ARIES
TAURUS
GEMINI
CANCER
VIRGO
SAGITTARIUS
AQUARIUS
SCORPIO
CAPRICORN
PISCES
LEO
LIBRA
DORIUS

THE CREATORS

Author
Julia DeVillers is the author of books including TRADING FACES and THE AUDITION with Maddie Ziegler. Her book became the Disney Channel Original Movie READ IT AND WEEP.

Co-Author
R.R. Wells is a writer, producer, and director of animated short films. He has a passion for graphic novels and jumped at the chance to write one.

Illustrator
Rafael Rosado is the illustrator and co-creator of the graphic novel series GIANTS BEWARE, MONSTERS BEWARE, and DRAGONS BEWARE. He is currently a storyboard artist for Warner Brothers, Disney, and Cartoon Network.

Inker/Penciler: Dan Root
Colorist: John Novak
Penciler: Josh Tufts
Production Manager/Letterer: Kylie Lovsey
3D Artist: Patrick Danber
Producer: Jeremy Hughes
Executive Producer: Joe Niedecken
Cover Designer: Kylie Lovsey

Assistant Visual Designer: Josh Jackson
Assistant Visual Designer: Anna-Grace Blackburn

Special thanks to Lece Lohr, Sara Tervo, Kendra Stokes, Traci Graziani, Emily Reichert, and Meghan Kerr!!!

MAKE SURE TO KEEP UP WITH ALL THINGS ULTRASQUAD (AND FIND BOOK #3!) AT YOUR NEAREST JUSTICE STORE!

FIND OUT WHAT HAPPENS TO THE STRANGEBOW AT THEULTRASQUAD.COM/STRANGEBOW

**

For information regarding the CPSIA on this printed material, call: (203) 595-3636 and provide reference #RICH - 826015.

Copyright @ 2019 by Justice Studios. All rights reserved. No part of this book may be reproduced or transmitted in any form or by any means, electronic or mechanical, including photocopying, recording or by any information storage and retrieval system, without written permission from the publisher. For information, write: Justice Studios, 8323 Walton Parkway, New Albany, OH 43054.

Printed in the United States of America.

First edition.

ISBN-978-1-7327030-2-5